PENGUIN BOOKS

923

BULLETS FOR THE BRIDEGROOM

DAVID DODGE

OTHER BOOKS BY DAVID DODGE

*

Death and Taxes
A Drug on the Market
Plunder of the Sun
Shear the Black Sheep
The Long Escape
The Red Tassel
To Catch a Thief

BULLETS FOR THE BRIDEGROOM

*

DAVID DODGE

PENGUIN BOOKS

IN ASSOCIATION WITH
MICHAEL JOSEPH

Penguin Books Ltd, Harmondsworth, Middlesex

CANADA: Penguin Books (Canada) Ltd, 47 Green Street,
Saint Lambert, Montreal, P.Q.

AUSTRALIA: Penguin Books Pty Ltd, 762 Whitehorse Road,
Mitcham, Victoria

SOUTH AFRICA: Penguin Books (S.A.) Pty Ltd, Gibraltar House,
Regents Road, Sea Point, Cape Town

—

First published 1948
Published in Penguin Books 1953
Reprinted 1955

THIS IS FOR

ELVADEE

Made and printed in Great Britain
by Hazell Watson and Viney Ltd
Aylesbury and London

CHAPTER 1

THERE were four men in a dark little room. One of them had been shot several times in the chest and was about to die.

The room was bare except for a rickety table, a couple of chairs to match, and a number of heavy packing cases. The dying man lay sprawled on his back across a couple of the packing cases, and blood bubbled in the back of his throat as he breathed. The other men stood by silently, waiting.

The smallest of the three men who watched the unconscious body on the packing cases had a face like a weasel. One of the others was stocky, heavy-set and middle-aged, with greying hair and very pale blue eyes. The third was younger, of average height, average weight, average colouring, average looks. He and the heavy-set man could have been a couple of plumbers or a pair of mechanics from the nearest garage. Both wore overalls, and their hands were grimy with grease and dirt.

The dying man, except for the blood that soaked his shirt and coloured the saliva at the corner of his mouth, was just another chubby man with a bald spot. His clothes were more expensive than most, but that was all that distinguished him, although he had more stamina than most chubby men with bald spots. He was dying hard.

Weasel-face said, 'He's sure taking his time about it.'

'He's going.' The heavy-set man did not shift his eyes from the face of the man on the packing cases. 'He's lost too much blood to pull out of it. We won't get anything from him.'

Weasel-face said, 'Maybe he's got something in his pockets.'

'I searched him once.'

Weasel-face said nothing for a while. After a moment he suggested hopefully, 'Maybe he'd wake up if you stuck a pin under his fingernail or something.'

The third man looked at weasel-face sharply, frowning. But the heavy-set man shook his head, as if he had considered the idea and discarded it. 'He's too far gone. If you hadn't been so free with that gun of yours, we could have made him talk.'

'Well, what was I going to do – let him get away?'

'One shot would have been enough.'

'I didn't know I hit him with the first shot. Anyway, he had a gun. Suppose —'

The heavy-set man turned his pale eyes towards weasel-face. Weasel-face shut up. The heavy-set man said, 'Never mind explaining again. It's too late to do anything about it now. Next time you get ready to shoot somebody, remember what I told you.'

Weasel-face muttered, 'I was just trying to stop him.'

'His eyes are open,' the third man said suddenly.

The man on the packing cases had come to the end of the road. For a short moment before he died, the fog lifted and he saw the three faces above him. They watched his eyes come into focus. He looked directly at the heavy-set man, and one corner of his mouth twitched up in what might have been a spasm of pain and might have been an attempt at a derisive grin. Then the bubbling stopped in his throat, his eyes closed, and he was dead.

'That's that,' the third man said. 'We don't know any more than we did an hour ago.'

'*He* knows a lot less.' Weasel-face nodded at the body. 'If he'd got away, we'd have had something to worry about.'

'We've got plenty to worry about,' the heavy-set man said. 'If he was after us, he wasn't doing the job by himself, and they're not going to stop looking because we kill one of them. All you did was complicate things.'

'Jesus, he saw you guys working, didn't he?' weasel-face said plaintively. 'I had to stop him, didn't I? I don't see why you have to act like I should have let him get away. You told me to stop anyone that came prowling around, and I did. Now I'm dumb because I plugged him.'

'You're dumb because you're dumb,' the heavy-set man answered. 'You try to think with your gun. You could have brought him in without killing him, and I'd have made him talk. Then we would have known whether he was looking for us or whether he just stumbled in here by accident.'

'You don't know that he would have talked.'

The heavy-set man turned his head. 'Don't I?'

Weasel-face looked away from the pale eyes. There was no real doubt in his mind. Even when he had his hand on the gun in his pocket, the heavy-set man could scare hell out of him just by looking at him.

6

The third man said, 'What do we do now?'

'Go on where we left off. I don't think he was anyone we have to worry about; it's too soon for them to have trailed us here. And even if he was looking for us, he didn't know he was going to find us or he wouldn't have come alone. They haven't located us yet.'

'Yet.' The third man repeated it. 'You sound as if you're pretty sure they're after us. As far as I can see, there isn't any real reason to think they even know we're operating.'

The heavy-set man said, 'Of course they know we're operating. It's their business to know. He may have been one of them or he may not, but they'll find us sooner or later. It's up to us to know about it before they get ready to close in, that's all.'

The heavy-set man bent over the body on the packing cases and began to strip off its clothes. As he removed each garment, he went systematically through the pockets, felt the lining, and examined seams for signs of re-sewing. He found nothing that interested him.

The third man watched the search thoughtfully. He said, 'Someone will be looking for him, whoever he was. He's been around Reno for a month, and every time I saw him he was spending money. There'll be a lot of people interested in what happened to him. Maybe we ought to move along.'

'No one will be able to find anything.' The heavy-set man did not look up from his work. 'We're as safe here for a couple of weeks as we'd be anywhere, if we're careful.'

'The trouble with that is, we're not safe anywhere.'

'That's right. Did you think you were going on a picnic when you got into this?'

The other man did not answer. The heavy-set man looked at him for a moment and went back to his job.

After the body of the dead man had been stripped, the heavy-set man went to a corner of the room and came back with a gunny sack, which he threw over his shoulder. Before he bent to pick up the body, he had one or two more words to say to weasel-face.

'You aren't being paid for your brains, so I don't expect you to have any. But try to remember that whether this man was searching for us or whether he wasn't, somebody else is. A lot of people are. They're twice as harmless to look at as anyone you ever saw and five times as smart, and they don't wear tin

7

badges on their chests to advertise themselves. The only way to beat them is to find out who they are before they find out who you are. That means I want the next visitor alive and in good shape, so he can talk. Do you get it?'

Weasel-face muttered something under his breath. The heavy-set man said, 'I didn't hear you.'

'I said O.K.'

The heavy-set man bent over the packing cases and hauled the limp body to a sitting position. With the help of the others, he got the body up and across his back, and lumbered towards the door with his burden. Blood soaked the gunny sack on his shoulder.

'Come along,' he said. 'It's dark enough to get rid of this.'

The third man said, 'Are we going to work any more to-day?'

'We'll clean up the traces. Then I want to get back to the old place and pack the rest of the stuff. We'll move it to-night.'

The two men followed him from the room.

CHAPTER 2

THE chubby man with the bald spot had been dead five days.

At four o'clock on the morning of the sixth day, James Whitney drove his car around the last of the winding curves that led down from Donner Pass and stepped on the gas as the road straightened out in front of him. He was travelling faster than he should, in view of the condition of his re-caps, but it was late and he wanted to get to Reno. He knew a man there who would perform a matrimonial welding job on him and the beautiful creature who sat beside him, and he wanted the job done before the beautiful creature had too much time to think seriously about what she was getting. She had a keen sense of values, in addition to her good looks.

The bride-to-be put her nose over the collar of her fur coat and looked around.

'Where are we, Whit?'

'I don't know. We ought to be nearly there, unless they've moved the town.'

'What time is it?'

'Four o'clock.'

8

The bride-to-be yawned. 'How did you talk me into this?'

'Into what?'

'Driving to Reno in the middle of the night on five minutes notice, with a borrowed gas ration book, a trousseau in one suitcase, and not even enough to drink to make it seem sensible.'

'We decided we didn't want to wait for a California licence. Either you had more drinks than you think or your memory is failing.'

'My memory is good enough to remember that you proposed to me a year and a half ago, and it turned out to be a proposition instead of a proposal. You waited eighteen months before your conscience began to bother you. Why all the fuss now?'

Whit shrugged. 'You know how it is.'

'I don't know how it is, and I'm curious. What happened?'

'My God, Kitty. I just want to marry you, that's all. You ask the silliest questions.'

Kitty said, 'I keep on asking them, too. Something happened, and I want to know about it. What was it?'

Whit did not speak while a quarter of a mile of highway rolled by under the tyres. Kitty waited. He said abruptly, 'I'd have to tell you sooner or later, I guess. I'm going to be drafted.'

It took a moment for it to soak in. When it did, Kitty sat up straight, and anger made her voice shake. 'Draft dodging is certainly a romantic reason for marriage. You can turn around and drive back to San Francisco, as far as I'm concerned. The wedding is off.'

Whit reached over to pat the nearest bulge in the fur coat. 'Take it easy, honey. Whether I'm married or not doesn't mean anything to the draft board. You've got too much money to be a dependent, and it wouldn't make any difference, anyway. Getting drafted is my own idea. I wanted to sew you up tight before I go down to the draft board and turn myself in. You're too good-looking to leave lying around loose while I'm in an army camp.'

Kitty said, 'You're not volunteering.'

'No. I'm getting drafted.'

'But you were deferred.'

'I'm going to be undeferred.'

Kitty stared at him. He gloomily explained.

'There isn't anything less essential to a war than an income-

9

tax consultant, unless it's a piano player in a cat-house. I should have known there was something funny about my deferment when I hadn't asked for it, but I was making a lot of money and I wanted to keep the business going. So I just figured I was pretty important after all and let things ride. Then to-day – yesterday – I was talking with a client and he spilled the beans. He's Mr Big on the draft board, and I've been fighting a fifty-thousand dollar tax case for him that's going to drag on for another year or so. The son of a bitch had me deferred.'

'So you're mad at him,' Kitty said.

Whit looked at her in surprise. 'I told him to take his tax case and jump into the bay with it. What would you expect me to do – tip my hat and say thank you kindly, mister?'

Kitty shook her head. 'You're weird. What did he say?'

'He said if I felt that way, he'd see to it that I was in uniform in a couple of days. Then I said that's the way I felt and I'd see to it myself. Then I kicked his pants and threw him out. But I figured I could be spared from the army long enough to take a honeymoon, so I wrote the draft board a letter, told them I'd be available in a week, and here we are. If you still feel like it.'

He sounded unhappy.

Kitty slid across the seat, lifted his arm from the wheel, and draped it around her neck. She said softly in his ear, 'I could be persuaded.'

Whit persuaded her, giving it up just in time to drag the car back on the road by main strength. When they were once again on an even keel, he said, 'I should have told you before, but I didn't want to spoil your honeymoon. I'm afraid it's going to be kind of short.'

'A week is better than nothing. I wouldn't have liked it if you had gone away *without* marrying me.'

'Not me. I got no faith in you. Anyway, it'll be a nice peaceful week. I'm going to stop worrying about income taxes for the first time in ten years. Nothing but rest and relaxation for seven whole days.'

'I won't like the eighth day,' Kitty said.

'Neither will I. Keep your mind off it until it gets here.'

The next signpost they passed marked a wide place in the road called Verdi, and Whit knew where he was. The town was ten or eleven miles from Reno. They should be there by four-thirty.

'You'll be a bride in less than an hour,' he said. 'How does it feel?'

'It thrills me,' Kitty said, yawning. 'You don't expect to find anyone to marry us at this time of night, do you?'

'Sure. I've got connexions with a man named Pop Foster. He's a justice of the peace.'

Kitty thought it over. 'How did you develop connexions with a justice of the peace? You told me you'd never been married.'

'I lied,' Whit said. 'I've been married eleven times. Pop gives me wholesale rates.'

Kitty sniffed.

Whit said, 'He and my old man used to be in business together, years ago, before Pop got to be a J.P. I don't know what kind of justice he hands out, but he can marry us as well as the next man. And he's a nice guy.'

'He must be, if you expect him to marry us to-night. Anyone who came around knocking on my door at this hour of the morning would get the hose turned on him.'

'People are used to it in Reno. It's illegal to sleep.'

Reno was living up to Whit's promise when they arrived. All the gambling joints were open, and even at that late hour there were enough suckers out to make business good for those on the right side of the tables. Whit, for the first time in several trips to Reno, did not immediately join the suckers. He found an all-night drug store where he could get directions. Kitty waited in the car.

Whit returned in a few minutes with his directions written on a piece of scratch paper, and a package that could only contain a quart bottle of something. He turned the car around and headed back in the direction from which they had come.

Kitty said, 'Now what?'

'Pop's moved since I was here last. He's living out at that village we passed coming in – Verdi. A gallon and a half of gas gone to hell, just like that.'

'What's the bottle for?'

'A little bribe. I know Pop won't take anything for marrying us, but he's never been known to refuse a drink.'

It was five o'clock before they reached Verdi. Whit's scratch-

11

paper map took them away from the highway and left them high and dry on a back road where any of several houses could have been the one they were looking for. They finally found the right place by examining mail boxes along the road with a flashlight until they came to one with the name Foster on it. The house belonging to the mail box was set back some distance from the road in a neat yard surrounded by white pickets. They found a gate and started up the gravelled path.

At the first sound of their feet on the gravel, a dog began to bark from the rear of the house. It was an unusually dirty bark, and it said clearly that the dog wouldn't waste his breath making noise if he could only get at them. They heard a chain rattle as the dog lunged at it, howling.

Kitty clutched at Whit's arm. 'He sounds mean. I hope he's tied tightly.'

'So do I. With the meat situation what it is, I wouldn't want —'

Whit stopped, blinking.

A flood of light had come on, surrounding the house. Not only was the wide porch ahead of them lighted, but the entire yard inside the picket fence was illuminated brightly by unshaded light globes hanging from wires which radiated from the house to the surrounding trees. One light burned almost directly over their heads. Behind the house the dog kept up his howling, jumping at the chain.

Whit said, 'I guess that's the welcome sign. Pop sure likes plenty of light, doesn't he? You could play night baseball under those things.'

'Why doesn't he turn on a light inside?' The house itself, except for the porch, remained dark.

'You got me. Let's find out.'

They continued down the path. The gravel crunched under their feet, and the unseen dog barked furiously.

The door of the house was open about six inches when they reached the porch. They could see a man's face looking at them, but the light did not shine through the doorway and Whit could only tell that it was not Pop Foster. The man inside the house said flatly, 'What do you want?'

'We're looking for Pop Foster,' Whit said. 'We saw his name on the mail box out in front.'

'What do you want with him?'

Whit didn't like the guy's attitude. Before he could make up his mind whether to answer politely or ask what the hell business it was of anybody's why he wanted to see anyone, there was a movement in the dark and a second voice said something in a low tone. Another face appeared in the doorway and looked them over. After a moment the door opened and a light came on inside. They went in.

Two men faced them as they entered. The man who had opened the door was stocky, heavily built through the chest and shoulders, grey-haired, and pleasant-looking except for his eyes, which were a peculiar pale blue. He had a dressing-gown over his wrinkled pyjamas, and wore bedroom slippers. The second man was smaller, thinner, younger. He had a weasel's face – long nose, small eyes, and not much chin – and his rumpled hair was greasy. He wore pyjamas also, but they weren't his own; the legs had been turned up at the bottom so they wouldn't drag on the floor. Instead of a dressing-gown and slippers, he had on a black overcoat, buttoned across his waist, and unlaced shoes on his bare feet.

The heavy-set man smiled with the bottom part of his face. His eyes didn't change. 'Good evening.'

Whit said, 'Evening. Is Pop Foster here?'

'What do you want to see him about?' It was the question they had heard before, only the tone was a little more polite. The politeness was as superficial as the smile.

Whit said pleasantly, 'It's personal.' The heavy-set man could make something out of that, if he wanted to. Whit didn't feel like handing out his birth certificate every time some strange mug asked him to.

The man looked him over for a moment, then briefly at Kitty, and made up his mind. He turned towards the stairs leading from the hallway to the second storey and raised his voice.

'Pop! Come down here. You've got visitors.' He motioned to the weasel-face. 'Go shut up that hound and turn off the lights.'

The weasel-face scowled suspiciously at Whit as he went out. Whit didn't notice the scowl. He was listening to the slapping noise of slippers coming down the stairs.

There had been no time for anyone to come to the head of the stairway after the heavy-set man had called. Whoever wore the slippers had been waiting there in the dark, listening to the conversation below. And if it were Pop Foster, he was taking orders from the heavy-set man. The call up the stairway had been a demand.

Pop came down into the light, tugging at the cord of a heavy woollen bathrobe. He feigned a look of amazement as he saw Whit. 'Well, Whit! This is a surprise, boy. What are you doing here?'

'Hello, Pop.'

Whit's own surprise was genuine. He had not seen the old man for two or three years, but he remembered him as a little round, jolly gnome with white hair, something like a clean-shaven welterweight Santa Claus, who liked to drink and tell tall tales of the bad old days – a pleasant sinner who laughed a lot and enjoyed life. Pop's hair was whiter now, and there was not so much of it. He had lost weight, too, and the lines in his face had not been there before. The most noticeable change was that his hearty welcome did not seem genuine. He had always been fond of Whit.

Pop pumped Whit's hand. The heavy-set man waited in the background. Pop said nervously, 'What are you doing here at this time of night? You didn't come all the way to Nevada just to call on old Pop Foster, did you?'

'I sure did.' Whit took Kitty's arm and urged her forward. 'I thought I'd give you a little business while I was here. This is Kitty McLeod. We want you to marry us.'

'Well, well.' Some of Pop's nervousness went away. He patted Kitty's hand in his own. 'I'm happy to meet you, young lady. Always knew Whit would get himself a winner.'

Kitty said, 'I'm happy to meet you too, Pop. I hope you don't mind callers at five o'clock in the morning.'

'I like callers any time. Particularly at five in the morning.' Pop patted Kitty's hand again. 'I wouldn't miss seeing you for a million. I told Whit years ago that when someone landed him I wanted to perform the ceremony. You're a lucky girl to get him. He's a great boy.'

'I think so too.'

Kitty knew that her conversation was not brilliant, but she couldn't help it. There was something in the air that made her uneasy. The heavy-set man in the background was watching Whit like a hawk.

14

Pop saw Kitty look at the heavy-set man. He said, 'This is Walter Gates. He's an old friend of mine.'

The heavy-set man smiled and nodded his head to acknowledge the introduction. His pale blue eyes did not change expression.

Kitty said, 'How do you do?'

Whit said, 'Hello.' He didn't care how Walter Gates did. He didn't like Walter Gates for sour apples.

The conversation sagged there. Kitty looked at the heavy-set man, the heavy-set man looked at Whit, and Whit looked at Pop. Before the silence began to grow uncomfortable, Pop said loudly, 'Well, we might as well go inside where it's warm.'

He led the way through a doorway and switched on the light.

The room was a big Victorian parlour, full of red plush furniture. There were gilt-framed pictures on the walls: The Lone Wolf, The Stag at Bay, The End of the Trail, and several more of the same breed. An enormous airtight stove and a wood-box took up one end of the room, and at the opposite end there was an old-fashioned red plush settee. A couple of blankets and a pillow were rumpled on the settee, and a man's clothes were tossed over the nearest chair. One of Pop's guests had been sleeping under a handicap. Whit guessed that it was the weasel-face, because Walter Gates would have overflowed the narrow couch like a double mattress on a single bed. And Gates looked like someone who wouldn't put up with discomfort if anyone else could be persuaded to do it.

The weasel-face came in while Pop was stirring up coals in the big stove. Pop introduced him as Sammy Kohler, without explaining his status. Whit didn't like Sammy any more than he liked Walter Gates, on general principles, and particularly because Sammy shook hands with Kitty, holding on until she pulled away. Sammy grinned when she disengaged her hand, and Kitty was flustered. Whit saw the by-play. He tucked Sammy away in his head for future reference, just in case an opportunity to rearrange the weasel-face should present itself some day.

Pop finished with the stove and stood up, rubbing his hands. 'Sit down, sit down. It'll warm up in a minute. Let me take your coat, young lady. Might as well make yourself comfortable.'

15

'No, thank you. I – we aren't going to stay long. I'll —'

'Nonsense. Can't get married in a fur coat.'

Pop helped Kitty take it off. She looked unhappily at Whit, and he smiled encouragement. He didn't like the atmosphere any more than she did, but he didn't know what to do about it – not until he found out what was wrong.

When Pop came to take Whit's own coat and hat, Whit discovered he still had the bottle of whisky under his arm. He said, 'Here, Pop. I brought you something for your arteries.'

'That's nice of you, boy.' Pop took the package and disposed of the coats on a chair. 'I guess we've got something to celebrate. You don't get married every day. I'll go find some glasses and we'll all have a drink to warm us up.'

He started towards the door through which Sammy Kohler had entered.

Gates, leaning against the wall near the other doorway, said, 'Sammy will do it, Pop. You don't have to trouble yourself.'

Pop stopped obediently. Gates nodded his head at Kohler, and Kohler took the bottle from Pop's hands and left the room. Pop came back and poked unnecessarily at the fire in the stove.

Gates said to Whit, 'Just arrive to-night?'

'Yes.'

'Where from?'

'We drove in from San Francisco.'

'Pretty hard to get enough gas to drive that far, isn't it?'

'It sure is.'

Gates should have been discouraged, but he wasn't. He said, 'Just come up to get married?'

Whit's only wish was to get married and get the hell out of the place. Gates irritated him, Pop irritated him, and the whole set-up irritated him because he didn't know what was going on. He felt more like asking questions of his own than answering them, but Kitty was already uneasy. If he pointed out to Gates that Gates was being entirely too nosey, something would probably happen to disturb her further.

He said, 'Mostly that. We thought we'd try some of the gambling joints in Reno for a few days, do a little horse-back riding and look over the country. Combination vacation and honeymoon, more or less.'

Gates turned to Kitty, 'Do you like to ride?'

'What?' Kitty had been watching Pop's nervous putterings. 'Oh, yes. Very much.'

'You'll find some very interesting country around here. It's a little wild, though. You have to be careful where you go.'

'I imagine so.'

Sammy broke up the conversation by coming back with the opened bottle and whisky glasses. There was no ice and no mixer. Pop proposed a laboriously gallant toast to the bride, and they all drank.

Gates' hands, as Whit saw when the man lifted his glass, were those of someone who had worked with tools. The nails were broken and discoloured, and the skin around the nails was darkly engrained. The hands were not dirty from lack of soap and water, but the grease had worked in too far to come out with a scrubbing.

Whit looked at the hands and wondered why Mr Gates, who clearly gave orders, was a worker, while Pop and Sammy Kohler, who just as clearly took the orders, had such nice clean cuticle. He poured a second round of drinks, putting as much whisky in the small glasses as they would hold. Someone might loosen up and talk before the bottle was gone. But Pop, for the first time to Whit's knowledge, was not interested in another drink. He said earnestly, 'Not now. Not now. Let's get on with the wedding.'

Gates and Sammy Kohler were to be the witnesses. Pop bustled around nervously, placing Whit and Kitty together in front of the stove and Gates and Kohler on either side. When they were all set, he produced a Bible.

'There we are,' he said. 'Now let me have the licence, Whit. You've got the ring?'

Whit said blankly, 'I've got a ring. I didn't know we needed a licence in Nevada. That's why we came here.'

He was looking at Pop as he spoke, and he saw fright spring into the old man's face. Then Pop's eyes skittered sideways towards Gates. Whit turned his head.

Gates said slowly, 'I'm afraid that's a pretty serious mistake.' The menace in his voice could not be mistaken.

CHAPTER 3

WHIT'S normal disposition was inclined to curdle anyway at five in the morning, and he had put up with all the hocus-pocus he wanted for one night. He took three quick steps and came face to face with Gates.

'All right,' he said. His voice was ugly. 'I've had enough of this.. What are you driving at?'

Gates did not give an inch, although Whit stood over him by half a head. His pale eyes looked searchingly into Whit's face. 'So you want to be married?'

'Yes. And I'm damned if I can see what business it is of yours or anyone else's.'

Behind Whit's back, Sammy Kohler said, 'Don't try to —'

'Shut up.' Gates' eyes did not move. 'You came here at five in the morning to get married, without a licence?'

'That's what I said, and that's what I mean. What's it to you?' Whit was aching for something to start while his anger was hot. He stood spraddle-legged, his feet solidly planted, ready to belt Gates with both hands when the ice broke.

'Ah, Walter,' Sammy Kohler said pleadingly. 'Let me —'

'Shut up,' Gates repeated. 'Pop. Did you know he was coming?'

'No. No.' Pop's voice behind Whit was a shaky croak. 'He's telling the truth, Walter. I know he's telling the truth. Let him go.'

Whit whirled around. 'Nobody has to let me go any place. I'll go whenever I get good and ready. Pop, you old fool, straighten up. For God's sake, what's the matter?'

Pop shook his head miserably. He did not look up.

Nobody moved for a moment after that. Except for Pop, slumped in a chair with his head in his hands, they all watched Whit. Sammy Kohler was facing him now. He had his hands in the pockets of the black overcoat, and Whit knew all of a sudden that whatever was going on, he was into something too deep and too dangerous to handle by slugging people. Weasel-face had a gun in his overcoat pocket. It didn't bulge the coat perceptibly, but Whit knew it was there. He could practically smell it. And from the sudden cold feeling just below his navel, he knew where it was pointing.

It chilled his fury instantly. He had to get Kitty out of this. He could tell from her pale face how scared she was, but she had not caught the significance of Sammy's Kohler's position. Whit counted to ten as slowly as he could manage, being careful not to look again at Kohler, counted five more so the transition would not be too quick, and turned back to face Gates.

'I give up.' He was the picture of a man whose will-power controlled a hot head. 'What's it all about?'

'What's what all about?'

The question encouraged Whit. He might be able to talk himself and Kitty out of it after all. Whatever Gates had believed a moment ago, he was not sure now.

'Why, the excitement because we forgot the marriage licence.'

'Nobody is excited but you,' Gates said. 'I'm just surprised that you'd forget anything that important. You're sure you didn't overlook the ring, too?'

Whit said pleasantly, 'Ah, now you're ribbing me.' He smiled. His face felt stiff, like a pumpkin-head with a broad grin cut into it.

It seemed that Gates would never answer. Whit kept the pumpkin-head smile on his face with an effort, conscious of Kohler behind him and the small cold spot that had moved from under his navel to the middle of his back. He tried to make his breathing sound normal. Gates finally opened his mouth.

'I guess you'll just have to wait a while for the wedding.'

The cold spot turned into a drop of sweat and ran down Whit's backbone. It was a great relief. 'I guess we will,' he said. He turned around, not too quickly. 'We might as well get along, Kitty.'

As the tension broke, Pop began to talk aimlessly about nothing. No one paid any attention to him, but the sound of his voice eased the atmosphere while Whit collected Kitty's coat and his own. Sammy Kohler stayed where he was, his hands in his pockets, still watching Whit.

'— plenty of people to marry you in Reno,' Pop was saying. 'Get a licence in three-four hours when the county clerk's office opens, and have the knot tied in ten minutes. 'Course I'd like to do it myself, but there's no sense in you driving all the way out here again. Besides —'

'You don't sound very hospitable, Pop,' Gates said. 'Mr Whitney came all the way from San Francisco to have you perform the ceremony. Maybe he doesn't want anyone else to do it.'

The fright came back into Pop's face. He shut up.

Whit said, 'We've disturbed you enough for one night, Pop. We'll be married in town.'

'I – I'd be happy to do it,' Pop said nervously. 'I just thought —'

'I know, Pop. Thanks, anyway.'

That was the end of their jolly little visit to an old friend. Pop came to the door with them, but Walter Gates was right behind him, and Whit did not have a chance to talk to the old man. Pop's lined face showed a mixture of misery and relief as he switched on the porch light – the yard lights did not function this time – and said good-bye.

'You – won't be coming back?' It was almost a plea.

'Not to-day, Pop. Maybe soon. What time does the county clerk open up?'

'Nine o'clock, I think. I'm not sure. My – my memory isn't so good any more. I'm getting old, Whit.'

The plea was there again – for forgiveness and understanding.

'Well, we'll wait up for him. Good-bye. Good luck.'

There was nothing else that could be said. Whit slipped Kitty's hand under his arm and they left the porch. The dog in the back of the house barked loudly as they walked up the gravelled path.

The porch light went out as they got in the car. Kitty was very quiet. Whit did not pay much attention to her as they drove away, because he was too busy watching the rear-view mirror. He did not drive fast, but after five minutes there were still no headlights behind them. He heaved a long sigh of relief.

'I guess they aren't coming after us. God, what an experience.'

He looked at Kitty as he spoke. She did not answer him. The light from the dashboard was enough to let him see her face, and he stopped the car quickly at the side of the road. When he reached for her, she came limply towards him, and he slipped his arms around her body inside the coat and held her close.

After a long while she said something into his lapel. He turned her head to one side and kissed her. Her lips were cold. He said, 'What?'

'I was scared.'

He kissed her again. Her mouth was not so cold this time. He said, 'We were both scared.'

'What was it about?'

'I'm damned if I know.'

He bent his head to kiss her a third time, and was pleased to find a reasonable amount of fire in her response. Everything was going to be all right.

'I thought you were going to hit him. You were so mad.'

'I intended to hit him. I changed my mind when I turned around and saw rat-face. He had a gun.'

'Whit!' Kitty jerked her head up from his shoulder.

'He sure did. It was staring me right in the belly-button, too. I damn near fainted.'

Kitty said shakily. 'Oh, my. What a wedding night. Let's get out of here, quick.'

Whit released her and started the car. 'They're not after us. You don't need to worry now.'

'I'm not worried. I want to get back to Reno.'

'Sleepy?'

'I'll never be able to sleep again. I just want to go to some place where I can see people – a lot of nice, plain, ordinary people.'

*

Walter Gates gave Pop Foster a bad few minutes after the visitors had gone, but although he hammered questions at him mercilessly he could not shake Pop's story that the old man had not seen Whit nor heard from him for two or three years. Pop was wrung out like a rag when Gates finally dismissed him and sent him to bed. Gates himself stayed downstairs. He had to think.

Sammy Kohler did not know how to think, but he had ideas and he liked to talk. Gates gave him no encouragement. He answered Sammy either in monosyllables or not at all. Sammy eventually gave up, wrapped himself in his blankets, and went to sleep on the red plush settee.

Gates sat for a while looking at the flicker of flames in the isinglass peephole of the stove. When Sammy had begun to breathe noisily through his mouth, Gates went to the back of the hallway, where there was a telephone in a cubby-hole under the stairs.

The bell rang several times at the far end, after he put in his call. Finally a man's sleepy voice said, 'Hello.'

'This is Walter Gates, Jess. I want to talk to you.'

The man at the other end of the line woke up quickly. 'What's happened?'

'Not on the phone. I'm coming into town right away. Wait up for me.'

Gates hung up, without waiting for an answer, and went to get his clothes.

There was a Ford delivery truck in the garage at the back of the yard, behind the cottage. The dog chained near the house lifted his head and growled as Gates came out of the back door, but Gates spoke to him sharply and the dog was quiet. Gates got the delivery truck out of the garage and drove away in the direction of Reno.

The light truck made good time on the empty highway. Twenty minutes after he left Verdi, Gates parked near an apartment house on the heights overlooking downtown Reno from the south side of the river. The neighbourhood was much too swank for a shabby delivery truck. Gates did not stop directly in front of the apartment house, but left the truck around the corner, where it would be in the shadow. He walked back to the apartment house and looked around carefully before he pressed one of the buttons under the bank of mail boxes in the doorway. The electrically controlled door-latch clicked open immediately.

An automatic elevator took him to the apartment on the top floor of the building. The man who waited for him there in pyjamas and a dressing-gown was the man who had been with Gates and Sammy Kohler when they watched the chubby stranger die on the packing cases six days earlier.

There were no greetings exchanged. Gates said, 'I think we're going to have trouble.'

'What happened?'

22

'A young fellow came to Foster's house with a girl, about an hour ago. They said they wanted to get married. He knew Foster, and Foster swears he's known him all his life, but when it came to the ceremony they didn't have a licence. It looked to me as if they might have come to see what information they could get from Foster, not expecting to find anyone else there, and thought up an excuse on the spur of the moment when they saw what they were up against.'

'They're clever enough not to send anyone without a more convincing story than that.'

'They're clever enough so that we can't take chances. I want you to pick up this fellow – his name's Whitney – and see what you can learn.'

'Where is he now?'

'Here in Reno. He and the girl left Foster's house an hour ago.'

The other man's face showed his surprise. 'Why didn't you stop them?'

'I'm not going to stop anything or start anything until I have more to go on. They said they were coming into town to kill time until the county clerk's office opens, and if they do you'll be able to find them somewhere on Virginia Street. I want to know if they get married.'

'A wedding wouldn't prove anything. They'd go through with it to keep up the bluff, if they thought they had to.'

'They might. But if there *isn't* a wedding, I'll know what to do about it. We could get some useful information from Whitney if he's what I think he is.'

'Have you talked to Renzo? He gets most of the luxury trade in town when it's this late.'

'I'll call him while you're getting dressed. Hurry it up.'

Gates went to the telephone across the room. The other man hesitated, as if he were going to protest against being dragged out in the middle of the night. Then, as Gates made an impatient gesture, he went into the bedroom.

Gates had to give his name when his call was answered, and wait a few minutes until his man came to the phone. He said, 'This is Walter Gates. I want you to watch for a man and a girl who may turn up there this morning. He's big – six feet or better, heavy, dark hair, clean shaven, about thirty-five. He's wearing a brown sports coat and slacks. The girl is a brunette, pretty, looks like money and class. Fur coat and black dress.'

The man at the other end of the line said, 'I'll look for them. But I've got a girl of my own here who might develop into something entertaining, Walter. I don't want to —'

Gates cut him off. 'Forget about your floozies and do what you're told. If you see these people, keep them entertained until Jess gets there to take over. This is important.'

'All right, all right. What's up?'

'Trouble.'

Gates put the phone back in its cradle and went into the bedroom.

CHAPTER 4

THERE were not very many towns where Kitty could have found a lot of nice plain ordinary people to mingle with at the shank-end of the morning. Reno was one of the few.

The joints lining Virginia and Centre streets had adopted twenty-four-hour-seven-day operations long before other and more essential industries had got around to it as a result of the war effort. Most of the loot that flowed across the gambling tables into the hands of the local operators came from the transient trade, and the transient trade often didn't have much time to waste losing its money. Since all of the games were reasonably honest, only time and the house percentage worked against the customers, and every hour that a gambling joint shut down was money out of pocket. As a result, there were no shut-downs.

Whit and Kitty picked the dive nearest to the spot where they parked the car upon their return to Reno. They headed first for the bar. Kitty was not a drinking woman ordinarily – not at such an uncivilized hour, anyway – but her nerves were still twanging from her experience with the mysterious Walter Gates and company, and she needed something to tune them down. Whit would drink anything, any time, and particularly after strange weasels had just finished poking guns at him, so they sat on a couple of nice plain ordinary stools at the nice plain ordinary bar and ordered a couple of double highballs from a bartender who looked like a nice plain ordinary cut-throat. The bar was not very well patronized at that hour, but there were plenty of people nearby at the dice-tables and the blackjack layouts. It was just like being home again.

Neither of them had anything to say until the first drink began to get in its foul work on their stomach linings. Then Kitty looked around the smoky room and said contentedly, 'Oh, my, this is lovely.'

'It's an improvement.' Whit motioned to the bartender. 'Do it again, will you? Put some liquor in them this time.'

It hurt the bartender's feelings. He took the empty glasses away, filled them with whisky, sprayed the whisky with a thin film of seltzer water, and brought the glasses back. Whit tasted the drink and nodded.

'That's better. Here's to your bonny blue eyes, Mrs Whitney-to-be.'

'I'll drink to my bonny blue eyes. But I'm not going to be Mrs Whitney if we have to go back to that place to be married. I'd rather live in sin.'

'We won't go back.'

'Have you any idea what it was all about?'

'Nope.'

'Did that nasty little man really have a gun?'

'Yep. He wanted to use it, too. He was waiting for the other guy to give him the word.'

Kitty shuddered. She drank half of her second drink in a gulp, without tasting it.

Whit said, 'I sure wish I could figure it out. The whole set-up was funny; those lights, and the dog, and the way what's-his-name – Gates – watched us all the time. And Pop was scared silly. He's changed a lot since I saw him last, Kitty. Something has been going on for a long time, to make him look so bad.'

'He was certainly frightened, poor man.'

Whit contemplatively twirled his glass. 'I ought to try to find out what's bothering him.'

'Whit, if you go back to that place again, I'll leave you.'

'You can't leave me legally until you marry me. And I didn't say I was going back. I just thought I ought to try to help Pop out of whatever spot he's in, if I can. He and my old man were pretty good friends.'

'Don't talk about it to-night,' Kitty said. 'I'm just now getting over the jitters. Let's go play roulette for a while, until it's time to get the licence. We can think about Pop afterward. Please.'

'O.K.'

They had another drink and left the bar, mildly cockeyed. They both felt much better for it.

The roulette wheel took twenty dollars of Whit's money and paid it over to Kitty with a little extra to boot. Whit was disgusted. He played roulette with an accountant's eye on the percentages, while Kitty chunked her money in on any number that struck her fancy, and the longer the odds the better. Whit finally came to the conclusion that the wheel hadn't heard of the law of probabilities. He left Kitty optimistically stacking chips on the double zero, and wandered away to the nearest crap table.

The dice hadn't heard of the law of probabilities either. After another twenty dollars' worth of bad luck, Whit went back to gather up Kitty and her winnings. She was ahead considerably more than he had lost, and he spent a futile few minutes trying to convince her that since they were practically married, the money was community property under Nevada law and therefore half his. She wouldn't fall for it. They moved down the street to the next place.

It was the same story there, only it didn't take so long for Whit to lose his money with the dice, or for Kitty to hit a preposterous seventeen-to-one shot at the wheel. She baulked at being dragged away while she was winning, but Whit was determined to find a pair of hot dice somewhere. As a C.P.A. and a mathematician, he knew he would lose his shirt sooner or later if he bucked the house percentage, but as a confirmed gambler he was sure that he could find the right combination if he kept trying. Also, the place they were in didn't have a bar attached, and he was getting dry.

The sky was beginning to turn grey in the east when they got out in the street. Their next stop was at an ultra-ultra dive flaunting the name LORENZO'S CLUB. The management went in for thick carpets, evening clothes on the bouncers, a dance floor for those customers who wanted more exercise than they could get pulling the handle of a slot machine – there were none at that late hour – and a hat-check girl in very short skirts. The skirts were justified by the most elegant legs that Whit had seen in years of research. He whinnied gently under his breath when the girl gave him a check and a smile and went away with the coats.

Kitty said, 'Stop it.'

'I didn't say anything.'

'Stop acting like a goat every time you see something female.'

'I wasn't acting like a goat. I was just thinking.'

'Well, stop thinking.'

'Yes'm.'

Kitty headed for the roulette table, over his protests, and the vicious circle began again. Whit's money moved from his hands into the croupier's bank and back to Kitty. It didn't make him feel better because she won more than he lost. She wasn't scientific but she was hot. Whit finally gave up his scientific betting and put his chips where Kitty put hers, just to see if he could capitalize on her streak. They both lost. She chased him away.

He made a detour to the change booth for more working capital and arrived at the dice games with a pocketful of silver dollars. Two tables were open to crap shooters. One of them was run by a henna-haired female with a hard face who was getting a play from three or four night-owls when Whit arrived. The other was unpatronized, possibly because the house-man was a house-man and not a woman. The red-head was no glamour girl, but Whit didn't want to take a chance that Kitty would accuse him of acting like a goat again. He picked the unpopular table.

The house-man without customers was a slim young fellow with slick blond hair, a pool-room pallor, and a short apron. He was killing time by flipping a pair of dice along the side of the boxed-in table so that they spun like tops on the green felt. He looked up as Whit approached.

'Morning.' The dice danced across the table and spun to a stop in front of Whit. 'Crowd right in, mister. It's your turn.'

'Heavy business to-night?'

'It's usually slack about this time. The night-hawks are folding up, and the morning crowd comes in after breakfast.'

'I'll give you a little trade for a while. How about fading a couple of bucks?'

The house-man patted the rack of coins in front of him. It held two or three hundred dollars in silver. 'I guess I can handle it. Roll them out.'

Whit rolled them out.

He had an entertaining few minutes for his pocketful of dollars, but the law of probabilities was still suspended. The dice did everything but bite his fingers. When he had lost his pocketful of coins and another pocketful he got in exchange for a bill, the house-man bought him a drink and joined him with a coca-cola.

'That's quite a streak you had there, mister,' he said. 'I never saw anyone lay so many eggs in a row before. You must have done something real bad in your lifetime.'

'I'm lucky at love,' Whit said drearily. 'I can't win.'

'I thought that just cooled you off at cards.'

'Cards, dice, matching pennies, mumbly-peg, it's all the same.'

'She must be a queen, to make you that salty.'

'She is.' Whit jerked his thumb over his shoulder. 'Over by the roulette wheel, if you're curious.'

The house-man looked over by the roulette wheel. 'The brunette in the black dress?'

'That's her.'

'She's worth losing money for. But if I were you I wouldn't crowd my good luck too far, mister. Not around here. The guy she's talking to is a wolf.'

Whit turned around.

He hadn't been keeping an eye on Kitty while the dice were growling at him, and meanwhile things were going on behind his back. The roulette table had become very popular since he left it. Kitty had been joined by two men and a girl in evening clothes, and seemed to be on friendly terms with all of them. The dice-man's critical comment had been directed at one of the men, a Latin menace in a white-tie and tail-coat.

Whit wasn't worried about anybody poaching on his territory – Kitty had pinned back wolf-ears before, without help – but he was mildly curious. He said, 'Who's the pretty boy?'

'He owns the place. His name's Lorenzo Colusa, and I wouldn't trust him within twenty feet of my seventy-nine-year-old grandmother. If you know what I mean.'

'Uh huh. Who are the others?'

'The guy is one of the regulars. The girl I've seen around a couple of times. I don't know their names.'

'Your boss probably just came around to see what had gone

28

wrong with his roulette wheel. My girl has been milking the house all night.'

The dice-man shook his head. 'I wouldn't count on it. Lorenzo kind of likes the way he gets along with the ladies.'

'I'm not worried. Look, I'll show you.'

Whit took the remaining coins from his pocket, dropped them on the line, and simultaneously threw the dice he held in his other hand. They came up six-six at the far end of the table. The dice-man raked in the money.

'See what I mean?' Whit said. 'Lucky at love, damn it. Fat chance your boss has against that.'

He walked away. The dice-man watched him join the group around the roulette wheel.

Kitty's hot streak was still holding up, and she had forgotten all about her experiences earlier in the evening. Her eyes sparkled with the excitement of gambling. She pointed to her stack of counters and crowed as Whit came up.

'Look at that, I'm breaking the bank.'

'That'll help. I just lost enough to start a new one.'

The Latin menace flashed his teeth at Whit. 'That's what keeps us in business.'

Kitty made the introductions.

'This is Mr Colusa, Whit. Lorenzo of Lorenzo's Club. He groans every time I win. Miss Warren, Mr Caldwell. Mr Whitney.'

'I haven't groaned yet, but I may get to it.' Lorenzo of Lorenzo's Club flashed his gorgeous teeth again as he shook Whit's hand. 'I'm happy to meet you, Mr Whitney.'

Whit said something polite, shook hands with the second man, and bowed to the girl.

His reaction to everyone but the Latin menace was favourable. Lorenzo was too handsome. In addition to the teeth, he had beautiful wavy black hair and a profile. The other man seemed like a fair kind of Joe Doakes; not handsome, not homely, not big, not little. The person who impressed Whit most was Miss Warren. He wondered what Kitty would do if he whinnied.

Miss Warren was a pocket-size taffy blonde with an amazingly beautiful figure encased in an evening gown that fitted her like the skin on a weenie. She was moderately drunk. Her face didn't quite go with the figure; it was a doll's face, and it was easy to see that she wouldn't be a stimulating conversationalist during the long winter evenings. But for long winter evenings *without* conversation —

' . . . have, Whit?' Kitty said.

'I beg your pardon?'

'I said, Lorenzo wants us to have a drink.'

Whit brought his mind back from the long winter evenings with Miss Warren. The Latin menace might be something of a wolf at that, if he could get Kitty to call him by his first name in the time he had known her.

'Thanks.' He calculated his losses quickly. 'How about some champagne? I feel like celebrating.'

'Certainly. We'll all celebrate. What's the occasion?' Lorenzo raised his hand, beckoning to a waiter.

'I'm about to be drafted.' Whit hadn't expected his suggestion of champagne to be taken seriously. 'You order, but it's on me. I'll buy it out of my losses.'

'Not at all. This is with the compliments of the house. Nothing is too good for the armed forces.'

Lorenzo gave an order to the waiter who had come up in answer to his signal.

At that point Whit's low suspicious mind began to make ticking noises. He was willing to believe that there were gamblers who either didn't mind having the suckers win once in a while or who could put up a front that it wasn't breaking their hearts. But champagne for a pair of strangers, when one of the strangers had already tagged the bank for a couple of hundred dollars? A mickey finn, maybe, not champagne. Not unless there was a reason for it. Maybe the guy *was* a wolf.

The waiter arrived with the bottle in an ice-basket. It was good champagne, and very expensive. Whit took a closer look at Kitty's new acquaintances while they drank.

Caldwell and the blonde girl were bucking the wheel, following Kitty's plays and making money at it. The blonde giggled at something Caldwell said as he reached across the table to stack counters on a number. Whit's eyes followed Caldwell's hand. The fingers showed the same scrubbed griminess that Whit had seen on Walter Gates' hands, earlier that evening.

Things began to make a hazy sort of picture after that. It was hard to tell what the picture meant, but Walter Gates and Caldwell were together in it somewhere. Two non-labouring men in the same evening, both with dirty hands and both interested in the same strangers, seemed like more than a coincidence. In San Francisco, it would have been an even chance that they were both patriotically handling a shift in the shipyards in their spare time. But in Reno there were no shipyards. And even if there were some legitimate dirty work they could have had their hands in, why free champagne?

Whit looked at Lorenzo's hands, one of which was then resting on Kitty's arm. The nails were clean and beautifully manicured.

The croupier spun his wheel and the little ball went round and round. Kitty laughed as Lorenzo pretended concern over his losses. Whit smiled mechanically and thought, God, I'm getting imaginative. I guess I need some sleep.

He drank another mouthful of Lorenzo's good wine.

Sleep or no sleep, the champagne was the real McCoy. It was too good to give away without an equally good reason for it. But what reason was there? Whit and Kitty were harmless; people had no cause to get itchy trigger fingers because of them, or buy them champagne either. Yet in the last three hours Walter Gates, his man Kohler, Lorenzo and Caldwell had all developed sudden interests because an accountant and his girl had come to Reno to be married. Something was very smelly somewhere.

Whit listened carefully to the talk around the table for a while, and kept his eyes open. Nothing was said or done that meant anything. He did learn that the blonde's name was Gladys, that she didn't like the way Lorenzo was bending his profile at Kitty, and that she was counter-attacking by turning her glamour loose on Caldwell, whose name was Jess and who was stone-blind to glamour, in a polite way. Gladys couldn't understand it. Neither could Whit. If Gladys were to blink her big beautiful eyes at him the way she did at Jess Caldwell, he would at least be gentleman enough to give her some encouragement. But Caldwell, damn him, did nothing at all. He was polite with everyone, his conversation was amusing and without significance, and he did nothing. He was just there, with his dirty fingernails.

It began to get tiresome after a while, waiting for something to happen that didn't happen. Whit looked at his watch and put his empty glass in the ice bucket.

'You've made expenses for one night, Kitty. Let's move along. It's after eight o'clock.'

The objections were immediate and unanimous from the other roulette players. A rabbit's foot like Kitty didn't turn up every night. If Whit took her away, he would be taking money right out of their pockets.

'It's the first time I've won in years,' Gladys complained. 'I don't see why you have to go now.'

Jess Caldwell joined in with his protest. 'Oh, wait a while. In another hour I'll get back all I've paid Lorenzo in the last three months.'

'Maybe I should go before we take all of your money, Lorenzo,' Kitty said apologetically.

Lorenzo shrugged and smiled. 'It's there to take. A good gambler never leaves while he's winning.'

Kitty looked questioningly at Whit.

'Me or the roulette wheel,' he said. 'I've been up two nights in a row. If you want to accomplish anything to-day, you'd better move. We've got to get a licence and find a justice of the peace before I fall asleep on my feet.'

'So the secret is finally out,' Caldwell said. 'You're getting married.'

'That's the general idea.'

'In that case, I withdraw my objection. And to make sure you don't get led astray. I'll go with you.' He pushed his counters across the table to the banker. 'Cash me in.'

Gladys said promptly, 'Lorenzo isn't much fun any more, and I love weddings. I'm going, too.'

There was no way to avoid them without being deliberately nasty, so Whit said nothing. Kitty did not seem to mind. Lorenzo was sorry he had to stay behind, but he had a business to take care of. Whit rather thought he had hoped to take care of the blonde as well, before the party was over. Lorenzo gave Caldwell a dirty look as Gladys attached herself to Caldwell. But Lorenzo was a good loser, as far as money went. He flashed his teeth at Kitty and invited her – and her husband, of course – to come back and take more of his money whenever she felt like it. He would be glad to see her any time – and her husband, of course.

Whit said, 'Yeh, sure.'

Kitty was still full of life when they left the club with their new friends. Whit did his best to liven up a bit, but it was a hard job. He was dog-tired, the drinks had worn off, and he felt a gloomy premonition that Caldwell had a reason for clinging to them like a limpet on a rock. Every time he looked at Caldwell's hands he thought of Gates, and every time he thought of Gates he saw weasel-face Kohler with his hands in the pockets of the black overcoat. It was a hell of a state of mind for a man about to be married.

The coloured doorman outside the club tootled his whistle for a cab as the party came down the steps, and grinned and bobbed his head as Caldwell put a bill in his white glove. Whit's car was a block up the street. He weighed the number of gas tickets in his ration book against the possibility that he and Kitty were about to be snatched by Caldwell and the cab-driver, and decided that if there was going to be a snatch there was going to be a snatch. There was no sense in wasting his gasoline on his own kidnapping.

He felt faintly amused by his own morbid thoughts while he stood with Kitty waiting for a cab in the bright early morning sunshine. Another hour without sleep and he'd develop a persecution complex. Then the pair of cowboys who were clumping up the street in high-heeled boots would be carrying poisoned lollipops to ram down his throat, the sad-looking tart down the block would be a Japanese spy in disguise, and the frowsy bum loafing in the sunlight across the street —

Whit's wandering eyes jerked back to the frowsy bum across the street. He was staring intently at the man when their cab drew up to the kerb and cut off his view. He disengaged his arm from Kitty's with a mumbled excuse.

Kitty said, 'Where are you going?'

'I'll be right back.'

The shabby man across the street was walking away as Whit came around the front of the cab and started towards him. Whit was still twenty feet away when the shabby man turned into a doorway and was gone. He had not looked back.

Whit was right at his heels. The doorway led into a dingy bar smelling of stale beer and cigar-butts. The only person in sight when Whit entered the place was a pale man swamping the linoleum floor with a mop.

'What happened to the guy that just came in here?' Whit asked.

The pale man looked up. 'Huh?'

'What happened to the guy that just came in, five seconds ago?'

The pale man jerked an indifferent thumb towards the back of the bar-room and went on with his swamping.

Whit followed the thumb, but it was too late. A door in the back of the place opened on to an alley, and the shabby man was nowhere in sight.

Whit said thoughtfully, 'I'll be god damned.'

CHAPTER 5

WHIT walked back to the cab pondering over a new mystery.

Casey Jones was the rounder's name. That was how the song went, about the brave railroad engineer who whistled for the crossing with an awful shrill and found Number 4 staring him right in the face. It had been on the Reno hill, too. Quite a coincidence. The Casey Jones Whit knew had been an engineer also; not an engine-driver, but an electrical engineer and a good one. Whit had known him well in San Francisco, up until two or three years before. They and a newspaperman who was a kindred soul had lunched together occasionally, played handball at the gymnasium, and caroused more or less regularly. The combination had broken up when the newspaperman went to New York and Casey gave up a good private practice to accept some kind of a travelling job that took him away from California. Whit hadn't known exactly what the new job was, although Casey had been pretty hot for it. It had a future. But the future hadn't panned out so well, because Casey either had a double wandering around loose or Whit had just seen him on the bum in Reno.

He was still puzzling over it when he got back to the cab. Kitty said, 'Why did you suddenly lope away like that?'

'Thought I saw someone I used to know.'

'Oh?' Kitty's normal curiosity was bothering her.

'I was wrong.'

Sure he had been wrong. It was just a chance resemblance. Casey, whatever might happen to him and however he might go to the dogs, would never end up as dirty as the tramp had been.

34

Casey was a soap-and-water fiend. The guy across the street hadn't even shaved for four or five days.

'I thought the groom was leaving you in the lurch,' the blonde said to Kitty. 'My third husband almost did that. He got cold feet.'

'Your third husband?' Kitty looked at the blonde in surprise. Gladys was still on the green side of thirty.

Gladys giggled. 'I think it was my third. I lose track sometimes.'

Whit said, 'I won't run away. But there's a good chance I'll pass out unless we get started. Get going, driver.'

'Where to?' The driver was patient with him. 'I ain't psychic, mister.'

'The county clerk's office.'

The cab took off. Kitty and Gladys got into a discussion of the subject of trousseaux, with Caldwell arguing the male critic's point of view. Whit closed his eyes and thought about Casey Jones.

After all, there was still something wrong with the theory that the tramp hadn't been Casey. Why had he turned away when Whit started across the street? That disappearance into the saloon and out the back door could only have been for the purpose of getting away from Whit, and why would a stranger give a hoot because somebody came across the street in his direction? It was damn queer. Everything about this trip was queer. First it was Pop and his two thugs, then Lorenzo and the Caldwell limpet who seemed determined to accompany Whit and Kitty right to the nuptial bed, then the tramp who couldn't be Casey Jones but was. It was a hell of a situation, all around.

Whit yawned.

He was almost asleep when the cab stopped. The driver said, 'Here y'are. D'you want I should wait? I can find you a J.P. faster'n anybody in town.'

'I thought you weren't psychic,' Kitty said. 'How do you know we're going to be married?'

The cab driver grinned at her as he opened the door. 'You just don't look like you'd be interested in anything the county clerk can sell you except a marriage licence, mam.'

'Time is of the essence,' Whit said. He yawned again. 'Stick around. We'll be right out.'

The wedding ceremony was performed by a cadaverous justice of the peace with bad breath and a falsetto voice. He had a working arrangement with the cab driver which made them both quite a bit of money, partly because the J.P.'s place of business was two good miles from the county clerk's office and partly because he put so much bogus enthusiasm into his work that brand-new husbands felt guilty if they gave him less than ten dollars.

'Oh, fine, fine,' he piped, jockeying Whit and Kitty into the proper position for the operation. 'Now the witnesses, please.' He pointed a bony finger at Caldwell and the blonde. They stepped forward. 'That's fine. Just fine. Now, let's see. The licence? Fine. The ring? Fine.' He produced a worn prop Bible, let it fall open at random, and cleared his throat.

'Now if the bride and groom will clasp hands, please. Fine, fine.' His voice dropped two octaves in honour of the solemn occasion. 'James Whitney, do you take Kathryn McLeod for your lawful wedded wife? . . .'

They were married.

Whit kissed Kitty, then Gladys, and then Kitty again to make sure that she still tasted better than anyone else. She did. She was inclined to weep when she looked at the ring on her finger, and had to blow her nose once or twice. Whit wished that Gladys and the limpet weren't around so he could say something nice to her. He compromised by inconspicuously patting her bottom. She smiled tearily at him.

'Fine, fine,' said the justice of the peace, not referring to the pat. His voice was back to its normal squeak. 'Congratulations. I'm sure you're going to be the happiest pair in the world.'

'We are.' Whit gave him twenty dollars. 'Thanks a lot.'

He hurried Kitty away while the J.P. was looking at the twenty and trying to figure out what he could give them in the way of an encore.

Their driver still waited for them, contentedly listening to the ticking of his meter. They all got into the cab. The driver said, 'Happy landings, chums. Where to now?'

'An hotel.' Whit was having trouble with his eyelids.

'Which one?'

'Any one. Use your own judgement.'

Gladys said, 'You might as well go to the Truckee, then. That's where I'm staying. I'm beginning to need my beauty sleep too.' She batted her eyes at Caldwell. 'You don't mind, do you?'

'Of course not. It's time we all went to bed.'

Gladys looked disappointed. She and Caldwell didn't see eye to eye on the subject.

Whit said, 'Where can we drop you, Caldwell?'

'I'll go to the hotel with you and take the cab from there, thanks.'

Whit had expected the limpet to struggle more when it was pried loose. It surprised him that Caldwell had lost interest in clinging to them, now that they were married. Caldwell was still as friendly and pleasant as ever, but his attitude was indefinably different. He dropped them at the hotel with a cordial good-bye and congratulations, and left without even trying to sign up the blonde for a date. Gladys was so indignant that she flounced away to her beauty sleep with hardly a farewell for the bride and groom.

The bride and groom came very near to being thrown out of the hotel before they even got in it. First of all, their bags were still in Whit's car, several blocks down the street, and the clerk naturally thought the worst of people without luggage. Whit got around that by giving the clerk his keys, describing the car, and asking that somebody be sent to pick it up. But the clerk's eyebrows went up again when he looked at Whit's signature on the registration card.

'The lady, sir. Do you wish two rooms, or —?'

He let the question hang delicately in mid-air.

Whit flushed a dull red as he retrieved the card and added 'Mr and Mrs' before his name. Kitty looked off in the distance. The clerk eyed them knowingly, shook his head at the clumsiness of people who thought they could fool an old hand, and rang for a bellhop.

At long last the newlyweds were alone in their room. The hotel stood on the bank of the river that bisected the town; five storeys below their window the stream made a murmuring noise as it flowed between the carefully kept grassy lawns that were Reno's pride. A warm breeze stirred the curtains of the window, and a patch of sunlight lay across the carpeted floor. It was quiet and very peaceful. Whit yawned tremendously.

'You certainly made a fool of yourself with the registration,' Kitty said as she took off her hat. It was a new hat, and she was proud of it. Whit thought it looked like a banana-split, but he hadn't said so.

'My mind was on something else.'

'What?'

'Guess.' Whit leered at her.

Kitty scoffed. 'You acted like a schoolboy sowing his first wild oat. I'll bet you never took another woman to an hotel in your life.'

'Bet I have.'

'You have not.'

'I have too. You're just one of dozens.'

Kitty's smile was strained. 'I'm the nicest one, though.'

'Oh, I'm not so sure. You're just the latest. Next month it'll be someone else.'

'Is that so?'

'Yep. I get tired of 'em soon. I think maybe I'll make a pass at that little blonde next. What a figger.'

Kitty's smile had completely disappeared. 'Nice and dumb, too. Just what you'd like; someone with an empty head and a crowded brassière.'

Whit reached out from his seat on the bed and pulled Kitty down on his knees. He wrapped both arms around her and put his face in the hollow of her shoulder.

'Honey, I won't even joke about it.' He nuzzled the skin of her neck. 'I've got what I want. Other girls are just a bunch of washerwomen to me.'

'You need a shave,' Kitty said. She didn't try to pull away from the whiskers. 'And you smell sweaty. But I prefer you to anybody else.'

'Even Jess Caldwell.'

'Yes.'

'Even Lorenzo?'

'Yes.'

'He kind of likes you.'

'Why shouldn't he?'

'No reason. But he had the blonde until Caldwell took over, and he could have kept her if he hadn't got off base in your direction.'

'He wouldn't have kept much.'

Whit chuckled at Kitty's scornful tone. 'After I've had some sleep, remind me to tell you the plot I evolved for a meller-

38

drama about Caldwell and Walter Gates. It's called "Dirty Work Is Hard on the Nails." '

'Tell me now.'

'Uh-uh. Nothing interests me now but a pillow.'

Kitty's cheek was resting on the back of his head. She said softly. 'That sounds like a challenge.'

Whit grunted. He was nearly asleep.

The bellhop with their bags knocked on the door at that point. Whit did not move. Kitty went to the door, took the bags, and sent the boy on his way with a tip. Whit still sat slumped on the bed with his eyes closed. Kitty picked up the smaller of the two bags and disappeared quietly into the bathroom.

When Whit finally lost his balance and toppled sideways, it woke him enough so that he dimly realized he was on a bed of some kind. He didn't care what kind or where. He struggled out of his clothes without getting to his feet, dropped them on the floor, tossed his shoes on top of the pile, and crawled gratefully between the clean cool sheets. He was fast asleep in twenty seconds.

Kitty found him that way when she came out of the bathroom some time later. She had bathed, cleaned her teeth, brushed her hair, applied new make-up, and dabbed lavender water behind her ears, and her whole beautiful clean self was clothed sketchily in a disgraceful black chiffon nightgown woven of spiderwebs and moonbeams. She was a beautiful girl even without the aid of artifice, and as she looked then she would have made any man in his right mind light up like a match. But her husband of less than an hour lay sound asleep on his back, making noises in his throat like a toy steam engine.

Kitty's face was pink when she came through the door to present herself to the happy groom. The pink faded as she stood and looked at him. She said unhappily, 'Oh, you great big clown!'

*

'They were married, all right,' Jess Caldwell said to Walter Gates. 'I was one of the witnesses. It was the real thing.'

Gates scowled at his muscular, grease-stained fingers. He had been asleep on the davenport when Caldwell came into the apartment, and now he sat with his hands hanging loosely between his knees, listening to Caldwell's report.

'It doesn't prove anything one way or the other,' he said. 'We've still got to watch them. Where are they now?'

'We took them to an hotel. The Truckee.'

'Who's we?'

'Renzo's latest girl and I,' Jess said. 'Renzo had plans for her, but he paid too much attention to Whitney's woman and the girl got her feelings hurt. She went with us when we left. Renzo thinks I stole her from him.'

'What Renzo thinks doesn't matter,' Gates said. 'I don't like him getting involved with these local tarts. Tell him to forget the women and stick to business.'

'He'd pay more attention if it came from you, Walter. He's going to be upset because I took his girl.'

'Was she something special?'

Jess made a negative gesture. 'You know Renzo.'

'The girl was with you at the wedding?'

'She was the other witness.'

'I think you're going to have to see more of her,' Gates said. He took his hat from the floor by the davenport and stood up. 'I'm going back to Verdi. I want you to spend all the time you can with Whitney, and it may be easier if you make it a foursome. Find out everything you can without giving yourself away. I'm not satisfied yet that he came to Reno just for a honeymoon.'

Gates put on his hat and left the apartment.

CHAPTER 6

'OH, who will kiss them ruby lips,' Whit sang lustily in the shower. 'Oh, who will kiss them roo-hoo-hoo-bee lips, when I am dead and gone.' He soaped himself thoroughly, rinsed the soap off, and turned the shower regulator from hot to cold. As the chilly water hit him, his song changed.

'Oh, God! Get m-me out of here!'

Kitty came running into the bathroom and yanked the shower curtain away. 'What is it? What's the matter?'

'The w-w-water.' Whit's teeth chattered. The shower was bringing goose-flesh out on his arms and legs.

'Is that all you were yelling about?'

'I always y-y-yell in a cold sh-shower. I c-can't help it.' Whit shivered violently as he turned off the water and reached for a towel. 'I-I'll be all right in a m-m-minute.'

'You almost gave me heart failure, screaming like that. Why do you take cold showers, if they hurt so much?'

'It f-feels so good after it's over.' Whit rubbed briskly at his hair. 'B-r-r. You ought to try it some time.'

Kitty dropped the shower curtain in disgust and went back to the bedroom to manicure her nails.

Six hours of sleep had done wonders for Whit. Once more he was back on top of the world. The events of the night before – not counting his wedding – seemed remote and not very important. His imagination had been bothering him; imagination and lack of sleep. All he could think of now was the week with Kitty that lay before him. He was not concerned with what might come after, nor with what had gone before. The next seven days were enough.

'Oh, who will kiss them roo-hoo-hooby lips.' He sang as he lathered his face in front of the mirror. Marriage was wonderful. Kitty was wonderful. Reno was wonderful. Everything was wonderful.

In the other room the telephone rang. He heard Kitty answer. She called through the doorway. 'It's for you,' and he strode naked and half-lathered from the bathroom, soapily kissing the roo-hoo-hooby lips as he passed. 'Hello,' he said into the telephone.

'Whit?'

'Yep. Who is it?'

'Pete Weston. I hear you just got married.'

'Pete!' Whit was startled. 'Where are you calling from? I thought you were in New York?'

'I'm in the lobby. I represent the Associated Press in the State of Nevada now. Can I come up and meet the bride?'

'Sure, sure.' Whit looked down at his bare shanks. 'Give me enough time to put on a necktie. Make it about fifteen minutes?'

'O.K.'

Whit replaced the telephone receiver and stared at it thoughtfully.

'Men are certainly ugly with their clothes off,' Kitty said, cleaning the shaving soap from her face. 'Who was it?'

'Newspaperman I used to know in San Francisco. He's coming up.'

Kitty said, 'Oh?' Whit's expression indicated that there was more to it than that.

'There are strange things going on in this town, Kitty.'

'Oh?'

'Come into the bathroom while I shave. I want to tell you something before Weston gets here.'

She followed him into the bathroom and sat on the edge of the tub with her manicuring doodads.

'I thought I was having a pipe-dream up until a minute ago.' Whit went to work with the razor as he talked. 'Do you remember that tramp I chased across the street from Lorenzo's Club this morning?'

'What tramp?'

Whit told her about the man who looked like Casey Jones. 'I thought it was Casey at first. Then I convinced myself that it was only a resemblance and forgot about it – until Pete Weston called. Now I'm not so sure.'

'What changed your mind?'

'Weston and Casey were thick as thieves when I knew them. Casey is supposed to be travelling somewhere, and Pete had a good job in New York the last I heard. Now I bump into Pete the same day I see a bum who looks more like Casey than Casey does himself. Something is going on.'

'It could be a coincidence.'

'Oh, sure. It *is* a coincidence. That's what bothers me. Casey was one of the best electrical engineers in the country and Pete Weston once won the Pulitzer Prize for reporting, so they both end up in Reno – one on the bum, one holding a job that he would have laughed at two years ago. And there are a lot more coincidences rearing their ugly heads around here. Like you manicuring your nails right now. Did you notice Walter Gates' fingers when we were at Pop's place last night?'

'I was too scared to notice anything at Pop's house.'

'Did you notice Jess Caldwell's hands while you were playing roulette?'

'They were dirty, if that's what you mean. As if he had been working with something greasy.'

'Gates' hands were the same way. And I don't think that was

42

only a coincidence. Gates was interested as hell in what we were doing at Pop's house, Kitty. I don't know why, but he and his weasel came awfully close to giving us trouble last night. When we left, they didn't try to stop us and they didn't follow us, but as soon as we hit town we were picked up by Lorenzo and Jess Caldwell. And right now I'll bet Walter Gates knows everything we've done since we left him.'

'Oh, I hope not.' Kitty finished the manicure job on one hand and held it out to admire it. 'Is this the melodrama you were promising me this morning?'

Whit laughed. 'All right. It does sound like a dime novel. But I didn't imagine what went on at Pop's house last night. Don't forget that.'

'I'm going to try to forget it,' Kitty said. 'I wish you'd hurry up and put on some clothes. I can't get used to the idea of watching a naked man shave himself.'

Whit wiped his face and went to look for his pants. He was respectably dressed when Pete Weston knocked on the door a few minutes later.

Weston was a tall, pleasant young man who wore collegiate clothes and a bow-tie and would always seem much younger and more innocent than he was. He and Whit pumped hands and called each other foul names to indicate how glad they were to see each other after a long time.

'Pete Weston, of the Associated Press,' Whit said. He cleared his throat. 'My – uh – wife, Pete. Mrs Whitney. My – uh – wife.'

'Your – uh – wife,' Pete repeated. He shook Kitty's hand. 'I'm happy to meet you, Mrs Whitney. I know how he feels. I was married myself once, and it took me a week to get used to it.'

'I hope you didn't convince any hotel clerks that you and your wife weren't married, the way he did.' Kitty had already looked Weston over and decided that she liked him.

Whit said, 'How did you find us, Pete?'

'Part of my job. Reno's a fine place to begin a marriage or finish one. I keep an eye on the vital statistics – who marries who, who divorces who, and who does what with who in between. I saw your name on the list this morning and checked the hotels.'

'It doesn't sound exciting for a man with your background. What happened to the New York job?'

'I got a promotion.'

'To Reno?'

'It's a step up. I'm in charge here. In New York I was just another legman.'

'Is that the only reason you came here?'

Weston looked at him with a puzzled expression. 'I don't get you.'

'Let it go,' Whit said. He took his coat from the back of a chair. 'How about having breakfast with us?'

'Sure. But what about dinner first. It's six o'clock.'

'Breakfast,' said Whit. 'We're night-owls. Where's a good place to eat?'

Pete had to make sure they were really starting the day before he would suggest a restaurant. He had eaten around town so long that he had places picked out for particular meals. When he was convinced that they wanted breakfast and nothing else, he took them down the street to John's Grill.

'It's a Greek joint,' he explained on the way. 'John's the best fry-cook in town, and he can cook eggs and hamburger like nobody's business, or fried potatoes. But as far as he knows, a green vegetable is something you take out of a can and use for garnish around a steak. Breakfast is fine. Only don't ever order the blue plate dinner.'

The Greek joint was small and clean. There was a big range and a steam table between the window and lunch counter, and four or five booths for people who didn't like to sit at the counter. The prop., according to the printed menu, was John Masilikos. He turned out to be cook, as well as prop., and the entire working force of the grill except for one waitress. Pete called him away from the steam table to meet the Whitneys.

John was happy to know any friends of Pete. He was a tremendous ape of a man with a close-cropped head, and a bull neck growing from a thicket of black fur on his barrel chest. The black hair covered his forearms and the back of his hands, which were the size and shape of fielder's mitts. He wiped them carefully on his apron before shaking hands with the newlyweds.

'We want the best breakfast you can throw together,' Pete said. 'Something extra special, John.'

John smiled broadly. 'Breakfast at six p.m. Try the blue plate dinner.'

44

'I've tried it,' Pete said, without enthusiasm. 'We want break-fast. Nice thick ham steaks, a lot of eggs, some of those good fried potatoes with onions —'

'Ham steaks? Where would I get ham steaks, with meat what it is? I can give you bacon, maybe.'

' Ham steaks.' Pete brushed John's objections away. 'I know you've got a ham hidden away some place. Do I complain about the Annie Oakley situation when you want to go to the wrestling matches?'

John looked at Kitty and winked. 'That's a newspaperman for you. Nothing for nothing. All right, maybe I can find some ham. Go sit down.'

He turned back to the range and began rattling frying pans.

Pete gave the Whitneys the local dirt while they waited for food. His business was news, and he had lots of it. Two movie stars were in town to arrange an official switch of wives as soon as they had established residence, although a *de facto* switch had been made the day they arrived; a banker from Chicago, in Reno to dispose of a wife through the Nevada courts, had disposed of a hundred thousand dollars at poker while he was waiting; what's-his-name was sleeping with what's-her-name. And so on.

'You're better than Walter Winchell,' Kitty said. 'Do you do anything else besides run a gossip column?'

'That's only incidental. My real job is clearing war news through the censors. And I earn my salary, believe me. They're tough cookies.'

'What war news is there in Nevada?' Whit asked.

'Plenty. There's a big army command here, a couple of training bases within a few miles, the largest Navy ammunition depot in the country is down the road a few miles – there's a lot of activity. The difficulty is getting any of the news on the wires. All the censors will let us print is what comes from the O.W.I., and human interest stuff about the army home-away-from-home.'

'I suppose you want to give the public the details of the secret bomb-sight.'

Pete shrugged. 'If the secret bomb-sight is news, I'm sup-posed to get in on the wires. That's my job.'

'Nice patriotic attitude,' Whit said. 'Talking about news, I've got some for you. Guess who's in town.'

45

'I'll bite.'

'Casey Jones.' Whit watched Pete's face.

'Casey Jones?' Pete's expression was completely blank. 'I don't know — Oh, Casey. You're crazy. He's in Washington.'

'He's in Reno. I saw him this morning, looking like he hadn't had a bath or a shave for a week.'

'Where?'

Whit told him. He continued to watch Pete while he talked, waiting for some indication that it was not all a surprise to the newspaperman. Pete simply looked incredulous.

'You're full of beans,' he said, when Whit had finished. 'I can believe anything except Casey needing a bath.'

'You didn't know he was in town?'

'I still don't know it. You've been seeing things.'

Whit shrugged. 'O.K. Have it your way.' He would get nothing from Pete, whatever the newspaperman knew or did not know about Casey Jones.

The waitress arrived with their breakfast, and Pete democratically introduced her to the newlyweds while she tossed cutlery around. Her name was Evelyn. It was quite a coincidence for her to meet the Whitneys that day, because she was celebrating an anniversary herself.

Kitty said, 'Oh, that's nice. How long have you been married?'

'A year. And it was a divorce, not a wedding.' Evelyn looked Whit over critically and nodded to Kitty. 'You'll do better than I did, dearie. Mine was a heel.'

'So is mine.'

'Pass the marmalade,' said Whit. 'I can't live on compliments.'

The breakfast was all that Pete had led them to expect. John came through generously with the ham, and everything was cooked with the loving touch that a Greek chef gives to things which require frying. Whit and Kitty had not stopped for food since leaving California, so they made up for it until their eyes bulged.

Pete did most of the talking during the meal. He knew Reno inside and out, and he told more stories of some of the things that went on, mostly the scandal that did not get into the papers. From his lurid descriptions, Reno was a Bad Town.

'I'd like to try some of the dens of vice you mention,' Kitty said. 'Now that I'm a married woman, I'm entitled to see life in the raw. Why don't you be our guide for the evening, Pete? Whit will pay the bills.'

Whit choked on his last bite of toast. Pete said, 'It's a fair division of responsibility. Let's go.'

John was the cashier, as well as cook and prop. He beamed when they told him how good the breakfast was, and invited them to come in any time. Pete's friends were his friends. He might even find them another slice of ham. They promised to return.

Outside in the street Pete said, 'John's a good boy. Used to be a professional wrestler. He'll give you his shirt if he likes you.'

'What if he doesn't?' Whit said.

'He's liable to toss you out on your ear. He did it to a local hot-shot the other day; threw him all the way across the side-walk and into the gutter, like a sack of potatoes.'

'What started it?'

'I don't know. I was in one of the booths. It wouldn't have taken much, though, because the guy was an Italian and John hates 'em. He had a couple of brothers in the Greek army when Mussolini tried to take over, and they were killed. I don't know what this guy did, but John got mad, and – boom! Out he went.'

'John looks like he'd be tough if he got upset about something.'

'He's mild as a lamb most of the time,' Pete said. 'Well, where shall we go first?'

'You're the guide,' said Kitty. 'I want vice.'

'Vice is what you are about to stare right in the eye, then. Follow me.'

Whit said, 'Let's stare Western Union in the eye first. I left town without telling my partner where I was going, and I want to send him a wire before he has the Boy Scouts out looking for me.'

They stopped at the telegraph office, and Whit gnawed at his pencil trying to compose a satisfactory telegram. His partner was a solid citizen and a fine accountant, but he wasn't used to having his hand on the helm and he liked Whit around to tell him what to do. And Whit had an idea that the ex-client whose pants he had kicked might be unpleasant enough to try to hurry the draft board. He used extra-special finesse in writing a night letter. In its final form it read:

JUST MARRIED AND SPENDING HONEYMOON IN RENO.
WILL BE BACK IN ONE WEEK. CAN BE REACHED HERE AT
TRUCKEE HOTEL IF ABSOLUTELY NECESSARY BUT WANT
PEACE FOR A FEW DAYS. IF YOU ARE QUESTIONED, AM IN
NEW YORK AND CANNOT BE REACHED. LOVE TO ALL.

The 'Love to All' was a superfluity, but the wire rate covered fifty words and Whit felt friendly. With that off his mind, he was prepared to wallow in whatever sin Reno had to offer.

Kitty was sniffy about the dens of iniquity Pete led them to. He had a big touring car with a C-sticker, and he chauffeured them from one end of Reno to the other with the willingness of a real estate agent transporting a hot prospect, but it was no sale. The vice was too high-class for Kitty's taste. She had in mind a cross between an opium den and an apache joint, with rugged characters lurking in the shadows and a little shooting whenever things grew dull. Pete did his best, but he couldn't please her.

'I give up,' he said finally. 'There isn't any place as tough as you want, outside of the redlight district.'

'Let's try the redlight district, then.'

'It's closed. The army put its foot down.'

'Well, if this is all you can offer, we might as well go to Lorenzo's Club and win some money.'

Pete said, 'Lorenzo's Club?'

'Haven't you ever been there?'

'Once or twice. Why do you pick that particular place?'

'Why shouldn't I?' Kitty asked.

'No reason,' Pete said. 'Lorenzo's Club it is.'

Whit said nothing, but he was as curious as Kitty. Pete had something on his mind.

Lorenzo's Club was beginning a big evening when they arrived. The casino was crowded, the tables around the dance floor were full, and an orchestra was grinding out dance music. A different hat-check girl, just as leggy as the one of the night before, took their hats and coats, but no one else seemed particularly concerned about their presence. They worked their way to the bar for lubrication before tackling Lady Luck.

The lubrication came in tall satisfying instalments. Over the second one, Whit said, 'Do you know Pop Foster, Pete?'

'The J.P.? Sure. Everybody does. He's a local fixture.'

'How about Walter Gates? Or Sammy Kohler? They're –
uh – friends of his.'

Pete shook his head doubtfully. 'I don't think so. Not by
name. Why?'

'We stopped in to see Pop last night and met Gates and
Kohler there. They seemed like a queer couple of turnips.'

'Do you mean queer? Or queer?'

'Strange,' Whit said. 'It isn't important. I just thought you
might —'

'Oh, *hello,*' Kitty said. Whit and Pete turned around.

Gladys the blonde had got her man after all. She and Jess
Caldwell were together. Gladys wore a different dress this time,
but it was mounted on the same wheelbase as the night before
and was just as effective. Pete took one look and jumped off
his stool, brushing his hair into place with his hand.

Whit made the necessary introductions and moved over to
make room for the newcomers at the bar. He said, 'We're
celebrating something or other again. Have a drink.'

Jess Caldwell said, 'We don't mind if we do, since it's a
wedding day. How about it, Gladys?'

'It's a little sudden.' Gladys giggled. 'But if you really think
we'd be happy —'

'A drink,' Jess said. 'Not a wedding. I was talking about the
Whitneys.'

'Oh. Well, just one. I'm going to win some more of Lorenzo's
money to-night, if somebody doesn't get me drunk.' Gladys
batted her eyes tentatively at Pete to see if he'd like to try getting her drunk. He reacted properly.

'You'd better persuade Mrs Whitney to gamble with you,
then,' Jess said. 'I'll play myself, if she does. A horseshoe
doesn't turn up very often in this place. Do you mind being a
horseshoe, Mrs Whitney?'

'I don't mind, but Lorenzo might. Here he comes now,' said
Kitty.

The Latin menace was approaching through the crowd, nod-
ding and smiling to the regular customers, stopping briefly to
radiate a bit of glamour for some of the women, and bending
once to kiss a female hand extended for that purpose. He did
it well. He was a perfect picture of the suave city slicker in

49

tailcoat, white tie, gardenia, and – to Whit at least – stuffed shirt.

Lorenzo ran the gauntlet at last and greeted them with the same professional syrup. Gladys got only nominal attention, since she had shifted her interest to Caldwell, but Kitty came in for an extra-special flash of the beautiful teeth and some hand-patting. Lorenzo was enchanted to see her back so soon – and her husband, of course. They *were* married, weren't they? Congratulations. It called for more champagne. He raised a finger at the bartender.

'Make mine beer,' Whit said grumpily. Even if he hadn't suspected Lorenzo of being tied up with Walter Gates in some manner, he was beginning to think he could dislike the bastard without half trying, the way he kept slobbering over Kitty. Why didn't Kitty dust him off, instead of simpering like a schoolgirl?

Lorenzo said pleasantly, 'And your friend?'

'Ask him.' Whit dug Pete in the ribs to distract his attention from Gladys, with whom the newspaperman was making progress. 'Meet Mr Caruso, Pete. He wants to buy.'

'Colusa,' Lorenzo said. The professional smile disappeared for a moment and his dark spaniel's eyes were hot with a flash of anger. It was gone immediately, but it made Whit feel better to see it. Lorenzo had a temper, and the 'Caruso' hit home.

Whit had asked for beer, and he got beer. He didn't like the stuff much anyway, except for curing hangovers, and it didn't taste any better because the rest of the party were sharing another bottle of Lorenzo's good champagne. Whit knew he was being neglected, damn it. On one side of him Kitty was carrying on a sprightly conversation with Lorenzo and Jess Caldwell, and on the other Pete was monopolizing Gladys. Whit was left in the middle with nothing but a glass of beer and a smouldering grouch. It was a hell of a note when a man couldn't get a word in edgewise with his own wife.

By the time the drinks were gone, the grouch had matured to a point where Whit didn't like anybody. When Kitty said, 'Now I want to play roulette. Come along, Whit,' and clambered down from her stool, he answered grumpily, 'Go on and play. You've got plenty of company.' He saw her hurt expression, but he wouldn't meet her eye, and after a moment she went away without him. Gladys, Jess, and Lorenzo followed to see

50

if Kitty's luck was still holding up. Pete stayed. He said, 'Hurry back, toots,' to Gladys as she left, and she gave him a quick promising smile over her shoulder.

Whit said sourly, 'Go along with little hot-pants and play roulette. You don't have to worry about me.'

'I'm not worried about you.' Pete was finding something very funny. He shook his head and snickered. 'I was afraid I'd bust out laughing if I looked at him again.'

'Who?'

'Your friend Caruso. The hand-kisser.' Pete snickered again. He made a swinging gesture with his arms. 'You should have seen him when John took him by the scruff of the neck and the seat of the pants and chucked him into the street. What a sight!'

So Pete had to tell the story again in detail, and once more Whit felt that life was real, life was earnest. Pete's description of John's enormous hands fastening themselves in Lorenzo's collar and the seat of his elegant breeches was a beautiful job of reporting. It chased away Whit's grouch like a ray of sunshine.

'I wish I could have seen it. I wish I could arrange for a return match. You don't know what started it, Pete?'

'No. But you'd never get Lorenzo back there for a repeat performance, whatever it was.' Pete made the swinging gesture with his arms and they both burst into laughter.

'Lorenzo the Flying Roman,' Whit said. 'You've made my honeymoon a success, boy. The only thing that could add to my pleasure now would be to take a few hundred dollars of his money out of here. Let's go tangle with the crap-game.'

'Not me.' Pete shook his head. 'I gave up gambling after I turned my first month's pay over to the blackjack dealers. You tourists can contribute all you want. Me, I'll stick to something I know how to handle. Like that little blonde teaser, for example. I'm going to see if she knows how to dance.'

'You kind of like Gladys, don't you? If I weren't a married man, I'd show you how to shake her loose from her boy friend.'

'I can shake her loose,' Pete said. 'I could shake her loose from better men than Caldwell.'

'How do you know how good he is? What do you know about him, Pete?'

The newspaperman raised his eyebrows at Whit's question. 'Why, nothing. He just doesn't impress me as being much competition.'

'Has he been around town long?'

'I don't know. I never met him before to-night.'

Whit said, 'Uh.'

'What about him?'

'Nothing much. I was wondering why he has dirty fingernails.'

Pete heaved himself off the bar stool. 'You should worry about Caldwell's fingernails. He probably works in his victory garden. Let's go see what's doing at the roulette table before the blonde forgets about me.'

The law of probabilities had caught up with Kitty when they arrived at the wheel. She had put most of her winnings back into the bank, and Gladys and Jess Caldwell were with her in the red. Lorenzo had gone back to his syrup-spreading with the cash customers, so there was no one around to act as the fly in Whit's ointment. He came up behind Kitty and put his arm around her waist.

'I can't understand it,' she said. 'Nothing works right for me. I wonder if this gadget is honest.'

'Sure it's honest. It wins, doesn't it?'

'But I had a perfect system last night, and I haven't changed it. I think there's something wrong.'

'You're married to me, that's what.' Whit tightened his arm. 'Lucky at love, unlucky at roulette. Last night was different.'

'Oh, twaddle,' Kitty said. 'And while we're on the subject, you owe me seventy-five dollars.'

'*I* owe you seventy-five dollars?'

'Certainly. You explained it yourself last night. Now that we're married, everything we win or lose is community property, half mine and half yours. I just lost a hundred and fifty dollars, so you owe me half. Give it to me.'

In all of Whit's career as a successful tax practitioner, he had never argued so eloquently and so futilely as he did in the next fifteen minutes. He cited legal decisions from memory, invented precedents, quoted the law, fled to the principles of equity, and ended up still owing his wife seventy-five dollars. At last, dazed and beaten, he found himself paying off. He could hardly believe it himself.

Gladys, Pete, and Jess Caldwell stood around and enjoyed the debate. It was more entertaining than roulette and less expensive – for them. To Kitty, it was only simple justice.

'Maybe I don't know the law as well as you do,' she said, counting the money carefully. 'But I know what's fair. Now I can play some more.' She extended the money to the croupier. 'Give me some chips, please.'

'Wait a minute,' Whit said hoarsely. 'What if you lose that?'

'Then you owe me thirty-seven and a half, of course. You said yourself —'

Whit hauled her away from the roulette table by brute force.

Jess Caldwell came close to overcoming Whit's suspicions and making himself a friend at that point by inviting them all to his apartment for more drinks and some boogie-woogie on the phonograph. It was still too early to go to bed, and Whit couldn't think of a place in Reno where Kitty wouldn't be able to lose money. His mathematical mind pictured an algebraic formula stretching to infinity; no matter how long you continued to divide a loss in half, there would always be something left, and he knew he could never talk himself out of the hole after he had paid once. He snatched at Caldwell's invitation.

'Swell. Fine. Good. That's just dandy.' He hurried his reluctant wife towards the cloakroom. 'Come along, dear. The kind gentleman has invited us to his home.'

'But I want to play roulette.' Kitty hung back.

'Not to-night, dear. Get your coat, like a good girl, or I'll break your neck.'

Pete had turned his car over to a flunkey when they entered the Club. They left the building by a rear entrance, and came out on the gravelled parking lot that was one of Lorenzo's free services for the suckers, besides the operations by which he relieved them of unnecessary weight in the pants pockets. A girl in white overalls came up to them, took Pete's ticket, and went to get his automobile

The party waited near the exit, talking about nothing in particular. The girl in the overalls found Pete's big touring car at the far end of the lot and drove it back in a scatter of gravel that made Pete wince for his tyres. The car's headlights, sweeping the side of the building, lit briefly the figure of a man who stood there in the shadow fifteen feet from Whit, watching the group in the light of the doorway. Whit's eyes met those of the other man for the short moment that the headlights were on him, and this time there could be no mistake. It was Casey Jones.

Whit did not wait to make excuses. Casey had already disappeared in the darkness when Whit started in his direction, but Whit saw a moving shadow outlined faintly against a white fence blocking the corner of the parking lot. He closed in quickly, confident that Casey was cornered at last, and was near enough to the fence to see his man duck through an opening close to the building wall. He followed. On the other side Casey was legging it away into the darkness of a dimly lit alleyway.

Whit's legs were longer than the other man's, and he could run Casey down if he did it before his wind gave out. Casey had a head start and ran hard, not looking back, but Whit pulled up on him. There was no sound except the pound of their feet on the rough surface of the alley. When only a couple of yards separated them, Casey dodged around a fence into a second alley, narrower and more poorly lighted than the first. Whit's lungs were labouring for air, but he continued to gain. He was almost within reaching distance when Casey turned his head for the first time, saw how short the gap was, and put on extra steam. Whit's wind was gone now; another twenty yards would finish him. He made a last effort and threw himself at Casey's legs in a desperate tackle, hands outstretched. One hand missed, but Casey's ankle chunked solidly into the open palm of the other. They both came down on their faces. Whit pulled himself on to Casey's legs, puffed heavily two or three times, and spat the dirt from his mouth.

'There, damn you.'

Casey said, 'What have I done, mister? What are you after me for?'

Whit puffed some more. 'All right, keep up the masquerade. Let me know when you're ready to stop playing games and I'll get up.'

'I don't know what you're talking about, mister. You've got me mixed up with somebody else. I ain't done nothing.'

'Oh, hell. Why don't you stop it, Casey? You can't talk me into thinking I don't know you.'

Casey lay still for a moment. When he spoke again the whine

54

had gone from his voice. 'O.K., you win. Get off.'

Whit let him up. They brushed the dirt from their clothes. Whit's hat and Casey's disreputable eyesore lay on the ground. Whit picked them both up, slapped the dust off against his leg, and handed the eyesore to Casey.

'Thanks.' Casey jammed the hat on his head. 'Now what?'

'What's it all about?'

'What's what all about?'

'What are you doing here?'

'Well, what are you doing here?'

'Stop stalling. I want to know what's happened. Don't give me all that double talk.'

Casey's eyes flickered. Whit saw him picking out the best direction in which to make a break, and he fastened firmly on to Casey's coat. 'None of that, now. Come clean. What are you doing in Reno looking like a tramp?'

'Things haven't been breaking right for me, Whit,' Casey said earnestly. 'I didn't want you to see me looking like this, so I ran.' He put his free hand on Whit's arm.

'Horsecollar. I've known you too long. Something is up.'

'It's the truth.' Casey's hand slid down Whit's arm to the wrist. 'I wouldn't lie to you.'

Whit felt the grip tighten, but he was too late. He flew gracefully into the air over Casey's head and came down with a thump that knocked the wind out of him. Casey had a tight hammerlock on him before he could move.

'I'm sorry. Take it easy, now. I can't tell you any more than I have.' Casey's low voice in Whit's ear was commanding. 'Where did you meet those people I saw you with back there?'

'Ow. Go easy on my arm.'

Casey eased the hammerlock slightly. Whit said, 'One of them is Pete Weston. He's working here in Reno. We picked the others up this morning – or they picked us up. What's it all about?'

'Who is we?'

'Kitty – my wife – and I. We just got married.'

'Is that why you're in Reno?'

'Yes. And I'm getting tired of having my nose rubbed in it. Get off.'

'I'll let you up in a minute.' Casey seemed to be thinking hard. Whit was getting ready to buck him off, broken arm or

55

no broken arm, when Casey came to a conclusion.

'Listen, Whit. I'm in trouble. I can't tell you what it is, but I've got to keep under cover. I'm not known around town at all, and if it got out who I am I'd be washed up – bad – worse than I can tell you. You've got to forget you ever saw me.'

'If you need help —'

'No. No. I'll work it out all right. Just don't mention me to anyone. Nobody at all. When you go back to those people, tell them you were sick or you had to go to the can in a hurry or something, but keep me out of it. It's important, Whit. I can't tell you how important it is.'

He was convincing. Whit said reluctantly, 'All right. But *I'm* not just going to forget about it. Do I have to run you down again as soon as I get up or will you tell me what's the matter, without an argument?'

Casey chuckled. 'Stubborn as ever, aren't you?'

'I sure am.'

Casey let him up. They brushed themselves for the second time. Whit said, 'Well, how about it?'

'Not now. Not here. It's a long story. I'll look you up when we can talk. Where are you staying?'

Whit told him and gave him the room number. He said, 'I'm going to get it out of you if I have to chase you all over town, so don't try to give me a runaround. I'll expect to see you at the hotel – if they let you in.'

He was looking at Casey's shabby clothes. Casey said, 'Don't worry about me. I'll get there. Just remember what I said about keeping your mouth shut.'

'I told you I'd keep quiet, didn't I? What do you want – an affidavit?'

Casey put his hand briefly on Whit's shoulder. 'Good boy. I'm sorry I can't talk just now, but I'll come clean later.'

'You'd better, by God.'

Whit limped away. He did not look back.

The others were waiting for him in Pete's car when he returned. Except for his hands, which still showed traces of alley-dirt, he was presentable enough in the dim light. He got into the car, apologized briefly for keeping them waiting, and offered no explanation.

He was on one side of Kitty in the back seat, with Jess Caldwell on the other. Gladys sat with Pete in front. While Caldwell leaned forward to give Pete directions, Kitty whispered in Whit's ear.

'Where did you go?'

Whit whispered back. 'I had to wee-wee.'

'It certainly came on you in a hurry.'

'I'm like that.'

Kitty was puzzled. But Caldwell had finished talking to Pete, and Kitty knew that Whit would elaborate his explanation loudly and publicly if she asked any further questions. She let the subject drop until a more opportune moment arrived.

Jess Caldwell's apartment could have been the den of vice that Kitty had been looking for, if sinful luxury would satisfy her. It was a beautiful suite in an apartment building on a bluff overlooking the river, upstream about half a mile from their hotel and away from the central part of town. A balcony hung over a garden sloping gently to the stream below, and the view of the city's lights was beautiful. It had taken money to furnish the place, and it took money to keep it up. Jess Caldwell's liquor supply was large, high in quality, and as freely flowing as the river below.

Whit did his best to dent the supply during the course of the evening, first because Caldwell really had some good dance music for them and the kind of struggle that Whit called dancing made him thirsty, and second because he had a hunch that Caldwell would like to see him drunk and talkative. He was willing to oblige at Caldwell's expense. Caldwell himself was too cagey to drink much, but he would have to ask questions if he wanted answers. It would be interesting to hear what the questions were.

So Whit obligingly emptied his glass as fast as Caldwell filled it, danced with Kitty, danced with Gladys, and had a good time. When he got too warm, he took the latest refill and went out on the balcony to cool off, feeling high, hot and happy.

The music broke off after a while. Caldwell came out on the balcony with two glasses, put one at Whit's elbow, and settled himself in a chair with the other.

'Nice night,' he said.

It was coming at last. Whit said, 'Swell. Hope the weather keeps up while we're here.'

'How long are you going to be in town?'

'A week or so. First vacation I've had in two years.'

Caldwell didn't follow the lead. Whit helped him out.

'Yes, sir, in my business nobody can afford to let go of the reins long enough to take a holiday. Things happen too fast.'

'Is that so? What is your business?'

'I'm a C.P.A. Tax consultant.'

Jess hitched his chair forward an inch. 'What does that mean?'

'Well, tax consultants are a low form of life like revenue agents, only in reverse. A revenue agent tries to get you to pay twice as much income tax as you should, a tax consultant tries to get you off for half as much as you ought to pay, and it's usually settled at about what would have been the right amount in the first place. Lots of good clean fun, nobody hurt, and we make a living.'

Caldwell laughed. 'Are you any good at it?'

'I'm reasonably successful, if that's what you have in mind. What do you mean by good?'

'Successful. Maybe you can give me some professional advice – for a fee, of course.'

'Sure. Be glad to. What's the trouble?'

'Oh, not while you're on your honeymoon. Let me have a card and I'll get in touch with you.'

Whit thought it was very neatly done, although it was shame to waste such an elaborate build-up just to get a business card. He produced one from his wallet.

'Here. But don't let the honeymoon bother you. I like to talk about taxes any time. What's the problem?'

'I'll write you a letter when you get back to your office.'

'Oh, the hell with that.' Whit waved his glass, spilling part of the drink on his pants. 'I must be getting drunk. You go ahead and tell me what's bothering you, and I'll bet I can give you an answer in two minutes. One minute.'

'I don't want to trouble you now.'

'It isn't any trouble, I tell you. Now what's the matter?'

'Well, it's – the government wants more tax.'

'They always do. What're the grounds?'

Jess Caldwell was in a corner. Whit didn't want to leave him there too long. When Caldwell couldn't think fast enough, Whit said, 'It isn't one of those back-year adjustments, is it? A lot of my clients have been getting hooked for additional taxes because the Treasury Department finally made up its mind to

58

disallow stock losses back in '33, '34, and those years.' He hiccupped. 'You wouldn't be the only one that got hurt, if that's why they're after you.'

Caldwell took the bait. 'I'm glad I've got company. I've been pretty badly hit.'

'Well, I guess I can't bail you out as easy as I thought, then. But you send me your papers when I get home and I'll see what I can do for you. My address is on the card.'

'I'll do that.'

There were no more leading questions. Caldwell either had got what he wanted or he had been scared off when Whit backed him into a corner. They talked for a while – Whit was careful to slur his speech slightly, not too much – and after a while they went inside to dance with the girls again.

Whit's drunk act was only about one-third acting. When he stumbled over the carpet for the fifth time, Kitty recognized the symptoms. She didn't want to spend the next day helping him with a hangover. Pete, who was thoroughly occupied with Gladys, made a half-hearted offer to drive them home when Kitty announced that they were leaving, and was grateful when she said they would walk. Her husband needed fresh air. Her husband was a man who had been behind the door when the brains were passed out, and he didn't know yet that one man couldn't drink the country dry. She said good night to their host and thanked him for a lovely evening.

Whit was full of love and good liquor as they walked back to the hotel, and he sang bawdy songs quietly to himself. He was so cheerful that it was a shame to light into him about his drinking, but it had to be done periodically, for his own good. When they came to a park bench near the river-bank, Kitty sat him down and lit in.

'I wish you wouldn't drink so much, honey. It isn't good for you. Besides, we're going to get up and go horseback riding in the morning, and you'll feel terrible.'

'I feel fine. Ragtime cowboy Whitney, that's me.'

'You won't feel that way in the morning.'

'That's to-morrow. Anyway, I had to get drunk to get Jess Caldwell to talk.'

'*You* had to get drunk so he'd talk?"

'Sure. The delicate approach. I found out what I wanted to know.'

'What?'

'He's a liar, for one thing. Not a very good one.'

'Why is he a liar?'

'I don't know. Why do people lie?'

'I mean, how do you know he's a liar?'

'He wanted to find out what my business was and where I had an office, so he handed me a lot of malarkey about his income tax troubles and how he was going to write me a letter about them, until I gave him a business card.'

'Maybe he really does want to write you a letter about his income tax troubles. That's possible, isn't it?'

'Not about stock losses disallowed in 1933 and 1934, it isn't. I gave him that as a suggestion and he bit. The trouble is that the statute of limitations has run against those years and the Government can't reopen them. He wants to check up on me, for some reason.'

'Why?'

'I wish I knew,' Whit said seriously. 'I wish I knew.'

CHAPTER 7

IN the middle of the night Abou Ben Adhem Whitney awoke suddenly, conscious that someone had dug him in the ribs with a hard thumb. It was the early hour in the morning when his mind didn't function very well. He investigated the situation and discovered that he was in bed with someone warm and obviously female. It interested him. While he meditated sleepily on an appropriate course of action, he heard Kitty's whisper in his ear.

'Keep still. Someone is in the room.'

He remembered where he was then, and that he was a happily married man with a fuzzy taste in his mouth and a desire for peace. But he had responsibilities. If he were still single he could pull the covers over his head and pretend to be asleep. Marriage made it different. He turned his head slowly until his mouth was free and his lips were near Kitty's ear.

'Where?'

Kitty's answering whisper was barely audible. 'At the window.'

Whit cautiously turned his head in the other direction. He

could see a motionless shadow against the pale curtains. He wondered what he ought to do about it. If he felt braver, he could jump out of bed and tackle the intruder, but it was a long way to go for a man who had to disengage himself first from a pile of bedclothes. And it was hard to be brave at that hour of the morning.

Kitty's lips moved against his ear. 'I'm scared.'

Whit laboriously turned his head again. 'My God, so am I. I'm going to switch on the light. If anything happens, roll out on the floor and scream your head off. Here goes.'

The lamp at the bedside table had a chain pull. The chain clicked faintly as Whit's fingers found it, and the man at the window had whirled and was facing them with a gun in his hand when the light came on. It was a big, efficient gun, but Whit's heart, after the first bound, left his throat and went back approximately to where it belonged. The visitor was Casey Jones.

Casey was not something that a bride of one day should have had to confront in her bedchamber. His face was unshaven and haggard, he was hatless, and his clothes had been stolen from a dustbin. The only clean thing about him was the gun in his hand, and that was clearly in first-class shooting condition. Kitty took a deep breath when she saw it. Whit barely had time to clamp his hand over her mouth before she woke the neighbourhood.

'It's all right, honey. He's a friend of mine.' He kept her mouth covered as a precaution. 'What's the cannon for, Casey?'

'I wasn't sure I had got into the right room.' Casey stowed the gun away in his coat. 'Put out the light. No use attracting attention.'

Kitty said indignantly under Whit's hand, 'Blug go.' He let go and reached for the lamp.

Casey stayed at the window for a moment after the light went out. Then his shadow moved across the room and a chair made faint noises. He said, 'Sorry to bust in on you like this, but I didn't want to be seen. Can you spare a cigarette?' His voice had an undertone of strain.

'Sure.'

Whit groped for his cigarettes on the bedside table and threw the package towards the voice. A match flared, cupped in Casey's hands, and was quickly extinguished.

'Just for the record, that's Casey Jones over there and Mrs Whitney over here,' Whit said.

They both said how d'you do. It was all very polite and sociable. Whit waited for a decent interval, but Casey did not open the conversation. Whit had to throw the first ball.

'How did you get in?'

'Fire-escape.' The strain was still present in Casey's voice. 'Have you told Mrs Whitney about me?'

'She knows who you are. You don't have to worry. She can keep her mouth shut.'

'Did you talk to anyone else?'

'I told Pete Weston I had seen you in town, after I chased you this morning. That's all. He didn't believe me.'

The coal of Casey's cigarette glowed in the dark. He said, 'I'm in trouble, Whit.'

'What kind of trouble?'

'I'm wanted for murder and desertion.'

'Go ahead.'

Kitty moved uneasily at Whit's side. He gave her a soothing pat.

'I was commissioned in the Army after I saw you last, and they sent me to a camp in Idaho as an engineering instructor. There was a shooting one night. Another officer was killed, and someone arranged to have it appear as if I had done it. I don't know why, but it looked so bad for me I had to run out.'

'Why Reno?'

'I followed a man here, a civilian. He was mixed up in the shooting. I'm trying to get something to clear myself before they catch up with me.'

'Anyone I know?'

'No.'

The room was quiet for a moment. In the remote distance a bell tolled four times. Whit said, 'You don't want to tell me anything about it, do you?'

'I don't want you to get involved. I can pull myself out if I'm lucky, and if I'm not lucky there's nothing you can do to help me except forget that you've seen me. Nobody else knows me in Reno, but if I keep bumping into you around town you'll give me away. How long are you going to be here?'

'A week. But don't forget Pete Weston. He's a permanent resident.'

'I'll look out for Pete. You're the one that I'm worried about.'

'I'll make you a deal. Tell me the whole story and I'll forget I ever saw you in my life.'

'I told you the story. What more —'

'No. Who are you after here?'

'It's nobody you know.'

'What's his name?'

Casey said flatly, 'I'm not going to tell you, so you might as well stop needling me. I don't want you mixed up in this. You probably won't see me again before you leave town, but if you do all I ask is that you look the other way. And don't mention my name to anyone, no matter who it is, or you'll get me hanged for a murder I didn't commit. I'll go back and clear myself when I get the information I need, but I've got to have time. It's God's truth, Whit.'

'Am I calling you a liar?' Whit asked irritably. The desperation of Casey's appeal was too real to ignore.

'I just wanted to make sure you know how important it is for you to keep quiet.' Casey's voice was more controlled now. 'That's all. I'm sorry I had to disturb you, Mrs Whitney.'

'Oh, heavens,' Kitty said. 'Don't apologize. I wish there were something we could do.'

'I'll be all right. Just forget about me. I'll see you again some time, Whit.'

The chair made its faint noise again. Casey's shadow appeared at the window.

Whit said, 'Wait a minute. You can't walk out like this. There must be something we can do to help.'

'No. I'd tell you.'

'Do you need money?'

'No.'

'You've got to let us know how you come out.'

'Some day.' Casey was trying not to appear ungracious. 'I'm sorry I can't tell you more, Whit. I'm just trying to save you trouble.'

'You know best.' Whit turned on his side and pulled the covers around his ears. 'Close the door behind you when you go.'

'I'm going out the window. So long.'

He had been making sure that his path of escape was clear

63

while he talked. He had one leg across the window-sill when Kitty said, 'Mr Jones.'

'Yes?'

'Would you feel safer if we left town right away?'

Casey was silent for a moment. 'I don't want to spoil your honeymoon. I'll keep out of sight until you leave. Just so you both forget you've seen me, I won't worry.'

'We will. I hope – everything works out right.'

'Why, thank you, Mrs Whitney, I think it will.'

There was a faint whisper of cloth on the sill. The shadow disappeared.

Kitty was out of bed immediately and on her knees at the window, peering into the dark. She watched for the time that it took the fugitive to descend the fire-escape. When he reached the ground and was gone, she breathed a long sigh of relief.

'He made it.'

Whit kept quiet.

Even when Kitty turned on the light and sat on the side of the bed, he kept his eyes closed and his mouth open, hoping that she would go away. She didn't. When he couldn't maintain the bluff any longer he said hopefully, still with his eyes closed, 'I'd rather talk in the morning, honey. I'm tired.'

Kitty continued to sit there, waiting. Whit did his best to go to sleep, but they both knew he was licked. Finally he gave up and struggled to a sitting position.

'O.K., O.K. Get me a cigarette. What do you want to know about him?'

Kitty, as usual, wanted to know everything. She pumped him dry. Before he got back to sleep she knew as much as he did about the life, loves, and ambitions of Casey Jones, and when they got up a few hours later to go horseback riding she had dreamed up more questions to throw at him. He did his best to play down her concern over Casey's difficulties. He was disturbed himself by his friend's trouble, but he knew Kitty's propensity for taking up the cudgels for anyone who seemed to be getting a raw deal. If she decided to fight Casey's battles for him, red hell and high water couldn't keep her from it, even though it was just what Casey didn't want.

Kitty was in the shower when she got her brilliant idea. She put her head around the curtain and yelled. Whit went into the bathroom.

'I've thought of something we can do,' Kitty said.

'So have I.' Whit ogled at as much of his wife as he could see. 'If you'll just get out of here and dry yourself —'

He jumped back, too late to dodge the handful of soapy water that caught him in the mouth. Kitty said, 'That'll cool you off. Now listen. Why don't we go to Idaho and find out about the murder? Nobody knows who we are. Maybe we can discover something to prove Casey is innocent.'

Whit's voice was muffled by the towel he was using to dry his face. 'Fat chance.'

'Why do you say that?'

Whit came out from behind the towel. 'We couldn't do anything in six days, and they'll be after me for draft-dodging if I stay away any longer. We don't know who was killed, whereabouts in Idaho it happened, or when – or anything else, for that matter. Besides, Casey knows what he's doing. We're going to stay strictly out of it.'

Kitty didn't like his attitude. 'You don't sound very eager to help him.'

'I can help him by doing what he wants me to do – nothing. Anyway, this is a honeymoon, and you're too cute to worry about murders.' Whit twitched the shower curtain aside. 'The burleycue never had anything like that. If I were you —'

He ducked fast enough this time, but he had to get out of the room to keep from getting a shower of his own. Kitty finished her bath in modest privacy.

They left the hotel half an hour later to have breakfast before going for the horseback ride they had promised themselves. Kitty wore jodhpurs, a sweater, and a bandana over her hair, and she looked pretty but respectable. Whit clumped at her side in high-heeled riding boots, blue denim pants, an orange-and-green chequered shirt, and a cream-coloured five-gallon hat. He whistled 'Home on the Range' all the way to John's Grill, feeling very rugged and western.

John was glad to see them back. He produced another magnificent breakfast and found time to come to their table and admire Whit's outfit.

'It hurts the eyes but it looks good,' he said. 'You must be going riding.'

'We are if we find the horses,' Kitty said. 'Can you recommend a good livery stable?'

John scratched his jaw with a forefinger the size of a tea-roll. 'I don't know. Where do you want to ride?'

'Anywhere.'

Whit waved his hand in a general westerly direction. 'In the hills.'

John's waitress passed the table with an armful of dishes. John said, 'Where can people rent horses around here, Evelyn?'

Evelyn looked critically at Whit's clothes. 'There's a place in Verdi, but I don't know that you'd have much luck, with those clothes. They'd scare me if I was a horse.'

'He wears them for protection,' Kitty said. 'Any horse that will let him come close enough to get in the saddle is tame enough for him to ride.'

'There isn't a horse tame enough for that shirt,' Evelyn said. She went on her way.

'Have your fun,' Whit said. 'I don't think much of a place where you're insulted by the waitresses. Hey, we met a friend of yours last night, John.' He winked at Kitty.

'Who?'

'Lorenzo Colusa.'

John scowled horribly. 'That son of a bitch. Excuse me, lady.'

Kitty said, 'It's all right. My husband's language has conditioned me to anything. What did Lorenzo do to you, John?'

'He didn't do anything. I don't like Eyetalians, and I don't like that Eyetalian particularly. He's got a place of his own to go to if he has to eat. I'm not going to have him around lousing up my restaurant.'

'You can't just throw people out in the street because you don't like them.'

John gave her a friendly grin. 'Is that so? You tell Lorenzo that, next time you see him. Maybe he'll come back.'

Whit laughed. 'Call me in when it happens, will you? I'd like to be around.'

Kitty was ashamed of them both and said so, which didn't spoil their pleasure in the least.

The Whitneys left John's and used some of their precious gasoline to drive to Verdi. Kitty expected Whit to suggest that they stop to see Pop Foster, and she was prepared to be the agreeable little woman even though it gave her the shudders to think of weasel-face and the stocky man with the pale eyes. But Whit was bearing in mind his own advice that they were on a honeymoon. There was no mention made of Pop Foster.

The livery stable was run by an old-timer named Alex Hotaling. Alex was there himself to do business when they arrived. He was a leathery little ex-cowpuncher, and he talked like a Zane Grey character. His hosses was the best hosses in Nevayda, if he did say so hisself. He brought out a couple for their inspection. They were the second and third best hosses in the state.

'What happened to the first?' Kitty asked.

'She was stole,' Hotaling said philosophically. 'It goes to show what comes of trusting people.'

'Oh.'

'Yes, mam. I had a big bay mare that was the finest hunk of hossflesh in the State of Nevayda, if I do say so myself. I let a fellow take her out one day, the same like I'm letting you folks take these, and —'

'I hope you don't think —'

'No, mam, I ain't worried about you folks. I ain't worried about the skunk that stole my bay mare, either. They'll git him, sooner or later. That hoss had my brand on her, big as a pie plate. I'm just telling you why you only git second and third best. But they're better than any of the crowbaits you'd git any place else around here.'

Hotaling's experience with the bay mare had not made him less trusting. He let them take the horses without even the formality of a deposit. He was a good judge of character, as well as of hossflesh, and he could see right off that they were honest or he wouldn't let them have his hosses at all.

Neither of his customers brought up the subject of the character of the man who had stolen the bay mare. They mounted and struck out across the countryside away from the river, heading west and north. The weather was beautiful; not too warm, not too cool. An air of peace hung over the foothills through which they rode, and as the horses ambled gently along, picking their way through the sparse growth of trees on the hillside, Whit began to sing – yippee-ti-yi-yo, git along little dogies, it's your misfortune and none of my own. After all, what was the use of worrying about the troubles of other people? The hell with it; he had six days of freedom and the

67

finest woman in the world. Yippee-ti-yi-yo, git along little dogies.

The second and third best hosses in the state of Nevayda were an educated pair. When they discovered, as they did very quickly, that their riders had no particular destination in mind, they winked at each other and took the Great Circle route that brought them back approximately to their starting-point in three hours. It was their standard treatment for visiting firemen, and it saved wear and tear on the hooves.

So it was by the whim of the horses and through no plan of the riders that they came back to Verdi by the road that led past Pop Foster's house. They might not even have known that it was Pop's house, never having seen it by daylight, had their attention not been attracted by the unusual collection of automobiles at the roadside and the stir of activity in the yard and on the porch. When they rode up to the picket fence and saw the big car with SHERIFF painted on the side, they knew that whatever had been brewing on the night of their visit had come to a boil at last.

A number of men, including several in uniform, were prowling around the yard and through the house. One uniformed man stood guard at the fence, holding the fort against a few curious people who stood in the road and rubbernecked. The guard stopped Whit and Kitty when they dismounted at the gate.

Whit said, 'We want to see Pop Foster.'

'You can't see nobody.'

'Why not? What's happened?'

The cop seemed like a reasonable guy. While he looked them over, trying to make up his mind whether to tell them anything or not, Kitty suddenly called, 'Pete!'

Weston had come out on the porch and stood talking to one of the men in uniform. He looked up at Kitty's shout and came down the path. He said to the guard, 'It's all right, Sam. I know them.' The guard opened the gate.

Whit said, 'What is it?'

Pete made an uncomfortable gesture. 'Pop's been murdered.'

68

PETE told them about it under a tree in the corner of the yard, near the fence where the horses were hitched. The sheriff's men were still too busy in the house and around the yard to pay any attention to them, and the rubberneckers outside the fence were too busy watching the sheriff's men and waiting for something to develop.

'It happened in the middle of the night. Pop had a couple of friends staying with him – a man named Walter Gates and another fellow, Sam Kohler —'

Whit said, 'We met them here. I asked you last night if you knew them.'

'So you did. Well, Gates had a hunting dog he kept tied out in back, and in the middle of the night the dog began to raise a fuss. Gates got up and turned on the lights. They're strung all over the place; Pop was nervous about living out here so far from neighbours.' Pete gestured at the wires in the tree over their heads. 'Gates couldn't see anything, but the dog kept howling, and pretty soon Pop came downstairs to see what was the matter. They took an old shotgun that Pop kept for skunks and they all went out to see what was bothering the dog.

'There's a creek along the back of the property, behind the garage. Gates said that he and Kohler were at one end of the yard and Pop was at the other, down near the creekbed, when they heard a yell and a shot. They ran around the house in time to see Pop fall and somebody making a getaway down the gulley. Gates let go with the shotgun but the guy took a couple of shots at him and Gates had to get out of the light. When they got back to Pop he was dead. Shot through the back. They took the hound and trailed the guy down the creekbed a way, but the dog lost the scent in the water. So they brought Pop's body back to the house and called the sheriff. That's the story.'

Whit thought, in a pig's eye that's the story. He said, 'Where are Gates and Kohler now?'

'They went into town with the body to give their statements to a stenographer.'

69

'They're lying.'

The newspaperman looked at Whit sharply. 'What makes you say that?'

'I told you last night there was something wrong with them. What I didn't tell you was that they had Pop scared green. I've known him since I was in kneepants, and I know what I'm talking about. They had him so tight under their thumbs he was afraid to move. And I'll tell you one thing more; the little weasel – Kohler – was carrying a gun. If Pop was shot in the back, Kohler was the man who did it. I'll bet my eyeteeth on it.'

'That's a pretty strong statement,' Weston said slowly. 'He didn't have a gun when we got here. What calibre was it?'

'I didn't see it. It was in his pocket.'

Weston's scepticism showed in his face. Whit said urgently, 'Pete, you can *smell* the bugs in the story they told. All that horsecollar about a mysterious stranger in the creekbed; why, it stinks from here to there.'

Pete shook his head. 'There was a man in the creekbed. I saw his footprints myself, and he dropped his hat getting away. The sheriff has it now. And Gates' story checks with what we got from the nearest neighbour. He's down the road a quarter of a mile, but he heard the dog howling and the shots. I think the story is pretty sound, myself.'

Pete took a notebook from his pocket and flipped the pages. 'Here's something else the sheriff got from Gates; a description of the man in the creekbed. About six feet, weight a hundred and ninety to two hundred, dark hair, clean shaven, good clothes.' Pete looked at Whit over his notebook. 'Pretty good for someone you just saw running away in the middle of the night, even with those high-powered lights overhead.'

Kitty said, 'Oh!'

Whit didn't notice her reaction. He said, 'It's too good. Why didn't they get the colour of his eyes and the way he combed his hair?'

'I thought about that myself,' Pete answered. 'I'm telling you this because I got the impression that they had a pretty good idea of the man they wanted to identify, whether they saw him or not. I thought you ought to know about it before the sheriff starts asking questions.'

'Why me?' Whit wasn't very bright.

70

'Don't be stupid,' Kitty said. She was worried. 'That's your description.

Whit said blankly, 'By God, so it is.'

They were all silent for a few minutes. Pete squatted on his heels and pulled at grass stems, while the horses shifted restlessly outside the fence. One of them scratched his flank gently against a picket.

Whit said, 'What time was the shooting?'

'Twelve twenty-five. We checked the time Gates gave us with the neighbours up the road.'

'Gates is making a mistake if he's trying to get me involved. I was at Jess Caldwell's apartment at twelve twenty-five.'

Pete shook his head. 'You left at twelve-five. I was there.'

'But we were at the hotel in half an hour,' Kitty said urgently. 'Certainly he couldn't have come all the way out here, sneaked around in the dark, and got back to the hotel in that time.'

'You were in the hotel at ten minutes of one,' Pete answered. 'I checked up on you this morning, as soon as I heard that description. It means you were nearly an hour getting from the Caldwell's apartment to the hotel – half a mile.'

'We stopped in the park and talked.' Kitty was getting more and more uneasy. 'Pete, you don't think —'

'I don't think anything. It would be hard for anyone to get out here and back in that time, but I know Whit has a car and I know how he drives. It *could* have been done. At least the sheriff may think so.'

Whit said, 'Maybe you think so yourself. You sound pretty god damn convincing to me. I suppose you've figured out why I'd want to kill Pop.'

Pete's face flushed as he stood up. 'I'm telling you what I know, that's all. One day you turn up in town and call on Pop in the middle of the night, and the next thing he's murdered, the witnesses hand out your description, and your alibi is lousy. I don't think you killed him, but if you didn't someone is trying hard to pin it on you and you aren't going to keep out of trouble by getting your feelings hurt when a guy tries to give you a hand.'

He walked away. Whit looked after him stonily.

Kitty caught Pete before he had gone far and brought him back. She would have preferred to draw Whit after him by the

71

ear, but Whit was too big and pigheaded for her to handle when he got his mind set on something.

'Now,' she said. She was angry. 'That will be all from you, Whit. You apologize, and then Pete and I will see if we can get you out of this before you make a bigger fool of yourself than you are naturally.'

Whit glared at them both. Kitty glared right back at him. At long last he said stiffly, 'Sorry. Shouldn't have said that.'

'O.K.' Pete was just as stiff. 'Forget it.'

'That's better,' Kitty said. 'Now we've got to find out what this is all about and do something. Whit, you tell Pete everything that happened when we were here the other night, and see what he thinks.'

So Whit recounted the story of Pop's strange behaviour the night they had called, the menacing attitude of his guests, the gun in Sammy's pocket, Gates' obvious scepticism in regard to their reason for coming to the house, and everything else of significance he could remember, including the dirty fingernails. That brought him to Jess Caldwell and Caldwell's nails, and to Lorenzo and the free champagne.

Pete listened intently, forgetting his huffiness as the story progressed. When Whit finished, Pete wagged his head wonderingly.

'It beats me. You're sure you never saw Gates or Kohler before?'

'Positive.'

'Then why in hell should they try to pin a murder on you?'

'That's not hard. To keep it from being pinned on them.'

'But there *was* a man in the creekbed, and whether he did the shooting or not, he's the natural suspect. So why not his description instead of yours? They didn't even know whether you had an alibi or not.'

'Maybe they knew that my alibi was no good. Caldwell could have told them. Or maybe they never saw the guy at all and thought I was the man. Don't ask me why. Or maybe he really looked like me. Or maybe they're crazy. It wouldn't surprise me.'

Kitty had been following her own trend of thought while they stumbled around in the blind alley. She said thoughtfully. 'The hat, now. We know it isn't Whit's, and we ought to be able to prove it.'

'The way things are happening, I wouldn't be surprised if it

72

is mine,' Whit said. 'But we might as well have a try at it. Is the sheriff here, Pete?'

'He's in the house.' Pete wasn't sure that they were doing the right thing. 'I guess it'll be all right if we talk to him. But don't tell him what you've told me, Whit. It would look bad if you began explaining things away before anyone accused you. He's a pretty smart old codger. I know him and I can handle him. You keep quiet.'

'Good enough. Just for the novelty of it, I won't say anything at all.'

The sheriff was a grizzled Bill Hart with a handlebar moustache and a Stetson bigger than Whit's. Pete called him Andy, introducing Mr and Mrs Whitney as a couple of Pop's friends who had been riding by and had seen the commotion. They had called on Pop only the day before, and they were naturally shocked to hear of his death. Mr Whitney had known Pop for years. He was particularly anxious to be of service if he could.

The sheriff said, 'Shore. I know how you feel. But I guess there ain't much you can do, thanks. We'll handle it all right.'

His eyes were measuring Whit all the time he spoke – not the vivid cowboy costume, but height and build, colour and complexion. Whit could see that the sheriff was as sharp as Pete's warning had indicated. He waited for the old-timer to get around to the questions.

They came when the sheriff said, ' 'Course, we like all the help we can get, now. We aren't shore about the man who done the shooting. We've got sort of a description. Maybe you could help identify him for us.'

'Glad to try,' Whit said. 'But I'm a stranger around here. What did he look like?'

'About yore size, I'd say. Yore weight, dark hair – guess he must have looked something like you. Don't know anyone like that, do you?' The sheriff smiled. His eyes were alert.

'No one in particular. It's a pretty general description, though. Might fit a lot of men.'

'Yep. Guess yore right.' The sheriff scratched his chin. ' 'Course we have to check up everyone who might be mixed up in it, even though there isn't no sense to it. Now you and the missus, for example. You were out here to see Pop, so we got to find out about you. No offence, you understand. Just business.'

73

Kitty said, 'Of course we understand. What do you want to know?'

'Well, I don't suppose you could tell me where yore husband was last night, say about twelve-fifteen or twelve-thirty, could you?'

Kitty, who had no morals at all and who could lie with bare-faced boldness when necessary, managed a blush. 'It was our wedding night. We – he was with me.'

The blush was enough for the sheriff. He chuckled. 'Guess I shouldn't have asked that. Come on inside. I want to show you something.'

They filed into the big cluttery parlour. On the red plush settee there was a paper bag which held something bulky. The sheriff took a dirty felt hat from the bag and held it out to Whit.

'Ever see that before?'

Whit took the hat and looked at it without expression, turning it over in his hands. 'No.'

'Try it on.'

Whit looked at him with the proper amount of surprise in his face. The sheriff smiled. Whit put it on.

He was afraid for a moment that it was going to fit, but it settled over his head like a lampshade. He had got a short hair-cut before leaving California, and the hat was a full size too large. It slid down to rest on his ears. Kitty giggled nervously. Whit took it off and handed it back to the sheriff.

'Guess it isn't yores.' The sheriff put it away in his paper bag. 'We found it down in the crickbed. Fellow that did the shooting dropped it. Shore like to know who it belongs to, but I guess there isn't much chance of tracing it. No lining or nothing – kind of hat you can buy for two bucks and a half anywhere.'

Kitty said innocently, 'Did you think it belonged to my husband, sheriff?'

' 'Course not, mam.' The sheriff looked from her to Whit, and the good-natured smile left his face. 'If I did, I'd shore put him in jail for his own good. Pop Foster had a lot of friends in this county. Some of them wouldn't mind stirring up a necktie party if they thought they knew who had shot Pop in the back.'

He let them go with that to think about, and the understanding – 'course, it was only a suggestion – that he'd shore appreciate it if they'd let him know when and if they were figuring to leave town. Might be a good idea if they'd plan to stay around for a while. Then he buttonholed Pete and took him away. Whit and Kitty went back to the horses.

Whit sang no more songs as they rode back to the livery stable, and he wasn't communicative. Kitty didn't press the conversation; he would talk when he got around to it. When they were at last in the car and on their way to Reno, he did get around to it.

'Damn it,' he said. 'I wish I hadn't seen that hat.'

'Why, honey?'

'It belongs to Casey Jones.'

*

When Walter Gates and Sammy Kohler had given their depositions to the stenographer at the sheriff's office, they were free to go. They walked back towards town. In the middle of the bridge that carried Virginia Street across the river, Gates stopped and leaned on the railing. It was a good place to talk without being overheard. Sammy stopped when Gates did, but not as if he were anxious to talk.

Gates said, 'Where did you hide the gun?'

'In the basement. They won't find it.'

'I hope you're right. It will be bad for you if they do.'

Sammy said hurriedly, 'I know you're sore, Walter, but I didn't know what else to do, honest to God. You told me a million times I had to stop him if he ever tried to get away, and there he was, beating it down the creek. What else could I do?'

'You could have stopped Whitney. Foster wouldn't have made it.' Gates spoke without any particular heat.

'I couldn't tell which was which. They were already out of the light when I saw them. I dropped the man nearest to me; I would have got Whitney too, if he hadn't ducked into the brush.'

A couple of pedestrians were coming along the walk. Gates waited until they had passed before he spoke again.

'How sure are you that it was Whitney?'

'Who else could it have been?'

'I asked you a question.'

'Well, it looked like him,' Sammy answered. His weasel face was sullen.

'I should have known it. Before the sheriff got there you swore it was Whitney, and now you tell me that the first time you saw him he was so far away you couldn't distinguish between him and Foster.'

'But —'

'Never mind.'

'But, Walter —'

'Shut up,' Gates said. 'I want to think.'

He stood with his elbows on the railing, watching the river roll along below. Sammy kept quiet, nursing thoughts of his own. Some day when Gates talked to him like that he was going to get a big surprise. Some day —

Sammy started nervously when Gates spoke.

'We can move out to the other place now, but we've got to have an address to give the sheriff. You go back to Foster's house, pack up our clothes, and bring them back to town in the truck. Rent a room somewhere and leave the clothes there. I'll meet you at five o'clock at the corner of Second and Virginia.'

Sammy said uneasily, 'I don't like to go back there, Walter. What if they've found something?'

'There isn't anything to find, unless it's your gun. You'll have to get that. Don't take any chances, but don't leave there until you have it. If you can't make it here by five, I'll come back at six and at seven.'

'Maybe it would be better if I waited till to-night before I went there, huh?'

'I've got a job for you to-night.'

Sammy reluctantly shuffled away.

Gates found a telephone booth in a drugstore down the street and called Jess Caldwell. The line was busy for a long time. He got through on his third attempt, and Caldwell had a report for him.

'I was just talking to San Francisco,' Caldwell said. 'I think you were right about your friend's credentials.'

'I thought so. Have you heard the news?'

'Nothing in particular,' Caldwell answered cautiously.

'I'll be up to see you in a few minutes. We're going to have to call him in and ask him a few questions.'

The line was quiet for a moment. 'Is it that bad?'

'It's always bad,' said Gates. 'Good-bye.'

CHAPTER 9

IT was early in the evening when Casey Jones took up his watch in the pool hall on the corner opposite Lorenzo's Club. The only action going on in the place was an unskilful game of rotation between a couple of Filipinos, but the temperature was higher inside than out and Casey's ragged coat was thin. Also it was not yet dark, and Casey was less conspicuous there than he would have been in the street. The pool hall's front window permitted him to keep an eye on the main entrance to the Club, as well as a slice of the parking lot in the rear, and if he had not been more interested in what went on across the street than in the pool game, he would not have seen Whit walk by.

Casey scowled when he saw Whit go into the parking lot and disappear behind the building in the direction of the opening at the end of the fence. When Whit came into sight again some minutes later he was at the far end of the lot near the few cars parked there. Casey saw him inconspicuously examine each car as he passed. He was looking for someone, and Casey had an idea he knew who the someone was. He didn't like it.

Whit seemed to be undecided what to do next when he came out of the parking lot. He walked around to the front of the Club and past the Club's entrance to the alley-mouth at the side of the building, where he stopped. Casey saw him light a cigarette. The cigarette was only half smoked when Whit threw it away and moved on as if he had made up his mind where he was going. He passed out of Casey's line of vision, crossing the street, and Casey moved to the door of the pool hall to bring him in view. Whit was working his way methodically down Centre Street, nosing through the early evening crowds for a needle in the Reno haystack. Such determination worried Casey. He continued to watch from the doorway as Whit progressed. His interest increased sharply when he saw Sammy Kohler inconspicuously following at Whit's heels.

Whit was not moving too fast to miss seeing everybody who passed him, and Sammy had to stall considerably to maintain

77

his distance. The stalling required Sammy to peer into a number of unentertaining shop windows. It gave him away – not to Whit, because Whit wasn't expecting to be followed, but to Casey, and it put Casey immediately in an uncomfortable spot. He was greatly interested in the people who might go in and out of the Club across the street and even more interested in the actions of Sammy Kohler, but he couldn't divide himself in half like an amoeba. It took him nearly ten seconds to make up his mind what to do.

He ducked back into the pool hall to find a scrap of paper and a pencil, and wrote a hurried note. The note contained a strange message to come from a skid-row derelict. It was addressed to a gentleman by the name of Jackson, it was signed 'Betty', and it indicated that Betty was terribly, terribly sorry but she would have to stand Mr Jackson up that evening for reasons beyond her control, although she hoped that Mr Jackson would be able to carry on by himself. Betty would be available the next night as usual, and sent lots of love and kisses.

Casey folded the paper into a small wad. For two bits cash he found a fellow scarecrow in the street who would deliver it to Mr Jackson. Casey pointed out to the messenger that Jackson was employed at Lorenzo's Club and Lorenzo's Club didn't permit scarecrows to walk in the front door, so the messenger had to be given a couple of tips on how to get the note delivered and maybe make another two bits if Jackson was feeling good. The whole enterprise took about two minutes, during which time Whit covered less than a block in his search. When the note was safely on its way, Casey hurried to join the parade. He fell unobtrusively into line behind Sammy.

The three men kept their relative positions for the next two hours, the time it took Whit to work his way up Centre Street, back down Virginia Street, and ultimately away from the bright lights to the shabbier joints along the railroad tracks, still hunting. He kept his attention on the people he passed and Sammy in turn watched Whit, so neither knew he was being tailed. Casey watched them both, but he kept an experienced eye on his own back trail as well, to be sure that he was the last man in the procession. Once he stopped long enough to take off a sock near a convenient sand pile left by some street repair crew, and when he took up the chase again he wore one

78

shoe on a bare foot and carried the sand-filled sock in his pocket, ready for contingencies.

The contingencies happened when Whit finished his job of prowling the town from hell to breakfast and turned down a side street which was a short cut back to Lorenzo's Club. He intended to start his search all over again from scratch, if necessary, and his mind was thoroughly occupied, so he paid no attention to the light footsteps behind him until he felt something hard nudge him in the backbone. He stopped and turned around.

'Keep moving, smart guy,' said Sammy. His weasel eyes gleamed. 'You and me are going places.'

Whit was too surprised at first even to move, but he recovered quickly. Sammy, whatever his plans were, was dangerous, and Whit knew the little gunman wouldn't hesitate to blow him in half if he caused trouble. But Sammy would be an easy handful if he could be persuaded to point the gun in another direction for just a moment. Whit stood still.

'What's the idea?'

'You've been putting that long nose of yours into too many things for your health. Turn around and keep walking.'

The gun barrel jabbed Whit roughly in the belly.

Casey, coming up behind Sammy, covered the last ten feet in a couple of jumps. He made no noise even then, but Whit saw the dark shape over Sammy's shoulder and his eyes flickered. Sammy might have been able to bring the gun around in time to take care of Casey, but as he swung on his heel Whit hit him a tremendous blow in the bread-basket a moment before Casey's home-made sandbag came down on Sammy's head. Sammy went to sleep.

Casey had the limp body under the arms before it could hit the ground, and was dragging Sammy across the walk and into the shadow of the nearest house. Sammy's gun had fallen to the sidewalk with a metallic clatter. Casey said, 'Pick it up and get in here before someone sees you. Hurry!'

Whit snatched up the gun and followed Casey into the shadow.

Casey wasted neither time nor breath. He went rapidly through Sammy's pockets, one at a time, quickly examining their contents and replacing everything as he had found it. Sammy's wallet interested him for a moment, particularly the amount of money it contained, but he put it all back before he stuffed the wallet in Sammy's pocket. In a matter of seconds he had examined everything in Sammy's clothes.

Not until Casey had taken the gun from Whit's hand and was sniffing at the barrel did Whit catch up with current events. Everything had happened too fast. He said, 'What are you doing?'

'Never mind.' Casey concentrated on his examination of the automatic in the dim light. 'Take a look down the street and see if anyone is in sight.'

Whit obediently took a look. 'A couple of guys at the corner. They're coming this way.'

'Damn.' Casey was undecided. The gun seemed to be a hot potato; he wanted to keep it and he wanted to give it back to Sammy. At last he dropped it in his own pocket and took Whit's arm. 'Let's get out of here.'

Whit didn't argue. The two pedestrians were coming closer, and the shadow hiding Sammy's body was inadequate. They had reached the far corner when there was a shout from the passers-by behind them. They doubled the next two corners at a run and did not stop to catch their breath until they were a safe three blocks away.

'Slick as a whistle,' Casey said cheerfully. He took the skull-duster out of his pocket and emptied sand from his sock. 'That rat will wonder what fell on him when he wakes up.'

Whit said, 'I've been wondering about a few things myself.'

'Is that so?' Casey occupied himself in replacing the sock where it belonged.

'Yes. What were you looking for in Kohler's pockets?'

'Anything I could find.'

Whit made an impatient gesture. 'No more run-around, Casey. I want to know what you're up to. I want to know how you happened to be there when he stuck me up. I want to know a lot of things.'

Casey finished lacing his shoe and straightened up. 'You ought to be grateful I *was* there.'

'I want to know why.'

'I'll make you a trade. Tell me why Kohler was tailing you and I'll tell you why I was tailing Kohler.'

'I don't know why he was tailing me, and I won't make any

80

trades with you.' Whit's attitude was neither friendly nor unfriendly. 'I've been looking for you all over town. I'm going to get one straight answer if I have to whale it out of you.'

'About what?'

'Did you kill Pop Foster?'

Casey's face was as cold as Whit's while they stared at each other. He said, 'What was Foster to you?'

'A friend. Did you kill him?'

'A friend?'

'Nothing else. Did you kill him?'

'No.'

They walked on.

'The sheriff found your hat in the creek,' Whit said after a while. 'I know you were out there last night.'

'I was there. I didn't kill him.'

'Who did?'

Casey didn't answer. When he spoke at last, he paid no attention to Whit's question. 'No one else would recognize that hat. Did you give me away?'

'No. But I will unless I'm damn sure you didn't have anything to do with the shooting.'

'That makes it tough,' Casey said contemplatively. Whit didn't respond. They walked for a moment in silence.

Casey said, 'I guess we ought to have a talk.'

'That's what I'm here for.'

'All right. But this isn't the place.'

They had circled back towards the heart of town and were now approaching Commercial Row near the railroad tracks, a district of flop houses, cheap stores, and one-arm beaneries. Casey said, 'I've got a place at the Magnolia Rooms. You can see the sign from the corner, in the next block. My room is on the third floor, last door down the hall on your left as you come up the stairs. It's a dump and there won't be anyone around, but I don't want to take a chance on somebody seeing us together. I'll go ahead. You come right along, and be sure that no one sees what room you go into.'

'Third floor, last room on the left. I'll be right behind you. Don't run out on me.'

'I'll be there.'

Casey went on ahead. Whit waited for five minutes before he followed.

81

The five minutes gave him plenty of time to realize he was a dope to let Casey give him the slip again, and when he was at last in the dingy third-floor hallway of the Magnolia Rooms with the smell of flop-house disinfectant in his nostrils, he expected to find no one in the room at the end of the hall. But a light showed beneath the crack of the door, and when he made sure that no one was around to watch him and knocked gently on the panel, the door opened immediately. He stepped in. Casey closed the door and turned the key.

The room was as Casey had described it; a dump. It contained an ancient brass bedstead, one chair, a rickety table, and a large shabby suitcase, no more. A cracked blind was drawn over the single window, and a bare light-globe hung from a cord in the middle of the room. The glare of the unshaded light brought out the room's ugliness, but it was the first time Whit had seen Casey in a good light. He sat on the cot and looked his friend over.

He had been fond of Casey in the old days. They had been close friends, and much of the feeling still lay behind Whit's suspicion that Casey had shot Pop Foster. It depressed him to see how badly Casey had gone to seed.

Casey was more than shabby. He was dirty; his clothes were dirty, his hands were dirty, his unkempt hair was dirty, the skin of his face under several days' whiskers was dirty – not just smudged but grimy, as if he did not wash regularly. There were hard lines around his mouth which Whit did not remember, and he had lost weight. As he slouched in the middle of the room and waited for Whit to say something, he was the picture of a down-and-out has-been. Whit scowled. Casey had been a good man once.

Casey smiled at Whit's expression. 'Pretty bad?'

'What's happened to you, Casey?'

Casey shrugged. 'One of those things. You didn't come here to tell me I looked like a tramp.'

'No. I want to know what you were doing at Pop Foster's house last night.'

'What if I don't tell you?'

'I'll turn you in to the cops.'

'Just like that?'

Whit looked him in the eye. 'Pop was a friend of mine. If you didn't kill him, you know who did and I want him caught.

You had some reason to be there when the shooting took place. What was it?'

Casey took a bag of tobacco from his shirt pocket and rolled a cigarette. When he had lit it, he said, 'We used to be pretty good friends, Whit. I told you last night what I was up against, and what will happen if I'm caught. Suppose I tell you that I didn't kill Pop, that his death was just as bad news for me as it is for you, probably worse, and that I can't tell you any more. What then?'

'It's not enough. I've got to know the rest of it.'

'You won't take my word for it?'

'No.' Whit shook his head stubbornly. 'The more you stall, the worse you make it look. I've covered you up so far to give you a chance to come clean. I could have turned you in to the sheriff this afternoon, but I kept my mouth shut. I'm not going to keep it shut for ever – not without some reason.'

Casey said, 'I've got a gun. I could shoot you and nobody would ever guess what had happened. You're the only person who knows about that hat. And nobody saw you come up here.'

Whit glowered at him. It wasn't true about the hat, but this was no time to suggest that Kitty would have to be killed too.

Casey said, 'Did you think of that possibility?'

Whit answered doggedly, 'That gives you three choices. Either you shoot, you talk to me, or you talk to the sheriff.'

Casey dropped his cigarette butt on the floor and put his foot on it. 'You always did talk turkey, didn't you? I sure wish you'd picked some place else for a honeymoon. But I've got to take a chance on you, I guess. Tell me a few things first.'

'What?'

'Exactly how much do you know about those two guys that were staying with Pop – the little monkey we laid out to-night and his partner. How long have you known Lorenzo Colusa and Jess Caldwell?'

It did not occur to Whit to be surprised that Casey knew the names, and he could see no reason why he shouldn't answer the questions. He told Casey all he knew.

Casey brought up the rickety chair and sat spraddling the seat, his arms on the chair back, listening closely to what Whit had to say. The story seemed at once to excite and amuse him. At the end, when Whit repeated Sammy's words just before the joint action of the solar plexus punch and the sand-bag put him to sleep, Casey smacked his hands together and laughed.

'It's almost funny, Whit. Do you know you've come as close to being killed as you ever will in your life, just because you turned up in Reno at this time?'

'You think that's funny? You've got some sense of humour. Have you any idea why these clowns are so anxious to cool me off?'

Casey stopped laughing. 'I know exactly why. They want to get me and they don't know who I am. They think I'm you – that you're me.'

'Clear as mud. Who are you?'

Casey reached unhurriedly above his head and snapped off the room's single light. Whit's muscles tensed instinctively in the dark, but nothing happened. He heard Casey move, there was a slight sound he could not identify, and then the light came on again.

Casey held in his hand a narrow envelope of oiled silk. It contained a piece of paper folded several times to fit in the envelope. Casey removed the paper, unfolded it, and silently handed it over. A tiny photograph was pasted in one corner. The picture showed Casey's face as Whit had known it – alert, intelligent, clean – above the collar of a business suit.

Whit read what the paper had to say about Kenneth C. Jones. He made only one comment when he had finished: 'I'll be god damned.'

Casey was grinning. The grin made his face young again, more like the photograph. He recovered the paper and returned it to its envelope. All that Whit could think of to say at first was, 'Kenneth, huh? Where did Casey come from?'

'Kenneth C, K.C., Casey.'

'A G-man,' Whit said.

'That's me. Special agent for the Federal Bureau of Investigation – until they find out I let myself get backed so far into a corner that I had to tell you about it. Then I'll lose my job.'

'Whatever that is,' said Whit.

Casey's grin went away. 'It changes. Right now I'm keeping an eye on your playmates: Gates, Kohler, Colusa and Caldwell. Sooner or later they're going to lead me to something I'm here to find.'

'What's that?'

'A radio transmitter. Gates is operating one somewhere in this neighbourhood, and he's sunk more shipping with it than the Japanese air force.'

CHAPTER 10

THE piece of paper that was Casey's identification had rocked Whit back on his heels, but he was game although punch-drunk. Before he let himself be further befuddled with stories of secret weapons and weird radio beams, there were some things which needed clarification.

'Hold on a minute,' he said. 'Let me get it gradually. What about the Idaho murder story you told me this morning?'

'I made it up to keep you from letting anyone know who I was. I could see that Jess Caldwell was sticking close to you, and I was afraid you might let something slip unless I convinced you that you had to keep quiet. I expected trouble because of Foster's death.'

'Who killed him, Casey?'

'Kohler.'

Whit nodded. 'I thought it would be Kohler. How did it happen?'

Casey took time out to roll another cigarette. He said finally, 'I'll have to tell you the whole story about Pop Foster, I guess. You won't like it.'

'Go ahead.'

Casey lit the cigarette and squatted on his heels. He used the charred match-head to trace a sketchy map on the bare floor.

'Here's the Pacific Coast.' He made a sweep with the match-stick. 'San Diego, Los Angeles, San Francisco, Portland, Seattle. This nail-head is Reno. A couple of inches to the left is the biggest naval ammunition depot in the country.' He traced radiating lines from a spot near the nail-head to the coastal points. 'Ships go out of these ports to supply the entire Pacific war theatre – Australia, South Seas, India, Hawaii, Alaska – carrying troops, guns, planes, tanks, equipment, everything it takes to win a war – if they get there. To make sure they have a chance of arriving, all the freighters are armed with light guns and carry gun-crews. When it's a big shipment, the ships travel in convoys, and destroyers go along to protect

85

them. The destroyers carry heavier guns and ash-cans – depth bombs – to take care of submarines. When it's a tremendous shipment, the convoys are accompanied by cruisers, sometimes even battleships, and they carry murder all over them – depth bombs, torpedoes, secondary anti-aircraft batteries, and the heaviest guns afloat. The size and importance of the convoy is in proportion to the armament that travels with it.'

Casey looked up. 'Are you beginning to get it?'

Whit shook his head. Casey went on talking.

'There's no advertising when a convoy is made up. Even the men on the ships aren't told until the last minute when or where they're to join the line-up, because information leaks out, and when there's a leak ships go to the bottom. You've heard of the submarine "wolf-packs" that have turned up off the coast lately?'

'I read something about them in the newspapers. The story sounded like a reporter's dream to me.'

'It isn't. It should be; they're Japanese submarines, and they're too far from their base to be able to do any more than get over here and turn right back before they run out of fuel. A submarine is no menace without enough fuel for a cruising radius – unless it knows exactly when and where it's going to have a chance to use its torpedoes, and arrives at the right spot at the right time. These submarines have been doing just that. We knew there was a leak, but we couldn't put our finger on it when only the higher-ups had information until just before our ships were ready to sail. Finally we found the source of the leak – two hundred miles inland from the nearest seaport.'

Casey's match came to rest on the nail-head.

Whit said, 'I'm well confused. Don't tell me Gates is a Jap spy in disguise.'

'That's almost the truth. He's a German, of course; he spelled his name Götz when he was a colonel in the German army. Do you know anything about the German General Staff?'

'Not much.'

'Well, they're the boys that do the long-range planning in Germany. When Nazis and other riff-raff like them quit once, they're through for good; the General Staff just starts getting ready for the next war. Right now they know Germany is washed up for the time being, but Japan is still carrying the ball in the Pacific, and the longer Japan keeps going the more it will weaken us and the Chinese and the Russians for the *next* scrap. So Götz – Gates – was loaned to the Japs, where he could do some good. The Japs couldn't plant a spy here with slant eyes and buck teeth, but they have Gates; clever, unscrupulous, well-trained, supplied with plenty of money, and ready to die if he has to but planning to live as long and do as much damage as he can first. With a list of the names of native fascist sympathizers and the money he brought with him, he bought, bullied and bargained until he had built up an organization that covered the entire Pacific Coast. Some of his men were picked up right away, of course. The smart ones were harder to catch, but eventually we ran them down too. We haven't pulled them all in because we wanted a string to the boss, and finally we got a lead on Gates himself. When we caught up with him we discovered who was sinking our convoys.

'It's a neat scheme. He has a man planted in the ammunition depot who reports all seaboard ammunition shipments to him, and with that information he can tell what is brewing up and down the coast without ever being near the ocean. He knows that ammunition is shipped so as to arrive at the same time as the vessels it's intended for. When regular shipments of three-inch and five-inch shells go to a port, he knows it's routine supply for armed freighters. If the shipments are larger than usual and include six- and eight-inch ammunition, a convoy is being planned, with destroyer or cruiser escort. If something special in the way of fourteen- or sixteen-inch shells goes out, there are battleships loading up. Gates receives reports from his men on the coast of actual ship movements as well, and he got so he could figure what ships would be where and when, better than the War Shipping Administration. All that, plus odds and ends of useful information picked up by Lorenzo Colusa and Jess Caldwell from the military personnel with whom they make a business of rubbing elbows, Gates sends out by radio to the proper parties across the Pacific.'

'Where did Pop Foster come into it?'

'I told you that you wouldn't like it, Whit.'

'You think he was one of them?'

'I know he was. Gates bought him. A little cash must have

87

looked good to Foster; he'd never had any, he was getting old, and the marriage fees he picked up didn't amount to much. He was a good front for them, because everyone in the country-side knew him and liked him. He had a house where they could hole up, he could set bail if one of them got into trouble, and as a justice of the peace he had access to useful information.'

'I can't believe it of Pop,' Whit said. 'You're just guessing.'

Casey shook his head, and his bearded face was grim. 'I'm not guessing. We had a man here before I came, working on the job I'm holding down now, and we got regular reports from him. He spent six solid weeks gathering bits of information and putting them together, and in that time he learned what I'm telling you. It was a tough job, because he didn't dare risk anything that would let them know we were on to them, but he did it. He got everything we were after except the most important fact – the location of the radio station. They jumped it around periodically so we couldn't get a fix on it. About a week ago they moved it for the third or fourth time, and they were shut down for four days. In his last report our man said he was working on a lead that might take him to the new location. He didn't say what the lead was. That was the last we heard from him.'

'He's dead?'

'Probably. I hope so. If he isn't, they've got him alive. That wouldn't be so good – for him or for us.'

Both men were silent for a moment. Casey rolled another cigarette while Whit stared at the crude sketch on the floor.

'You know who these men are,' he said. 'Why haven't you gathered them in?'

'The radio. We have to locate it.'

'Why not knock them over and let the radio take care of itself?'

'Because we want to take care of it. We can do things with it. We know their code, we know their signals, we know every-thing – everything but the location of the damn thing. And we've *got* to find it before we clamp down.' Casey smacked his fist into the palm of his other hand. His voice was sharp with excitement. 'Why, think of it, Whit! We could set the biggest trap, the biggest series of traps that were ever invented. We could butcher Jap submarines like fish in a barrel. Give me a

88

chance to send a few messages with that radio and I'd clean them out of the Pacific Ocean!'

Whit said, 'I see the point. But I thought there were gadgets you could use to locate radios.'

'Direction-finders,' Casey gestured with his thumb towards the big shabby suitcase in the corner of the room. 'I've got one there. The trouble is that Gates' messages don't last long enough to give me a fix on him. He codes them first, then steps up the speed either with a phonograph recording or a bug, so they're too fast to take down. His longest message is just a high-pitched whistle lasting about twelve seconds.'

'What's a bug?'

'A mechanical gadget to speed up code messages. His are so fast I have to pick them up on a record and slow it down to a crawl to decipher them. I know what his messages are, but I don't know where they're coming from.'

'How long have you been working on it?'

'Since I've been in town; four days. He's only been on the air twice in that time, from the new location, and I haven't got very far. But I'll get him, by God. I'll get him, and when I do —'

Casey didn't finish the sentence. His eyes were bright.

Whit said, 'Tell me more about Pop.'

'There isn't much more to it. Our man reported that he thought Foster would talk if someone could get him away from Gates. Gates must have thought so too, because either he or Kohler was with Foster all the time. I wasn't making rapid progress with the direction-finder, and after I saw you that first day I thought I'd better try to get to Foster before you spilled the beans. So last night I went out to Verdi and prowled around. I'd looked the place over before and I knew about the lights and the hound, but there was a wind blowing and I thought if I could come upwind on the dog I'd be all right. I made it, too; I got in the house and told Foster enough to get him to come with me. He was too scared to talk until I got him away. We were out of the house and almost to the creek before the dog smelled us and began to howl, and then those damn lights came on and they started shooting. I heard Kohler's bullet hit Foster, but there was nothing for me to do but run.'

Whit stared at his shoes. After a minute Casey said, 'I'm

sorry, Whit. I couldn't do anything. I think he'd rather have died than be caught.'

'I know he would. That's why I'm going to settle up with Gates and Kohler. I liked Pop.'

'Gates and Kohler are my babies. I'll take care of them.'

'I'll help.'

'No.'

'I said I'll help. You can give the orders.'

'My orders are for you to get out of Reno.'

'I'm not going until I get ready.'

They stared at each other steadily.

Casey said, 'Listen. I work for the F.B.I. They know what they're up against, and they spend a lot of time and energy planning things before they do them, so that everybody has his job and will be where he's supposed to be and do what he's supposed to do when the time comes. You're not included in the picture. I know you want to help, but you'd just gum things up.'

'I said you could give the orders.'

Casey paid no attention to him. 'And there's another thing to consider. Gates suspects you already. He sent Sammy to bring you in to-night – not to put a slug into you, but to bring you in. He wants to make you talk.' Casey put up a hand as Whit attempted to interrupt. 'Don't think he couldn't make you tell everything you know and a lot more besides. He's playing for keeps, Whit; there's nothing for him but a firing squad when he's caught, and he knows it. He'd give you a god-awful bad time while you were trying to convince him that you were just an innocent bridegroom on a honeymoon. You'd spill everything you ever heard in your life before he got through with you.'

'Let's look at the other side. He thinks I'm you. The more he's interested in me, the less chance he has of finding out about you and the more chance he has of making a slip. So I'm a decoy – live bait.'

'I don't need a decoy. And you'll be dead bait if you go on getting crossed up with Sammy Kohler. You get out of town while you're alive and I'll feel a lot happier.'

Whit stretched his arms lazily. 'Now I'm scared.'

'You damn fool. Do you think this is a picnic?'

'No, I don't think it's a picnic. But the sheriff wouldn't let

90

me leave town now if I wanted to, after that phony description Gates gave him. And I don't want to. I'm not asking you for any trade secrets. I'm just offering to stick around and attract attention away from you so that I can help bring Gates and Kohler in.'

'You attract any more attention from Gates and he'll bust you into little pieces to see what makes you run.'

'He'll do the same to you if he finds out about you.'

'It's different with me. It's my job. This is nothing to you.'

Whit's face flushed. 'The hell you say! Who do you think you are – Nathan Hale? Do I have to wrap myself in the flag and sing "God Bless America" before I can take a hand in this? I've got as much stake in it as you have.'

It was only a moment before Casey began to smile. He said, 'By God, you're as stubborn as you used to be.'

Whit muttered something surly.

Casey laughed at him. 'All right, I'm not arguing, am I? You win. You can stick around and be a decoy for me, and if you get killed I won't even come to your funeral. How's that?'

Whit said grumpily: 'O.K. I wouldn't want you around, anyway.'

They talked it over after that was settled. Casey said, 'I want you to be sure you know what you're getting into. They won't give up trying to get you just because we laid Sammy out tonight, and I can't give you any protection. I can't even be seen near you.'

'I'll take care of myself.'

'I'm not so sure that you can. A punch in the nose isn't going to stop anyone like Sammy Kohler. Can you shoot a gun?'

'Some. I'm not an expert.'

'That's bad. They won't take a shot at you if they can help it; they'll keep trying to get you alive. You'll have to be awful damn careful.'

'Suppose I get a bodyguard?'

Casey was doubtful. 'Who?'

'There's a plain-clothes cop in San Francisco I can borrow for a few days. He's an ex-pug and a gunman. He did the job for me once before.'

Whit rubbed the scar over his ribs and did not mention that his bodyguard had let at least one bullet get by which had nearly terminated his employment.

'How much would you have to tell him?'

'Not a thing. Absolutely nothing except that I needed to be covered.'

'Well, all right. You'd better get him here in a hurry. Sammy will be looking for another chance to get you when he recovers from his headache.'

'I'll telephone to the city to-night.'

'Good. In the meantime you'd better get back to your hotel and hole up. I've got work to do.'

Whit let himself be led to the door, but he still wanted more information before he let Casey get away from him.

'Are you working all alone in this, Casey? I mean here in Reno?'

'I'm not going to tell you any more than I have. If Gates does get hold of you – and I hope for your sake and mine that he doesn't – I'm the only one who'll go down with you.'

'You're still assuming that Gates could make me talk. I'm not so sure about it.'

Casey said seriously, 'Gates could make you talk. Gates could make you talk, or me talk, or anyone else talk, if he got us. Don't you believe what you read in the funny papers about the tough guys who die before they open their mouths. I've known men who have been tortured until they invented things to talk about because they had told everything they knew and were still alive. Any man will talk if it's made bad enough for him. That's a good thing to remember.'

Whit did not argue. He hoped he would never have the opportunity to find out if Casey were right.

Casey gave him one more warning before he unlocked the door. 'You'll have to keep this from your wife, Whit.'

'I'll try.'

'Try, nothing. Keep your mouth shut.'

'You don't have to worry about her.'

'The hell I don't. I have to worry about everything.' Casey turned the key and opened the door a crack. 'I ought to have my tail kicked for letting you catch me in the first place. The hall is clear; go on, beat it.'

'Tell me who I have to look out for before I go, Casey. I know Gates, Kohler, Jess Caldwell and Lorenzo. Are there any others?'

'None that I know of in Reno, but look out for strangers.

Kohler and Caldwell are the strong-arm men who'll be after you. Gates will stay in the background, and Colusa doesn't count for rough stuff.'

'Good enough. How will I get in touch with you if I pick up any useful information?'

Casey started to say that the amount of useful information Whit might pick up could be comfortably stuck in the corner of his eye, but he changed his mind.

'You can come here, if you're careful. You'll probably be followed.' He showed Whit a loose ornamental knob on one post of the old-fashioned brass bedstead. 'I won't be here often. Leave a message. If I want to talk to you I'll come to the hotel.'

Casey took another peek at the hallway. It was still empty. He took Whit's hand in a brief hard grip and thrust him into the hall.

'Good luck, guy. Don't take any chances.'

The door closed quietly behind Whit's back.

CHAPTER 11

WHIT avoided short cuts and stuck strictly to the bright lights on his way back to the hotel. He kept reminding himself of Casey's assurance that Gates and his pals would want to bring him back alive if they could and wouldn't take a shot at him, but the back of his neck nevertheless felt naked every time he passed a corner. The hotel looked like home sweet home when he got there at last, minus bullet holes.

There was a convenient telephone in the lobby. There was also a telephone in Whit's room, but it was not so convenient in view of Kitty's presence. Whit used the lobby phone to call San Francisco.

He was either lucky or he sounded like official war business to the telephone company, because his call took only fifteen minutes to get through. The voice with a smile and a clothes-pin on its nose finally said, 'Here is your party.' A second and sleepier voice grunted, 'H'lo.'

'Hello, Swede. This is Whitney. Wake up.'

A tremendous yawn crackled over the wire. 'What for?'

'I'm in trouble. I need help.'

93

'What jail are you in?'

'I'm not in jail, I'm in Reno. Now listen good. I've got a bunch of gunmen after me and I need a bodyguard. I can't tell you what it's all about now, but I'm not crossed up with the law and you don't have to worry about getting into trouble. Grab a plane in the morning and I'll pay all expenses.'

Larson said unbelievingly, 'You got a bunch of gunmen after you and I don't have to worry about getting into trouble. It's a joke.'

'Don't argue. Can you be here to-morrow afternoon?'

'Hell, no. I'm on the police payroll. I can't go hopping off to Reno just because you whistle. You know Lootenant Webster as well as I do. He'd blow a fuse.'

'Webster will let you go if you tell him I need help, and I do. Be a pal and stop arguing. I'll expect you to-morrow.'

'Whit, for God's sake!' It was a groan. 'You're crazy. I'd stop being a cop the minute I crossed the border; I couldn't —'

'I don't want a cop. I don't even want anyone with brains. I need someone who can shoot faster than anybody else if shooting starts, and you can do that. This call is costing me money and I haven't much time. Do you take that plane or do I step out on the street to-morrow and get myself bumped off?'

It was a dirty pool, but it got results. Larson groused, argued, swore and asked questions without getting satisfactory answers, but he liked Whit and had a lot more freedom of action in his job than he pretended. He had acted as Whit's bodyguard in an official capacity some years before when Whit was dodging bullets because of a little matter of half a million dollars in income-tax refunds. As a result of the little matter, Whit's former business partner had been knocked off by a client who had attempted to clean house immediately thereafter by having Whit knocked off as well. The client hadn't quite made the grade, partly because Larson was around to disturb the gunman's aim so that the bullet only messed up Whit's ribs instead of killing him. As a result, Larson felt something of a proprietary interest in Whit's carcass. After he had groaned and moaned for a proper length of time, he agreed to be in Reno the next day. Whit hung up quickly before he could change his mind.

It was after one o'clock when Whit cautiously opened the door to his room. The reading lamp burned by the bedside, and

94

Kitty was propped up with pillows and a book. She said immediately, 'Did you find him? What did he say?'

'Who – Casey? Oh, sure.' Whit's nonchalance was as corny a piece of acting as Kitty had seen in years. 'We had a nice long talk. It wasn't his hat after all. He'd never been near Verdi.'

Kitty said nothing. Whit went to the closet humming to himself, hung up his coat, and took off his necktie. When he turned around, Kitty was giving him the evil eye. He stopped humming.

'What happened?' she said.

'I told you. I just made a mistake, that's all.'

'You made a mistake if you think you can get away with a story like that. You'd better come clean if you want to get any sleep. I can sit up all night if I have to.'

For Casey's sake, Whit put up a good fight. It was nearly a quarter of an hour before Kitty could dig the truth out of him, and a quarter of an hour was a new record. She usually had him well mixed in the web of his own lies in five minutes. This time he stuck doggedly to his story of a good clean mistake, which was simpler than trying to invent a fairy tale, but the pressure Kitty put on him was too great. When he finally weakened and began to leak driblets of information at the seams, it was all over.

There was only one thing Kitty failed to get out of him that night, and that was a confession that he intended to continue acting as a decoy to keep attention away from Casey Jones. She didn't know about his call to Larson in San Francisco, and while he knew he would have to tell her his plans sooner or later, he wanted it to be later rather than otherwise. It was a hell of a thing to have to tell a bride on her honeymoon that her husband was putting himself in a position to be snatched by a bunch of goons, if they didn't shoot him first.

Except for that bit of information, Kitty pumped him dry. After the operation was over she said, 'Now why do you try to lie to me? It doesn't do you any good.'

'Nope.'

'Then why not tell me the truth in the first place?'

'Because I promised I wouldn't. This is a big thing, Kitty. If Walter Gates learns about Casey, Casey's life won't be worth a nickel.'

95

Kitty said indignantly, 'I'm not going to tell all I know to everyone I meet.'

'I know it. But Casey doesn't.'

'Hmp!'

The discussion rested there. Mr and Mrs Whitney went to bed. In the morning the discussion started all over again on a new tack. Kitty had done some heavy thinking while she lay abed, letting her husband have priority rights on the bathroom, and her thinking streak crystallized while Whit was brushing his teeth.

'Whit!'

'Ugh?' He was talking around the toothbrush.

'If weasel-face tried to shoot you last night because he thought you were Casey Jones, he'll try it again.'

'Gah blug —' Whit removed the toothbrush and tried again himself. 'He didn't try to shoot me. He tried to stick me up and take me along with him.'

'Well, whatever he was trying to do, nothing has happened to make him stop trying. You can't tell them about Casey Jones, so you're going to be in danger as long as we stay in Reno. We'll have to leave right away, before they try something else.'

Whit heard her heels thump the floor as she sprang out of bed. He put the toothbrush down and went into the bedroom. Kitty was already yanking suitcases out of the closet.

'Just pack your own, honey,' he said guiltily. 'I'm not going.'

Kitty turned around to stare at him. He felt like a wife-beater, but he went on with it.

'I think it might be a good idea for you to go home, as long as there may be trouble, but I – uh – promised Casey I'd stick around town to – uh – give him a hand. I telephoned Swede Larson last night. He's coming in by plane to-day to help me out.'

It took stuffing to make that speech. It took more stuffing to stand up under the oral beating that Kitty handed him for being a selfish fool, a brute, and a suicidal maniac. He agreed with her and said his mind was made up, and then prepared to weather out the storm. He knew that she would have her say and shut up about it.

His ears had been thoroughly pinned back before she finally ran out of breath. Once she had stopped talking she was through with the subject. She slammed her suitcases back in the closet, slammed the closet door, and began slamming herself into her clothes.

'I'd feel better if you went home,' Whit said meekly.

'I don't care how you'd feel.' Kitty's chin stuck out. 'This is my honeymoon and I'm damn well going to have it. If you're a big enough boob to get yourself into hot water and not have enough sense to get out, I'm staying. Hurry up and get dressed. I'm hungry.'

They had a meal in the hotel grill for the first time. It wasn't bad. It wasn't the kind of breakfast that John the Greek could throw together, but Whit's stuffing was not enough to make him unreasonably foolish about walking abroad. Not until Larson arrived. Although he was perfectly willing to tangle with any two or three of Gates' crew with his hands, catch-as-catch-can, he knew that Sammy Kohler could get within shooting range without being within catching distance. It seemed too one-sided. Whit spent the morning in his hotel room with his bride.

Kitty wrote letters, did some mending, and generally occupied herself, but the waiting got on Whit's nerves. He prowled moodily around the room, read a paper, threw it down, picked it up, threw it down again, and went to the window to see if Sammy Kohler was waiting for him in the street. Nobody was in sight. It was worse than if the little gunman had been leaning against a lamp-post below. When someone knocked at the door about noon, Whit jumped a foot straight up in the air.

The caller was Pete Weston. He had something on his mind, as both Whit and Kitty could see the moment he came in. He didn't seem to think it strange that he should find them there in the middle of the day.

'What's up?' Whit asked.

'That's what I want to know.' Pete looked contemplatively at Whit's suit, which happened to be the light grey number Whit had worn the night before. 'I thought maybe you could tell me.'

'About what?'

'Kohler.'

Whit's expression was politely curious. 'What about him?'

'He got rapped over the noggin last night.'

'You don't say.'

Weston said, 'Just for the sake of argument I'll pretend you don't know anything about it. A bank clerk named Robinson was walking home from a bridge game with a pal last night, and he sees a couple of guys run away from the front of a house and beat it down the street. The guys act strange. The bank clerk and his pal look around when they get to the place the two fellows have just left, and they see a body lying there. So they yell. The two guys run. The bank clerk and his pal take a look at the body and go through its pockets to see who it is. About the time they find out its name is Samuel S. Kohler and it doesn't seem to have a home, it comes to life. They try to take it to a hospital but it cusses them out and accuses them of stealing its gun. Finally it leaves, still cussing. The bank clerk, being a law-abiding citizen, tells the law about it this morning.'

'Interesting if true,' Whit said. 'Where do I come in?'

Pete still had his eye on Whit's clothes. 'The bank clerk gave a fair description of the men he'd seen running away. The sheriff had a similar description this morning, as far as one of them was concerned. He asked me to stop around and mention that he'd like to see you to-day. He wants to know where you were about eleven o'clock last night, who was with you, and if you were wearing a light-grey suit.'

Whit scratched his chest. The grey suit was an unfortunate thing. But the time, now – that wasn't hard, with a co-operative wife around.

'Hm. This fellow who looks like me certainly gets around. But luckily I was in bed at eleven o'clock. Wouldn't you say it was about eleven, Kitty?'

'Nearer ten-thirty, I think.' Kitty responded like a trouper.

Pete said, 'Why don't you come clean, Whit? I want to help.'

'You're crazy. I don't go around slugging people, even Sammy Kohler. If people keep seeing me at places where I'm not, then either they're lying or there's someone around town who looks like me. That's all I can say.'

'Suppose the sheriff finds out you weren't in bed at eleven o'clock last night?' Pete said slowly. 'Suppose he hears that you made a telephone call to San Francisco at twelve-thirty, from the lobby downstairs?'

'You're a nosey bastard, Pete.'

'I'm not a fool. I know you're doing more in Reno than en-

98

joying a honeymoon. The sheriff has his eye on you for Pop Foster's shooting, and he isn't going to forget about it. And he's smart, Whit. Don't let the hayseeds in his hair fool you. If you'll let me know what it's all about, I can help. He'll listen to me.'

'I didn't shoot Pop, I wasn't within ten miles of his house when he was shot, and I didn't bang Sammy Kohler over the head,' Whit answered truthfully, splitting a fine hair. After all, he had only paralyzed Kohler with a punch in the belly. 'Maybe I wasn't here at eleven o'clock, but the rest of it is the truth, so help me.'

'And you aren't going to tell me any more than that.'

'I can't, Pete. I wish I could. You'll have to believe me.'

Pete shrugged, picking up his hat. 'I'm not the one who counts. It's the sheriff you've got to worry about, and he isn't going to be satisfied.' He turned to Kitty, 'If you've got any influence with your husband, keep him out of trouble.'

'I'll do what I can,' Kitty said. 'It isn't easy.'

The telephone bell rang.

Pete had his hat and was ready to leave. He stalled near the door while Whit answered the phone.

The hotel operator said, 'Mr Whitney? A Mr Larson just asked for you. He's coming up to your room.'

'I can't see him now. Tell him to wait.'

'I'm sorry, sir. He's already on his way up.'

'Oh. Thanks.'

Pete still waited as Whit turned away from the phone. Whit thought fast. He didn't want Weston to meet Larson until he had a chance to warn his bodyguard to keep his big trap shut. But he couldn't think fast enough. Almost immediately there was a thump at the door, which opened before Whit could get to it. Swede Larson had landed and the situation was well out of hand.

Larson was a big man, a few years older than Whit and about Whit's size, although heavier around the middle. He had been a fair-to-middling pug at one time in his career, and the marks of the trade showed in his face. His nose was dished at the bridge and the flesh over his cheek bones and beneath his eyebrows was thickened with scar tissue. He grinned, shaking Whit's hand. The grin became a bit stiff when he saw Kitty smiling at him, and the obvious evidence in the room that

99

Whit wasn't staying there alone, but he and Kitty were friends of old standing. He carried it off like the gent he was.

'Oh, hello. I didn't know – Whit didn't say nothing – well, hello. I'm sure glad to see you.'

Kitty said, 'Don't look so worried, Swede. We're married. It's a honeymoon.'

Larson was relieved. 'Say, that's swell. Congratulations. I was wondering when you two would get hitched. But if it's a honeymoon, what's all this that Whit was telling me about —'

'Mister Larson, meet Mister Weston,' Whit said. 'Mister Weston represents the Associated Press in Reno and he has a long nose and big ears. Don't say anything in front of him that you don't want to read in the papers. Mr Larson is a friend of mine from San Francisco, Pete. Just flew over for a brief vacation. How was the trip, Swede? Uneventful, I trust.'

'Oh, sure.' Larson and Pete shook hands. 'Nothing to it. One minute you're in San Francisco, the next minute you're in Reno. The only thing that gets me is the hump over the mountains. Plugs up my ears.' He beat the side of his head with his palm. 'Plane rides always makes my head ache. I'd have took a train if you hadn't been so anxious. What's all this you were saying about —'

'Lunch,' said Whit. 'We've got to have food before we talk. Excuse us, will you, Pete? Mr Larson and I have some business to discuss.'

'Don't mind me,' Weston said agreeably. 'I'm hungry myself. We'll all go together.'

'Swell,' said Larson.

Whit felt like kicking Larson's pants for him. Weston smelled news, and he was going to stick around until he got it. And Larson, who was the salt of the earth but not too sharp between the ears, would have to be hit over the head before he would get the idea that Whit wanted him not to talk in front of the newspaperman. Whit knew he couldn't shut Larson off indefinitely. He thought, God, if Pete doesn't give me just one minute alone with the dumb ox, I'm cooked.

It was the lady of the house who saved the day. Weston had Larson's arm and was making chit-chat with him as they all left the room. Only Whit's desperate interruptions kept the conversation where it belonged. He carried on a running monologue as the party progressed down the hall, clutching one of Larson's arms while Pete held the other. They reached the elevator in that arrangement, Whit still talking, Pete waiting for him to run out of words, Larson faintly puzzled, and Kitty bringing up the rear. At the elevator Kitty said regretfully, 'Oh, dear.' She pointed back down the long hall to where her gloves lay on the carpet in front of the door they had just left. 'Pete. Be a dear, won't you?'

There was no way for Weston to avoid being a dear or he would have done so. He gave Kitty a nasty look as he hesitated, and then did his best to recover the gloves in nothing flat. But Whit had time to whisper savagely in Larson's ear.

'Keep your yawp closed in front of that guy. You're a visiting fireman here on a holiday, and that's all.'

'What —'

'Shut up!'

Pete was back with the gloves. He suspected that some message had been communicated while his back was turned, but he could not be sure. He fastened himself again to Larson's arm and took up where he had left off.

As the elevator dropped them to the lobby below, Pete got his first opportunity to fire a direct question at Larson.

'What brings you to Reno, Mr Larson? The Press is always interested in visitors.'

'Holiday,' Larson said.

'From business?'

'Uh – that's right.'

'And what is your business?' Weston was ready to make reportorial notes on the back of an envelope.

Larson looked desperately at Whit for help, but Weston was watching them both. Whit could do no more than bare his clenched teeth.

Larson gulped.

'I'm a fireman,' he mumbled. 'Just visiting.'

CHAPTER 12

'You didn't have to be so literal,' Whit said, two hours later. 'A visiting fireman! My God, you might just as well have told him your name was Joe Doakes.'

The Whitneys and their man Friday were back at the hotel.

101

They had given Pete the dust-off and sent him on his way, with no more information than he had when he started but a firm suspicion that something was very fishy about Larson. Larson himself was still in the dark. There had been no attacks, no shooting, and no sign of Kohler or any other of Whit's fans. Larson had faithfully kept his eyes open and prepared himself for trouble without knowing just what form the trouble might take or from what source it might arise. Now he thought it was time he learned what it was all about. He said so.

Whit had to agree, and he found himself in a bad position. He trusted Larson as much as he trusted anybody, but every person who knew the facts was one more potential weak link in the chain on which depended Casey Jones' life. The responsibility was too heavy to pass on. On the other hand, Larson could not be expected to risk his own life for Whit's benefit without knowing what he was up against. Whit had promised Casey that Larson wouldn't have to be told too much, and he had believed it when he said it. But now he knew he would have to give Larson at least part of the picture, and he couldn't see a dividing line between part of the picture and the whole thing. Whatever he did, he was wrong.

He bit a large piece out of his thumbnail.

Kitty had been watching him stew. She said, 'You have to tell him. It isn't fair not to.'

'I know it.' Whit gnawed at his thumb. 'Damn it all, I know it. But I promised Casey – oh, nuts. Swede, I've got a gang of saboteurs after me.'

'A gang of what?'

'Saboteurs; spies; fifth columnists. They're here in Reno. They've killed two men already, at least, and now they're on my trail. One of them tried to get me last night, but I was lucky. I don't know whether I can go on being lucky. That's why I called you in.'

Larson frowned. 'What are you doing, messing around with spies?'

'They think I'm here to keep an eye on them. I'm not – or I am, I guess, but not the way they think. Anyway, they're after me and I can't go to the cops for help. So what do you say?'

'So what's the rest of it?'

There was no way out. For the second time in twenty-four

hours Whit had to break his promise to Casey and spill the beans.

Larson's reaction to the bean-spilling was negative. He listened without comment. In the middle of Whit's story he produced a package of gum, gave a stick to Kitty, and chewed reflectively while Whit talked. Whit didn't think he was making the proper impression. He pulled out a couple of tremolo stops and switched from the danger that confronted his own skin to the danger that would confront the good old U.S.A. if Larson didn't get in there and help Whit pitch. It was quite a speech.

Larson said in some surprise, 'You don't have to sell me any war bonds. I'm in.' He looked at Kitty. 'Sounds like a recruiting sergeant, don't he?'

Kitty said, 'He wasn't sure you knew how important it is, Swede.'

'I know how important it is.' Larson went on chewing his gum, but his eyes were dark. 'I know how important it is to win the war, too. People call me Swede because anybody named Larson gets called Swede, but my old man was a Norwegian. He and my old lady went back to Norway ten years ago. My old man was killed when the Nazzies came in, and I haven't heard from my ma at all. She was pretty old.'

There was an awkward silence for a moment. When Kitty and Whit simultaneously tried to say something, Larson interrupted them.

'Anyways, I wouldn't want to see your honeymoon busted up, and this guy Jones sounds like he needs all the help he can get. So if you'll leave me to check in with the local cops, now, I'll —'

'Nope,' said Whit. 'That's out.'

'What's out?'

'Reporting to the police. No soap.'

'But I got to. I got a letter from the Lootenant to the county sheriff here. I don't even have a licence to carry a gun in Nevada, and if I don't report in they could pick me up for carrying concealed weapons and take my sling-shot.' He patted the bulge in front of his left armpit. 'I might need it, from what you tell me.'

'You can't do it, Swede. Maybe the cops are all right, maybe they aren't. I don't know and I don't want to take any chances. You're just here on a vacation, that's all.'

103

'The cops will be sore if they find out I've muscled in here. I still think —'

'No,' Whit said flatly. 'I'm sorry. You'll have to stay under cover.'

Larson shrugged. 'O.K. You're the boss. What do we do now?'

'First we go call on the sheriff. He wants to talk to me about the lump on Sammy Kohler's head.'

'He's the guy who stuck you up?'

'Yes.'

'O.K., let's go. Maybe we'll meet him again and give him another lump.'

'That's an idea,' Whit said. 'Kitty, you stay right here until we get back, and don't open the door without finding out who's knocking.'

'I'm not worried about me. You be careful, honey.'

'He's safer than a safe-deposit box,' said Larson. 'With me on the job —' He snapped his fingers. 'See you later.'

Whit described the whole cast of characters as he walked with Larson to the Sheriff's office – Sammy, Walter Gates, Lorenzo, Jess Caldwell, Casey Jones, the sheriff, even Gladys. He held Gladys out as a kind of deep-dish apple pie who might keep Larson's visit from being all work and no play, and his description, although simple, was sufficiently graphic to get Larson interested. From Gladys the conversation shifted to Pete Weston.

Larson said, 'Why was you so hot to keep him from knowing why I was here? Is he somebody to look out for?'

'I think he's O.K. But I don't know for sure, and I don't want to take any chances. He's a newspaperman, Swede, and newspapermen aren't like regular people. They'd sell their own mothers down the river to get hold of a good story, and this one is good. If anything leaks too soon – blooie!' Whit made a tossing gesture.

'Uh huh. Well, I've heard tell that a closed trap catches no flies, and I guess there's something to it. But this whole business sounds like a movie plot to me.'

'Never you mind what it sounds like.' They were crossing the street, and Whit tried his best to look in all directions at once. 'You just keep your eyes open. Remember I can't pay your expenses if anything happens to me.'

'How about an advance?' said Larson.

Nothing happened to Whit before they reached the sheriff's office, and they were both grateful, Whit because he was unpunctured and unmolested and Larson because he hadn't yet got the advance. The sheriff seemed reasonably well pleased to see Whit, glad to meet Mr Larson – Mr Whitney's fireman friend from San Francisco, just in town for a vacation – and not as menacing as Whit had expected. He waved at a couple of chairs, stoked up a blackened pipe with something that smelled like burning brake-bands, and asked Whit how he was doing. Whit said he was doing fine, thanks. The sheriff was glad to hear it.

'Pete Weston told me you wanted to see me,' Whit said.

'That's right.' The sheriff tamped the brake-bands with his forefinger. 'Got a couple of things to ask you about. Maybe Mr Larson wouldn't mind waiting outside.'

Larson looked at Whit.

Whit said, 'If you say so. I don't mind him listening if you don't.'

'All the same to me,' said the sheriff. 'Thought maybe you might want to talk in private, seeing as how I'm maybe going to have to ask some embarrassing questions.' He puffed earnestly at his smudge-pot.

'What questions?'

The sheriff blew out a cloud of smoke. 'I been doing a little investigating. Pete Weston says yore all right, as far as he knows, and I hold pretty well with what Pete says, generally. I'll tell you right now, I'm willing to give you the benefit of the doubt about Pop Foster because as far as I can see you didn't have any call to shoot him. But there's something going on here I don't like.'

He sucked on his pipe. Whit kept his mouth shut, remembering Larson's comment about the flies and the closed trap.

The sheriff went on. 'It ain't rightly my business what happens inside the city limits. There's a pretty good police force here in Reno to take care of those things. But if you were hanging around Pop Foster's house the night he was killed – and I think you were – and if you had a hand in slugging Sam Kohler in Douglas Alley last night – and I think you did – then yore either mixed up in the murder or you know something about it. I want to know what you know.'

105

He peered at Whit through the smoke cloud.

'I wasn't near Pop Foster when he was killed,' Whit said. 'You can check with Weston to prove it, if you like. He was with me that night. And all I know about Sammy Kohler is that I met him at Pop's the day I was married and didn't like him, plus what Pete Weston told me to-day about him getting pushed over in an alley last night. Personally I think he's more liable to slug somebody in an alley than to get slugged. I'll tell you what I told Pete to-day, when he said someone who looked like me had been seen running away from Sammy Kohler; if people keep seeing me where I'm not, either they're lying or someone around town looks like me. Furthermore, I haven't any use for a gun. If you think I —'

'Who said anything about a gun?' the sheriff asked gently.

Whit knew he had stumbled, but he recovered quickly.

'I've talked to Pete. I know Kohler was crying about losing his.'

'Uh huh. I suppose you've got an alibi for the time he was attacked.'

Whit was ready for him this time. 'I don't know. When was it?'

'I thought you said you talked to Pete Weston.'

'He wasn't very clear about the time.'

'It was around eleven-thirty.'

Whit looked thoughtfully at the ceiling. If Weston had talked to the hotel clerk, the sheriff could too – if he hadn't already. 'Hm. Eleven-thirty. I guess I haven't got much of an alibi, then. I was out prowling around the crap-games most of the evening, although I don't know just where I was at eleven-thirty. But why don't you talk to Kohler? It seems to me that you ought to pay more attention to guys that go around carrying guns than to people who mind their own business and keep out of trouble. Kohler would tell you that I didn't slug him.'

It was a safe suggestion. Sammy the weasel wasn't going to talk to the sheriff if he could avoid it, and if he had to talk Whit would bet he wouldn't say anything that had any remote connexion with the truth.

'I'm planning to talk to Kohler as soon as I catch up with him,' the sheriff said. 'I don't know that what he has to say will carry much weight, any more than what you say carries much weight. Yore both holding out on me.'

106

'If you can think of one good reason why I'd want to bust him over the head, I'll put in with you.'

The sheriff shook his head. 'That's what I'm trying to find out, son. I don't know. When I do, I'll have something to say to you.' He gestured with his pipe. 'Who did you telephone in San Francisco at one o'clock this morning?'

Whit gave himself a mental handshake for being smart. He nodded in Larson's direction. 'Mr Larson.'

'What for?'

'I wanted to know when he was coming on to Reno. We'd made arrangements to meet here.'

The sheriff lit a match and applied it to the half-consumed brake-hands, cocking an eye at Larson over the flame. 'That's right?'

'That's right.'

'Seems a little strange to me that a man on his honeymoon would be so anxious for company. What's the matter with you and the missus, Mr Whitney?'

Whit felt himself getting hot. He was about to pop off when he saw the sheriff's keen old eyes watching him, and he realized that he was deliberately needled so that he might give something away. His temper faded. The sheriff was a smart cookie.

'We like to play three-handed pinochle,' Whit said pleasantly. 'If you're all through with us, we'll go get a game started.'

The sheriff nodded. 'That's all for now, then. Except I'd like to get yore fingerprints for the record.' He reached for the phone on the table behind him and clicked a switch at the desk-corner. 'Send George in to take some prints.'

It was Whit's expression that prompted Larson to put his oar in. Whit didn't mind being fingerprinted, but he couldn't think of any reason why the sheriff should want the prints. While he tried desperately to remember where he had put his hands in the last few days that he shouldn't have, Larson saw the worry in his face and misunderstood its cause.

'You don't have to give him any prints, Whit.'

The sheriff raised his eyebrows at Larson. 'You a lawyer?'

'No. I just know that he doesn't have to give you any prints if he doesn't want to. He isn't charged with nothing.'

The sheriff said, 'Not yet. Everything's friendly so far, and I'd like to keep it that way. 'Course, if we have to get tough we can think up something to charge you with, son. Can't see any reason for you to be persnickety if you haven't got anything to worry about.'

'Neither can I,' said Whit. 'Stop arguing, Swede.'

They got away a few minutes later, after Whit had left his prints for the records and received the sheriff's usual warning to keep out of trouble. Whit didn't say so, but he was expecting trouble to come up and hit him in the face the minute he and Larson stepped out in the street, and he was surprised that it did not. Neither then nor during the time it took to walk to the hotel. Either his bodyguard had scared the wolves away or they had lost interest. Whit didn't understand it. He was beginning to think he would welcome a little action in place of the nervous strain of waiting for something to happen that didn't.

Kitty was playing a slot machine in the hotel lobby when they got there. She didn't seem to like the machine very much, from the way she slammed at the handle. The machine stuck momentarily as Whit and Larson approached. Kitty gave the stand a kick and swore in an unladylike manner.

'Having fun?' said Whit.

'Oh, lovely,' Kitty answered. She kicked the machine again. 'You can't imagine how much I enjoy waiting for my husband to be brought home on a shutter.'

'Now what's bothering you?'

Kitty turned on him like a cat.

'What do you think is bothering me? I'm supposed to be on my honeymoon, and we haven't had a peaceful moment together since we got here. Two days married, and I have to spend my time squandering nickels on this damn pig-bank while my husband walks the streets waiting for someone to try to kidnap him. Oh, it's wonderful!'

'Now listen, honey —'

'Don't honey me!' Kitty's eyes were strangely bright. 'I was a fool to let you talk me into staying here, but I'm not fool enough to go on being a fool. We're leaving to-day.'

'We are not leaving,' Whit said. 'Don't be silly.'

Larson mumbled something and began to edge away. Neither Whit nor Kitty noticed him go.

Kitty said in a choked voice, 'I want to go home.'

'I think you should go. I said so this morning. But you know I can't leave.'

'Please.'

'I can't. You know I can't. What's got into you?'

'If you don't come with me now, you needn't bother to come at all.'

Whit stared at her. She was holding her mouth tight so it wouldn't tremble, but she couldn't control her eyes. The brightness in them was beginning to run over the lower lids. Whit took her hand and led her to a quiet corner of the lobby where there were a couple of chairs. She let him put her in a chair, and then she dropped her head down on the chair arm and wept unhappily, like a child.

Whit held her hand. When she quieted down, he said, 'Now what is it, honey? What happened?'

'Promise I can go along, Whit.' She didn't lift her head. Her voice was muffled by the chair arm. 'I don't mind anything if I can be with you. I just can't stand waiting.'

'Where am I going?'

'Promise. I know you'll go but if I can just be with you —'

'I promise anything that's reasonable. Where am I going?'

Kitty lifted her head and mopped her nose. She said miserably, 'Jess Caldwell telephoned. He wanted to make sure that you would be at Lorenzo's Club to-night. I could tell from the way he t-talked that he's – that they're going to d-do something to you.'

CHAPTER 13

THERE were arguments later, of course, but Whit found that leaving his ever-loving wife behind, once he had made a promise, was like leaving his ever-loving right arm. In the end, when he left the hotel with Larson that evening on the way to their rendezvous with trouble, Kitty went with them.

They walked. Larson was on the right where his gun arm wouldn't tangle with anyone in the event that something started prematurely. Kitty was in the middle, and Whit held down the left wing. The newly-weds had nothing to say to each other as they went down Virginia Street towards Lorenzo's Club and whatever waited for them there. They were talked out.

Kitty and Whit had gone to the mat on the subject of his skin *versus* his principles, and although his principles had won out it had been a rough tussle. He had not been able to sound convincing, even to himself, when he explained his reasons for walking into an obvious trap, and he had ended up by shouting that he was going to do what he was going to do, by God, and Kitty would damn well have to do as he said if she wanted to come along. And that was that.

They exchanged their first calm words when they reached the street corner at which they were to turn to go in the direction of Lorenzo's Club. Whit gestured silently ahead. They continued towards the railroad tracks at the shabby end of town.

Kitty said, 'Where are we going?'

'Casey Jones' rooming house.'

'What for?'

'I want to leave a message for Casey so he'll know what's happening.'

'Thank you.'

'You're welcome.'

They reached Commercial Row near the tracks without incident. It was early evening, not yet quite dark, but the town's main industry was humming at full speed with a rattle of dice, the slap of cards, and the whirr of the wheels. Near the end of Virginia Street there was a big and popular gambling hell, appropriately named The Last Chance. The customers went in through a plushy entrance on Virginia Street and were faced with a double row of slot machines which led from one end of the building to the other. Plenty of other methods were available for dropping the rent money if the customer were interested, but the one-armed bandits were the easiest and most convenient. They started at a dollar near the entrance and got progressively cheaper as the customer moved along. At the end of the line a brace of machines accepted pennies, and on the other side of those a dingy exit opened on Commercial Row next to a two-bit flop house. It was a very convenient arrangement if the customer still had two bits.

The dingy exit was convenient to Whit just then for another reason. He had patronized The Last Chance before, at one time or another, and had spotted it and its location in relation to Casey's hideout when he left Casey the night before. The rear exit was less than half a block from the Magnolia Rooms. Whit did not think that they were being followed, but he remembered Casey's warning and he was taking no unnecessary risks of leading the hounds to the fox-hole. So the Whitney-Larson Mutual Protection, Benefit and Honeymoon Society turned in at The Last Chance instead of proceeding around the corner.

Whit explained his plans while he donated a silver dollar, a half-dollar, a quarter, a dime, a nickel, and three pennies to different slot machines. None of the machines paid off, but the contributions gave him time to talk and carried the party unobtrusively to the rear door of the casino.

'There's a flop-joint down the street. Magnolia Rooms. You'll see the sign when we get out on the sidewalk. That's where I'm going. I want you to wait here with Kitty, Swede, and keep an eye on me when I leave. If anyone follows me into the place, you follow right behind and keep your eyes open. Kitty will be all right here. I don't expect anything to start, but if it does I don't want to be caught with my pants down. If you don't see anyone come after me, wait fifteen minutes – no, make it ten – and come along anyway, because something will have gone sour. Try the last room on the left-hand side going down the third-floor hall, and be ready for trouble.'

Larson nodded. 'I got it. Let me have a cigarette, will you? I'm fresh out.' He wasn't worried.

Whit gave him a cigarette and turned to Kitty. 'I've got to go. I'll probably be back in five minutes. Don't make me argue with you.'

'I won't.' Kitty smiled at him. The smile looked as if it hurt, but it was a smile. 'Be careful. Be *awfully* careful.'

'I will.'

Whit gave a quick look around and led the way through the exit.

Larson had been thinking hard. As they came out into the street, he said wonderingly, 'Now how did I get so drunk all of a sudden?' and reeled against Whit, putting his arms around Whit's neck to hold himself up. There were people near them, but no one was too near or too curious about another drunk. Whit automatically clasped Larson around the middle as the other man's weight sagged against him, not sure what was going on. Larson mumbled in his ear.

'Reach under my left arm and take my gun. You might need it.'

'I don't want it.'

111

'Take it.'

Whit took it. The heavy automatic slid easily from its spring clip into his hand. He put it inside his coat, then slipped it down into the waistband of his pants.

Larson was still hanging to his neck. He said, 'The button on the left where your thumb rests is the safety catch. Press that first, then pull the trigger. You'll knock down anything you hit, but hold low when you shoot. She kicks up.'

He let go of Whit's neck and pushed himself upright. Whit walked away without a backward glance.

The gun barrel made an uncomfortable lump in his groin as he walked. He kept his forearm pressed against it so it would not fall down his pants leg. It was reassuring to feel the heavy weapon under his arm, yet he hoped he would have no need to use it. Guns were foreign to him, except as toys he had used to blow holes in a target or a tin can. They seemed much too conclusive to use on a man. A good smack on the chin, now, Whit could understand that whether he gave it or received it. And he felt better about it, either way, than if it were a bullet.

The gun stabbed his leg as he climbed the stairs of the Magnolia Rooms. No one had been around when he entered and no one was in sight when he reached the gloomy third floor. The hall still smelled of disinfectant. He took the gun out of his waistband and put it in his coat pocket.

The slit under Casey's door was dark. Whit knocked once, then again, and tried the door knob. The door was locked, as he knew it would be, but the keyhole was one that looked receptive to any key and Whit had several on a ring in his pocket. One was a ten-cent pass key he had bought in a dime store for general use on closets and what-not. He looked back down the empty hallway and tried the key. It worked.

There was no need to turn on the light when he was inside. Enough of a glow came through the window from the light-well to show him that the place was empty. He had a pencil and some odds and ends of letters in his pocket. He selected an envelope, tore out a section that bore no writing, and wrote a note without salutation. It read:

Thursday night 7.30. On my way to Lawrence's dump to meet J.C. He's got some kind of a surprise party planned for me. I don't know what he's cooking in the way of a birthday cake, but if anything happens you'll know where I went, and I expect you to pay him for his trouble. Keep the home fires burning.

He signed it with a W.

It wouldn't be cryptic to Casey. It wouldn't be cryptic to anyone who knew what was going on, but it might puzzle an innocent bystander or a chambermaid. Of course the Magnolia Rooms didn't have chambermaids, and anyone who might find the note in Casey's room wouldn't be an innocent bystander, but Whit's principles were not to take a chance if it didn't buy him anything. He folded the note, hid it in the hollow post of the bedstead, and left the room as quietly as he had entered. No one saw him go.

Kitty was staring so intently at her wristwatch that she didn't notice him coming down the street until Larson spoke. When he joined them in the doorway, she said shakily, 'My, you haven't changed a bit.'

Whit patted her arm. 'I wasn't gone long.'

'It was the longest eight minutes I ever went through. Was he there?'

'No. I left him a note.'

Whit shouldered Larson into the doorway and slipped the gun out of his pocket. 'Here. Thanks, Swede. I was just thinking that you would have been in hell of a bad fix if I'd run into trouble and you'd had to come after me without a gun.'

'Sure. And while you were doing all that thinking, did you figure what a lot could happen to you while I waited down here for ten minutes? I'd rather get there quick without a gun than be ten minutes late with one.' Larson settled the automatic comfortably under his arm. 'That's a forty-five, chum. You might not have hit anyone with it, but it makes a lot of noise. If you'd of pulled the trigger, I'd of known about it.'

Whit said, 'Maybe you aren't so dumb after all.'

'I get an idea once in a while. Where do we go from here?'

'Lorenzo's.'

They cased Lorenzo's Club carefully when they arrived. Kitty was persuaded to wait under the marquee at the brightly lit entrance, and Whit and Larson prowled the front and side of the building, the parking-lot in the rear, and the alley down which Whit had chased Casey two nights earlier. Casey wasn't

113

in sight. No one was in sight that Whit had ever seen before in his life. He didn't know whether to feel happy about it or not.

It was the same when they got inside. The check-girl took their hats and coats and they looked over the crowd from the vantage point of the doorway. The Club was going full blast. Everybody in Reno seemed to be there except the people Whit expected to see. No Jess Caldwell, no Lorenzo, no anybody that counted. It was a hell of a situation.

He said, 'I wonder what we're supposed to do now.'

'I know what I'm going to do,' said Kitty, gesturing at a waiter. 'You and your ideas that women ought to wear spike heels because they're pretty. My feet are killing me. I'm going to sit down and have three drinks before I budge an inch, whatever happens.'

'Swell idea,' Larson said. He buttonholed the waiter as the man came up in answer to Kitty's signal. 'Give us a nice quiet table in a corner and bring us a lot of highballs.'

'Champagne,' said Kitty.

Whit gloomily corrected both orders.

'Make it three beers. We're expecting company, Swede. Let's stay on our feet.'

*

Jess Caldwell spoke without turning his head from the spy-hole that looked down on the casino from Lorenzo's office on the mezzanine.

'He's here. He brought his wife and another man.'

Lorenzo did not answer. He sat loosely in a chair across the room, holding a brandy bell cupped in both hands. He was dressed in his uniform of evening clothes and white gardenia, and his face was sullen, flushed with liquor and bad temper.

Caldwell said, 'Did you hear me?'

'What do you want me to do about it – sing?'

Lorenzo's speech showed a faint thickness. Caldwell, still without turning his head, said, 'You're getting drunk, Renzo.'

'Never mind me. I'm all right.'

Caldwell turned to look at him.

'You're not all right. You're drunk as a pig.'

Lorenzo's sullen glare dropped. He swished the brandy around in the belled glass and drank it down.

114

Caldwell said, 'You're not only drunk, you're a damn fool,' and turned back to the spyhole to peer once more at the crowded floor of the casino.

The two men did not speak again for several minutes. Caldwell stayed at the spyhole, watching what went on below. Lorenzo sat in his chair and drank. As the glass emptied, he refilled it from a bottle at his elbow. Once he spilled some of the liquor. It made a brown spot on his beautifully starched shirt front, but he did not notice it.

Caldwell said abruptly, 'Come here. Who's the plug-ugly Whit has with him?'

It seemed at first as if Lorenzo were to pay no attention, but he thought better of it. He went to the spyhole, looked through it briefly, and returned to his chair, weaving slightly as he walked.

'Never saw him before.'

'I wonder if Whitney suspects something,' Caldwell said thoughtfully.

Lorenzo reached for the brandy bottle. At the clink of the glass, Caldwell turned around.

'That's about enough, Renzo. You won't be any help to me if you go on drinking.'

'I won't be any help to you anyway,' Lorenzo answered. His speech was thicker now. 'I'm not going to have anything to do with this.'

'What?'

'You heard me, I can't afford to get in trouble. I've got a good business here; I'm making money, giving you a front, getting information that Walter wants. I'm not going to do anything to throw it away.'

'*You're* making money,' Caldwell said. 'You dirty immigrant, you didn't have ten cents when we put you in here, or any prospect of getting ten cents. You're here to do what you're told. Don't forget it.'

Lorenzo glared at him from bloodshot eyes. 'I'm not going to have anything to do with it,' he repeated, biting the words out. 'I don't care what you do. Just leave me out of it.'

'Do you want me to tell Walter that?'

Lorenzo continued to glare.

'Do you want your orders direct from him? He'll tell you what you'll do and what you won't do, and you know what

115

else he'll do if you cross him. Think that over.'

Lorenzo did not have to think it over. He knew, and it was too much even for the Dutch courage he had taken. In a blind fury of impotent rage and frustration he lifted the half-empty glass over his head and smashed it to the floor.

'That's fine,' Caldwell said contemptuously. 'Now listen, if you can still hear. Whitney is drinking beer. Sooner or later he'll have to go to the lavatory, and I'll take care of him when he does. I don't know who that is with him, but I don't want him interfering. All you have to do is keep him and Whitney's wife occupied until I can get Whitney out of here. Do you think you can manage that?'

Lorenzo made a thick sound in his throat. Caldwell turned back to the spyhole.

*

Larson felt abused. Beer was a lousy drink for a guy on a vacation. He was taking an unhappy sip of the terrible stuff when he caught sight of something luscious approaching the table. His face lit up, and he nudged Whit with his elbow.

'Hot dog! Look what's coming! Does she really know us or am I dreaming?'

Whit and Kitty both turned to see if he was dreaming. Gladys was coming towards them.

For a half-pint, it was wonderful how Gladys could soften up big strong men. Whit could see Larson falling apart as the introduction was made. He hoped that Gladys was not going to stick around. He had nothing against her, but Larson was not going to be of any value as long as the blonde was there.

Gladys batted her eyes at Larson and was *awfully* glad to meet him. She loved firemen. She had on still another evening dress this time. Whit couldn't remember whether it was the third or fourth he had seen her in. It was a different colour from the others but the same old sure-fire racing model – nothing at all that was not necessary to cover the chassis, and the minimum of wind resistance. Larson got one look at her close up, smelled the expensive scent she wore, and was ruined.

Gladys said, 'How's the honeymoon?'

'Very nice,' Kitty said. From someone else the question might have sounded a bit personal. It was different coming from Gladys. She hadn't enough depth to develop a hidden meaning.

'I always enjoyed mine – all of them.' Gladys giggled. 'Have you seen Pete? He was supposed to meet me here to-night. I think he's stood me up.'

Whit said, 'We haven't seen him. We were sort of looking for Jess, ourselves. I haven't seen anyone we know. Not even Lorenzo.'

'I haven't seen Jess since the night before last, when we were all here. I don't think he likes me any more.' Gladys giggled again, giving Larson the eye just to keep in practice. 'Can I sit here and wait for Pete? I always seem to get picked up when I wait for anyone by myself.'

'Sure.' Whit wanted to kick Larson's shin so the oaf would close his mouth and pay attention to something else besides Gladys' figure. 'What will you have to drink?'

'Oh, anything. A little brandy, I guess.'

The little brandy changed the party. Kitty was not going to drink beer unless everyone else drank beer, and she thought Gladys was very wise not to touch it. Whit would have liked something besides hogwash himself, but he couldn't have a drink without letting Larson have one as well and he wanted Larson's co-ordination at its peak when whatever happened that was going to happen. He ordered two brandies and two beers, ignoring Larson's hopeful look.

Gladys graduated immediately to calling Larson Sweedy-pie as soon as she heard Whit address him as Swede. She had Sweedy-pie dazzled. He was enjoying his dazzlement so much that he didn't keep his mind on his business. When Whit felt the beer percolating and got up to leave the table, Larson let him go.

Whit wasn't thinking himself, because it had been a long time since he had asked anyone to take him to the bathroom. He excused himself casually and inquired his way from a waiter to what the waiter called the gentlemen's lounch.

Jess Caldwell had selected Lorenzo's Club for his trap because he knew of the long passage-way between the casino proper and the men's washroom. From his lookout on the mezzanine he saw Whit leave the table and speak to the waiter, and he had plenty of time to get down the back stairs before Whit left the gentleman's lounch. He was waiting in a convenient alcove when Whit made the return trip. Whit heard a brief swishing noise, and then a beautiful skyrocket exploded in his head and he lost interest in things.

CHAPTER 14

IT might have been the brandy, or the pleasant music of the orchestra, or Gladys babbling about those nasty Japanese whose only interest in life was to make it difficult for her to get silk stockings, or the fact that Kitty didn't know exactly how long it should take a gentleman to return from the rest-room, but even after Whit had been gone nearly ten minutes she did not think about his absence until she happened to look at Larson's face. Then her heart jumped so that it hurt.

'Swede!'

'Yes, mam,' Larson said. 'I'm worried. He shouldn't ought to of been gone so long.'

'Go after him! Quick!' Kitty had jumped to her feet, and fright made her voice shrill. Several people turned to stare.

'Yes'm. You two stay here. Don't move until I get back.'

Larson collared the first waiter he saw. The man had a tray-load of dishes, and he saved them only by a masterpiece of juggling. Before he could open his mouth to express his indignation, Larson said, 'Shut up. Where's the can? Hurry.'

The waiter knew enough not to argue when a guest asked that question in that tone of voice. He pointed with his free hand, and juggled his tray desperately as Larson pushed him away and ran. The waiter had seen gentlemen in a hurry before, but never anyone like Larson.

The hallway leading to the rest-rooms was empty. Larson burst through the door of the lavatory with the ·45 in his hand, ready for action, and found the place empty except for an attendant in a white coat. The attendant was a pretty young man who did a small but thriving business in towels, hair tonic and similar items with the gentlemen who came to call at his place of business. When he looked up in surprise at Larson's abrupt entrance and saw the muzzle of the automatic staring him in the eye, he quietly fainted. Larson paid no attention to him. He left the lavatory as he had come, cursing bitterly.

118

Back at the table Kitty was holding herself together with plain will-power. The strain mounted as time went on and Larson did not return, until fear for Whit held her so strongly that the music, Gladys' voice, the noise of the cabaret, the pound of her heart, all merged together into a dull roar without meaning. Gladys finally had to reach across the table and shake her before she got the sense of Gladys' repeated questions.

'What is it? What happened?'

Kitty was too far gone to see the alert intelligence in Gladys' pretty doll-like face. She said numbly, 'They've got him! Oh, God, they've got him!'

'Who has him? Why?'

'They have. I – you wouldn't understand. I'm afraid! I'm afraid! I don't know what —'

'Keep quiet!'

Gladys had whispered, but even the whisper carried enough authority to shock Kitty into silence. Before she had time even to wonder at the incongruity of such a tone from Gladys, Gladys whispered again, 'Bluff it out. Here's Renzo,' and immediately launched into another discussion of the nasty Japs and her silk stockings. In the middle of the babble she looked up, and her eyes widened happily.

'Renzo! You're just in time to buy us a drink.'

Lorenzo stood by the table, scowling at them. He was very drunk, and there were red rims around his eyes. He did not speak. Kitty smiled, holding to the smile with everything she had. It was the only way she could fight him until she knew what to do. Bluff it out. Who had told her that?

Gladys said brightly, 'Well, if you won't buy us a drink, you might at least ask one of us to dance. Our boy friends —'

'Shut up.' Renzo did not look at her.

'Why, Renzo! I don't think you ought to —'

'Shut up!'

This time Renzo swung around to scowl at her. He was so drunk that the turn threw him off balance and he had to clutch at the table. The girls watched him as he regained his balance, holding to the table edge with both hands. He said thickly, 'Get out of here. Don't want you in my place. Nothing but bad luck since you came here. Get out.'

If he hadn't been so ugly Kitty would have wept from pure

119

futility and fear for Whit. As it was, Lorenzo made her mad. She said, 'Who do you think you're talking to?'

The red in Lorenzo's bloodshot eyes darkened. He let go of the table, reached for Kitty's wrist, and yanked her to her feet.

It was his bad luck that Kitty was already angry, and that the one thing which could make her angrier was to be manhandled by a drunk. She had been manhandled before during her career, usually to the regret of the man doing the handling, and she was not a gentle soul. She let Lorenzo have the heel of her free hand in a jolting uppercut that snapped his head back and would have knocked him down except for the table behind him.

Lorenzo was blind with fury. He struggled to recover his balance, his face purple with rage, and charged at Kitty like a bull. He caught her with one hand, twisted her arm behind her so that she gasped with pain, and as she struggled, slapped her brutally across the mouth – once, twice, three times. The smack of the slaps was clearly audible, people turned to see what was happening, and one or two men rose from their chairs with the hesitancy of strangers who wanted to interfere but weren't sure that they ought to butt in.

The blows knocked most of the fight out of Kitty. Lorenzo still held her with one hand as her knees weakened and she began to sag. Behind him, Gladys had reached for one of the beer bottles and was preparing to brain him. She never had to swing her weapon.

It was Lorenzo's second piece of bad luck that Swede Larson returned, bitter with self-accusation and frustration, in time to see the slapping from across the dance floor. Larson's path by the shortest route from where he stood left a broad wake of disturbed guests and displaced tables, but it got him there quickly – so quickly that Lorenzo knew about it only when Larson nearly broke the arm that held Kitty as he spun Lorenzo around.

The butchering wasn't pretty to see. Larson wanted to cut Lorenzo up as much as possible, and he brushed Lorenzo's hands aside and hit at his face with both fists as fast as he could move his arms, hooking from the sides so that his knuckles would do the maximum damage without laying his victim out too quickly. Even then, four or five cutting blows were all that Lorenzo took before he sagged back against the table. Larson set him up again with a left hook and dropped him to the floor with a tremendous smash on the mouth. The whole thing took only ten seconds. Lorenzo would never look the same.

'Who's that son of a bitch?' Larson asked, panting. He rubbed his knuckles where Lorenzo's teeth had cut the skin.

Kitty shook her head. 'Where's Whit?'

'I couldn't find him. I looked all over the building. They must have got him out.'

Kitty's legs went back on her. She let herself slide into the nearest chair. Her face still showed the red imprint of Lorenzo's hand, and she was close to a bad attack of jitters.

'We'll have to get out of here,' Gladys said. A crowd had gathered around them. Lorenzo lay on the floor, half under the table, and a knot of waiters and house-men was assembling on the other side of the dance floor. 'Swede.'

'Yes, mam,' Larson answered automatically. He was used to answering automatically to a tone of authority.

'Here comes trouble. Can you get us out of here?'

'Yes, mam.'

'We can't go now.' Kitty was desperate. 'You don't under-stand, Gladys. They've got Whit, and Lorenzo knows where he is.' She dropped to her knees and shook Lorenzo's limp shoulder. 'Wake up, damn you. Where is he? Where have you taken him?'

'Do what I tell you,' Gladys said. The crowd around them was thicker, and the knot of waiters had started towards them. Gladys took Kitty's arm and tugged. 'Get up. Hurry. I know what I'm doing.'

Larson rubbed his hands and grinned a nasty grin as the waiters bore down on him.

The waiters were in a nice tight little flying wedge when Larson met them, but the wedge disintegrated quickly into its component parts. Two of the parts ended up in a horizontal position, one was draped on the bias over a chair, and the re-maining elements were reasonably vertical but anxious to get away. Larson was a dirty fighter; a knee here, a foot there, a thumb in the eye when it seemed appropriate. It wasn't cricket but it certainly discouraged the opposition.

They were out in the street before the police arrived, with

no marks to show for their trouble except more skin off Larson's knuckles and a cut on his cheek. Kitty and Gladys did not have their wraps, but they did not stop to think about it. Gladys hurried them away from Lorenzo's Club, herding Kitty along as a sheep-dog would lead a ewe who wanted to stop for her lamb. They were two safe blocks away before they heard the sirens of the police cars.

Larson mopped the cut on his cheek. 'I hate these clowns that wear rings,' he said. 'You never know where they're going to mess you up.'

'You did a little messing up yourself,' Gladys said. 'That was the dirtiest fighting I ever saw in my life.'

'Thanks. What do we do now?'

'We've got to find Whit,' Kitty said. 'I'm going to the police.' She shivered, partly from cold, mostly from fear.

Gladys took her firmly by the arm. 'You are not going to the police. We'll find him, but we've got to be careful.' She was trying to search in her handbag and restrain Kitty at the same time. She found a scrap of paper in the bag and scribbled an address on it. 'Swede, do you know Pete Weston?'

'Yes'm.'

'Go ask for him at this address. He probably won't be there, but they'll tell you where to look for him. Keep trailing him until you find him, tell him what happened, and bring him to Kitty's hotel. We'll be there.'

Kitty said monotonously, 'I'm going to the police. Let me go.'

'You're not going to do anything, if I have to sit on you,' Gladys answered. 'I want to find your husband as much as you do, but the police won't be any help. I know. Go ahead, Swede. Hurry.'

Larson looked doubtfully at the paper she had given him. 'It seems to me you're handing out a lot of orders all of a sudden. Who are you?'

Gladys moved closer to him, put her hand on his arm, and looked up, widening her eyes. 'Never mind who I am, Sweedy-pie. Do what I say because I tell you to. Maybe I'll do something nice for you some day.'

Sweedy-pie gulped. 'Yes'm.'

He hurried away.

'They'll kill him.' Kitty's voice was dull, without hope.

Gladys knew that Kitty was talking about Whit. She said, 'They won't kill him. They want him alive. Now come along with me and everything will be all right.'

'They *will* kill him. How do you know they want him alive?' Kitty's suspicion penetrated her fear. She held back as Gladys tried to urge her along. 'How do you know what they'll do?'

'Never mind how I know. He'll be all right.'

*

Whit was a long way from being all right at that moment. His head hurt, his mouth tasted as if it were lined with postage stamps, and he couldn't move his hands. He thought dimly, this is the worst hangover I ever had in my life – what have I been drinking? – arms are paralyzed. His eyelids came unglued and he laboriously opened his eyes.

He closed them right away. The bright light was painful, and he wanted to think. He realized it wasn't a hangover that bothered him; he had been belted on the noggin with something heavy, he was tied to a chair, and Walter Gates sat facing him six feet away.

He opened his eyes again, more carefully this time. Gates was still there. Sammy Kohler was also there, behind the standing lamp that glared in Whit's face. Sammy was grinning his weasel grin, and he held the lampshade so that it focused the light directly in Whit's eyes. He seemed to be enjoying himself.

Gates said, 'How do you feel?'

'Terrible. Do you have to shine that light in my face?'

Gates gestured at Sammy Kohler and Sammy reluctantly let the shade drop. With the glare gone from his eyes, Whit had a chance to look around.

He did not recognize the room in which he found himself. He knew from its shabby furnishings that he was no longer in Lorenzo's Club, but that was all he could determine. He examined the place as well as circumstances would permit, remembering what Casey had said about the hidden radio station, but he could see nothing particularly interesting. The room had a dusty look, as if it were not much lived in. It appeared to be, as far as furniture went, a shabby living-room in a small, shabby house. The blinds were drawn over the two windows in sight, and a light outside – it looked as if it

123

might come from a street lamp – cast the shadow of a bush or a tree on the shade. It seemed more like a bush, so Whit guessed that he was on the ground floor. That was the best he could do.

Gates said, 'How is your head?'

'It aches.'

'Get some aspirin, Sammy.'

'To hell with that,' Sammy replied. 'I should worry about his head. He didn't care about mine.'

'Get some aspirin,' Gates repeated. 'I want him able to think.'

Sammy made a bitter comment about Whit and his thinking capacities, but he left the room. Gates and Whit looked at each other silently. A breeze outside made the shadow of the bush move on the blind.

Sammy was back with aspirin and a glass of water immediately. He fed Whit the pills and jammed the glass to Whit's mouth as if he wished it were a mug of carbolic acid, but Whit didn't care about a small bruise or what Sammy thought as long as he got the water. It washed some of the postage stamps from his mouth, and the aspirin quickly changed the pounding in his head to a mere painful throb. He began to feel almost human.

After a while Gates asked, 'How is it now?'

'What's this all about?' Whit said. 'Who slugged me? What am I tied up for?'

'It isn't important who slugged you. And you won't gain anything by pretending you don't know why you're here.' Gates leaned forward, his pale eyes fixed on Whit's face. 'You're going to give me some information, Whitney, or whatever your name is. I'd rather you didn't make me dig it out of you, but that's up to you. I'll get it one way or another.'

'What are you talking about?'

Gates made a small impatient motion, lifting his hand from his knee and letting it drop. 'You're wasting time. What's your right name?'

'James Whitney. I'm a certified public accountant, and I came to Reno from San Francisco to be married. I don't know what's going on here, but I think you've got me mixed up with someone else. You'll save yourself trouble if you let me loose right now.'

It occurred to Whit while he spoke that, except for the statement that he did not know what was going on, he was telling the literal truth. There was something funny about being able to lie like a trooper while telling the strict truth. Or it would be funny if he weren't in such a difficult position. He wished his head would stop aching. He knew he was in for a bad time, and the headache didn't help.

Gates made the small gesture again, and Whit watched the broad hand move on Gates' knee. The fingers were thick and muscular. The blunt nails were still grimy, but not as grimy as they had been when Whit saw them last. He wondered vaguely if Gates were leading a cleaner life. It didn't seem probable.

Gates said, 'Just to save time, I'll tell you that we know your name is not James Whitney.'

Whit blinked. 'You – I'm – what?'

'James Whitney is now on a trip to New York. I had inquiries made in San Francisco. You got your wires crossed somewhere.'

Whit opened his mouth and shut it without speaking. Good old Carl Krebs, damn his literal soul. The wire had told him to say that Whit was in New York, and he was going to say that and nothing else until he was told to do otherwise. Whit thought, oh, what a tangled web we weave when first we practise to deceive.

He said, 'Well, then, who am I?'

'You're an agent of the Federal Bureau of Investigation.'

'That's news. What is it I know that you want me to tell you?'

'You're going to tell me everything you know and everything that has been reported to your superiors. Also the names of your associates and the means you use to communicate with them.'

Whit started to shake his head, but changed his mind about it when the anvil chorus began in his skull. 'I don't know what you're talking about.'

'Don't waste my time. I can make you talk if I have to.'

Whit licked his lips and shifted his weight against the ropes binding him to the chair. They were tight. He said, 'If I did have the information you wanted, it wouldn't do me any good to talk. You'd have to kill me anyway.'

'There are things worse than being killed,' Gates said. 'Stop stalling.'

Sammy Kohler looked like a ferret standing at Gates' side. He leaned forward. 'Go to work on him, Walter.' His voice was husky. 'Go on! Let's not waste time.'

Gates paid no attention. He waited, watching Whit's face.

Little beads of sweat began to prickle out on Whit's forehead. He licked his lips again.

If he just knew what had happened to Kitty he would know better how to act, but he was afraid to ask a question. They seemed to think that Kitty was just his stooge, and it wouldn't do to let them know that she was anything else to him. It would be another strong card in a strong hand.

He was in one hell of a bad spot. Even if he could prove that he was the man he claimed to be – and the prospects didn't seem to be very good – it would require that he turn their attention towards Casey Jones, and he wouldn't do that if they boiled him in oil. He *hoped* he wouldn't. The things that Casey had told him were coming back to his mind, and as he looked at Gates now and at Kohler leaning forward over Gates' shoulder, both intently watching him, one cold and implacable and the other hot with eagerness to see him beaten up, he didn't know. He didn't know what he would do or say when Gates went to work on him. But, by God, he was sure of one thing. Whatever they got they would have to drag out of him.

He had to lick his dry lips once more before he could speak.

'I've told you who I am and what I know. If that doesn't satisfy you, you can go to hell.'

Sammy released his breath in a long sigh. Gates stood up.

Whit's legs were free. He was watching Gates, waiting for the stocky man to come close enough for a kick to be effective, but the movement of the shadow at the window behind Gates' back distracted his attention so that Gates' first heavy blow caught him unprepared. It split his lip and knocked him backward to the floor, chair and all, as the window blind, released from its catch, snapped to the roller at the top of the window and the window pane shattered in a shower of glass on the floor.

'Don't move!' said the voice behind the gun muzzle pointing through the broken window.

126

THE voice at the window was heavenly music to Whit, but it was strangely harsh and artificial to come from an angel. Whoever held the gun was speaking in a deliberate grating croak from the back of his throat. It was an effective disguise. The voice was unrecognizable, and only the indistinct outline of a man's head and shoulders showed behind the screening foliage of the bush through which protruded the gun and the hand which held it.

Whit had seen the gun barrel come through the broken window as he was knocked over. Now he lay on his side, encumbered by the chair and kicking desperately to pull himself around so he could see what was going on. He managed it finally by hooking his foot around a table leg and levering the chair and his body around with his cheek as a pivot. It didn't help his schoolgirl complexion, but at last he got a worm's-eye view.

Gates and Kohler stood motionless where they had been when the blind snapped up, only now both faced the window. The gun barrel rested on the window frame. As Whit finally got himself swung around the gun moved slightly, pointing now at Sammy Kohler instead of at Gates.

'You, rat-face,' said the harsh croak. 'Get over there where I can see your hands and untie the guy on the floor.'

Kohler, staring at the gun in fascination, moved towards Whit.

Gates said, 'Stand still.'

The gun muzzle shifted again – not towards Gates, but upwards, so that it pointed directly at a spot between Sammy's eyes.

'You heard me,' said the croak.

The gun had Sammy hypnotized. He took another slow step towards Whit. Gates said sharply, 'No!' but Sammy was looking at something with even more authority in it than Gates' voice. He did not take his eyes from the gun as he fumbled with the knots that held Whit to the chair.

The croak spoke to Whit as the last few turns of the bindings came away.

'You on the floor. Don't come between me and the boy-friends when you get up. Find your way out of there and come out here. Make it snappy.'

Whit made it as snappy as any man could who had an egg-plant growing on the back of his head, a badly split lip, and no circulation in his hands. The first door he tried opened into a closet. The second one led through an empty kitchen – he saw capped piping fixtures where the cooking stove should have been, and the dust and litter of long disuse – and out of the house. The fresh air smelled good.

His pal with the bullfrog voice still stood at the window when Whit found him. Whit hadn't had time to begin to won-der who it was that was saving his life this time, but nothing would have surprised him, even an archangel in white robes and a halo. So when he saw Casey Jones' unmistakable crummy hat among the bushes that grew thickly around the house, it seemed perfectly natural. Good old Casey had come through again.

Casey did not move when Whit touched him on the shoul-der, but he gestured with his free hand behind his back and Whit came closer. Without taking his eyes from the peephole he had arranged in the shrub before the window, Casey whis-pered instructions.

'Across the street. Board fence. Wait for me on the other side and keep out of sight.'

'What are you —'

'Don't argue. Beat it.'

Whit knew that the game was dealer's choice and that he was listening to the dealer. He beat it.

The board fence fronted on a lot directly opposite the house which Whit had just left. The house itself was one of a block of small residences in a district he did not recognize. The street was quiet and empty, except for a dilapidated delivery truck which stood at the kerb in front of the house. A solitary street lamp furnished all the light for the neighbourhood.

Whit's hands and arms had still not entirely recovered their circulation, but he managed to scramble over the head-high fence across the street and down into a patch of artichokes on the other side. He had barely untangled himself from the arti-chokes and was searching for a knot-hole which would give him a view of the street, when he heard the loud crack of a single shot, followed shortly by the quick pound of running feet.

There were no more shots after the first. The running footsteps came towards Whit's hiding-place. He heard them leap the kerb, felt the fence tremble as the runner's weight hit it, and then a body came up and over the six-foot barrier in an acrobat's twisting plunge and Casey dropped beside him.

The artichokes in which the two men found themselves were a small portion of a flourishing victory garden which filled the lot behind the fence, and the owner of the garden had built himself a barrier intended to keep passers-by even from peeking at his vegetables. Casey and Whit together finally found one small crack.

There was no sign of life in the house across from their peephole. Down the street a couple of porch lights went on and the neighbours came out to discuss the shot for a while before deciding it was only an automobile backfire after all and to hell with it. Across the street nothing happened. No one came out of the house, no light showed, nothing moved.

Whit muttered, 'What's up, Casey? You didn't knock them both off with one bullet.'

'I shot out the light, that's all. They're lying low and I don't like it. I'd feel better if they'd come looking for us.'

'Maybe they're rounding up reinforcements by telephone.'

'They haven't got a telephone. They just took that house yesterday.'

They waited for another two minutes. Still nothing happened. Whit said, 'Well, if they won't come after us there's nothing you can do about it unless you want to go ring the doorbell. Let's get out of this vegetable plate lunch.'

Casey was still suspicious of the lack of interest shown by the men in the quiet house across the street, but there was nothing he could do about it unless he wanted to follow Whit's suggestion. After they had waited another full five minutes, he gave up. They made their way through the garden and adjoining yards out to the street at the far end of the block. They were trudging back towards the centre of town before Whit offered his thanks.

'I owe you a good cigar, Casey. Those boys were just getting ready to run me through the meat-grinder when you arrived.'

'Uh.'

'How did you happen to be there just at the right time. Did you get my message?'

Casey grunted again. 'I didn't happen to be anywhere. I've had my eye on that house since I found out that Sammy Kohler rented it yesterday. I was watching the place to-night when Kohler drove up in that delivery cart with you rattling around in the rear end like a sack of potatoes. How did they catch you?'

Whit put his fingers gently to the lump on the back of his head. 'I don't know. I don't even know who clipped me, unless it was Jess Caldwell. He telephoned the hotel and suckered me into coming to Lorenzo's Club to-night. I had an idea he might be planning something, so I stopped by your room and left you a note —'

'I told you to stay away from there.'

'Don't get excited. Nobody saw me. I had a hunch something was going to happen and I wanted you to know what was going on.'

'O.K. Then what?'

Whit told him the rest of it.

Casey thought Whit had been pretty dumb. He said, 'You ought to have known better than to go to the can by yourself, when you were expecting trouble.'

'I didn't think.'

'So because you didn't think, I have to bail you out of trouble, bitch up my own plans, and tip Gates off to the fact that he's being watched all the time. I swear to God, Whit, I wish you'd never come to Reno. I wish I'd let Gates take you apart back there just to teach you a lesson.'

Whit said stiffly, 'Well, why didn't you?'

'Because I didn't want to see him beat the living bejesus out of you.' Casey was bitterly angry. 'He'd have killed you, and it would have served you right. Damn it all, do you realize that getting you out of there to-night has kicked over the apple-cart? Up to now Gates didn't know for sure that he was being watched; he would have gone right on operating that trans-mitter until I got a fix on it, and then I could have buttoned the whole business up with one raid. Now he'll haul out for a new location and I'll have to report that I fumbled the ball. I might just as well hand in my resignation and give up.'

Whit hunched his shoulders and kept quiet. His head still ached, his split lip had begun to swell, and he felt low. They walked on in gloomy silence.

When they were within a few blocks of the business district and Whit was beginning to recognize his surroundings, Casey stopped him. He had got over his fit of temper by then, but he had a few final words to say.

'I'm sorry I popped off back there, Whit. I know you've been trying to help and I appreciate it. There's still a bare chance I can find that transmitter before Gates moves it again, but I've got to be able to work without interference. You can help by keeping out of trouble.'

'I'll do my damnedest,' Whit said. 'What are you planning to do?'

'I'm going back to watch that house.'

'What do you expect to happen?'

'I don't expect anything now; I'm just hopeful. Gates sends a message every forty-eight hours, at exactly three a.m. Once or twice he's missed his regular schedule but he's never skipped more than one message at a time except when he's had to move, and then he's always notified his listeners that he'd be off the air for a certain period. It's the only way he can keep the connexion from collapsing when he has to shut down, and he'll have to do it this time. So there'll be at least one more message before he moves his equipment again; either to-night or the day after to-morrow. If it's to-night, I'll try to stay with him when he goes to the transmitter. I've got nothing to lose now by tipping my hand.'

'Maybe he won't move. I don't think he scares easy.'

'He doesn't scare at all. But his business is to stay in circulation, not to show us how brave he is. He knows that we're closing in. He'll move, all right, and this time he'll probably end up a thousand miles away. But he's got to send a final message to let the other end know what to expect. If he tries to get the message off to-night, I might be able to trail him. If he waits for a couple of days – and I think he's too cautious to try to get clear to-night – I'll have forty-eight hours to work in. That's all.'

'How do you know he hasn't left the house already?'

'I don't. I think he hasn't for the same reason I think he won't leave until daylight, because he'd be taking a chance that

131

we're following him and he doesn't take chances. I'll listen in at three o'clock to find out for sure whether he's been too smart for me. So long.'

He turned to go.

Whit said, 'Wait a minute, Casey. There ought to be something I can do.'

'There is. Keep away from trouble so I won't have to drag you out again.'

'I'm willing enough. It's the trouble that comes after me that I can't do anything about.'

'Then lock yourself and your bodyguard in a room for forty-eight hours and don't open the door. After that it won't matter.'

Casey shuffled away.

If it had not been that Whit had worries of his own to occupy his mind, Casey's parting words would have hurt. As it was, he had something else to think about. His immediate wish was to bang somebody's nose to pay for all the pushing around he had been getting, but he realized that nose-banging would have to wait. First he had to make sure that Kitty was all right.

Gates hadn't mentioned Kitty at all. That was good. If they had picked her up they would have let Whit know about it. They would have tried to find out whether she was a weapon they could use against him. So, they didn't have her. So, she was either still at Lorenzo's – not probable, unless she and Larson were taking the place apart looking for him, but possible – or some place else. Nothing to it. Now, where was she?

At a drugstore in the next block he found a phone booth and called Lorenzo Club. An uninterested voice said that it would page Mrs Whitney if the gentleman would hold the wire. After a few moments a smoother voice with entirely too much honey dripping from it wanted to know who was calling and could he be called back in a few moments? Whit hung up without answering, chewed on his thumbnail for a while, and put through a call to the hotel, not expecting her to be there but on the bare chance that she might have left him a message. He got the shock of his life when the hotel operator put him through to his own room and the unmistakable voice of Gladys the bird-brained blonde answered, 'Hello.'

'Gladys, this is Whit. Is Kitty there?'

Gladys didn't answer his question directly. She said in a

surprised tone, 'Whit?' and then there was a yell in the background and Kitty's voice shouted frantically into the phone.

'Oh, Whit, honey! Are you all right?'

'Sure I'm all —'

'Are you hurt? Say something. Whit. I've been so worried. Where are you?'

'I'm perfectly —'

'Are you all right? Oh, say something!'

'That's what I'm *trying* to do,' Whit bellowed. 'I'm fine, except for a knot on my head. I'm in a drugstore, and I'll be at the hotel in a few minutes.' As he heard suspicious preliminary sounds he added quickly, 'Now don't start to cry. I'm O.K., and I'll be right home. Is the Swede there?'

'No.' Kitty made snuffling noises into the telephone. 'I've been so *worried*. I thought you were d-dead.'

'I'm not. Stay right there and I'll be home in five minutes. 'Bye.'

He hung up before she began to bawl.

It took him nearer fifteen minutes than five to get to the hotel. He had an idea that from then on he was going to be very careful of his skin, and he felt a lot safer slinking through alleys than he would have done stalking unarmed and alone through bright streets where anyone could pot him before he even had a chance to yelp. There were plenty of roundabout ways through side-streets if a man wasn't in a hurry.

He had to come out in the open only once, when he crossed the river. There were only a limited number of bridges available to him, and they were all well lighted. He felt as naked as an open oyster as he made the crossing, and he winced when a couple of cars passed him on the bridge. But he made it without trouble, and nobody shot at him in the hotel lobby or knifed him in the elevator. At the door to his own room he straightened his tie, brushed his hair with the flat of his hand, being careful of the melon on the back of his head, and walked in. He didn't have the door closed before Kitty was all over him like a sheet of flypaper, weeping big hot tears down his shirt collar.

Gladys had waited there for his return. Now she had other things to do. She helped herself to one of Kitty's coats from the closet, fixed her face in the bathroom, pulled her stockings

133

up and her girdle down, and said good night. By that time
Whit had given up trying to detach Kitty from his neck and
had sat down with her in his lap. He felt relaxed and quite
content to stay that way. He and Kitty both knew that someone was saying good-bye and they both responded in a vague
fashion without breaking their clinch. Gladys shut the door
quietly as she went out.

Ten minutes later it flew open again and Larson burst in,
out of breath from a vain search for Pete Weston that had
taken him over most of Reno. The reason for all of his effort
and worry of the last couple of hours was at that moment receiving extra-special treatment for a split lip, and neither the
patient nor the doctor, still sitting in the patient's lap, looked
up or interrupted the treatment at Larson's entrance, although
one of the patient's hands did manage to flap in the direction
of the door.

Larson said, 'Oh, excuse me. I – uh, excuse me.' He backed
out, closed the door, and went across the hall to his own
room, where he went to bed. He did not think he would be
needed any more that night.

Whit kept his eyes shut. He continued to brush with his free
hand until he heard the door close.

After a while, Kitty interrupted the lip treatment to say
dreamily, 'Did someone come in?'

'Someone left, I think.'

Two minutes went by.

'Who?'

'Don't know.'

Another minute passed.

'It's late. Let's go to bed.'

'Um.'

*

Some time later Whit's collection of aches and pains awoke
him from a sound sleep. His lip had swollen and was throbbing
painfully, and the cut in his scalp still hurt. He got out of bed
to get a drink of water. His watch said two o'clock, which was
a dismal hour in any language, but he was not sleepy. He had
his drink of water and a cigarette, feeling more and more wake-
ful. Kitty slept on peacefully, her dark hair spread on the
pillow and her head resting in the crook of her arm. Whit

didn't have the heart to wake her, but someone was going to have to talk to him. He put on his bathrobe, phoned the hotel desk to get the number of Larson's room, and went calling.

The Swede answered the door clad in the hair on his chest and a bleary look, although he was as obliging as any tired man could be when disturbed at two in the morning. At first he had difficulty in keeping his eyes open, but as Whit told him of what had happened in the course of the evening, Larson woke up.

'Boy, you was lucky your pal was around,' he said. 'I damn near took Lorenzo's Club apart hunting for you when you disappeared. I would of, too, but I had to plug that Lorenzo clown on account of Mrs Whitney, and his bouncers wanted to argue, so I had to rap a couple of them to get out. I would of gone back in again, only —'

'Wait a minute. What was that about Lorenzo and Mrs Whitney?'

'Why, he was slapping her around. Didn't she tell you about it?'

Whit's face took on a stiff look around the mouth. 'She didn't tell me anything. What happened?'

'I don't know what started it. I think the guy was drunk. I came back after I couldn't find you in the can, and he was holding her up and smacking her while that blonde twist got ready to bean him with a beer bottle. I got there first.'

Whit stood up and started towards the door. Larson said, 'Hey, wait a minute,' and jumped out of bed. He caught Whit in the doorway, hauled him bodily back into the room, and pushed him into a chair.

'Hold on now. You can't go anywhere without me, and I haven't got my pants on. What's the rush?'

'I'm going to find the son of a bitch,' Whit said thickly, struggling to stand up. 'Get out of my way.'

'At two o'clock in the morning?' Larson pushed him down. 'Don't be a chump.'

'I don't care what time it is.' Whit still struggled to get free, but he was handicapped by his position. 'Get away from me!'

Larson dug his toes in the carpet and pushed him back into the chair again. 'Simmer down. You wouldn't touch him if you saw him now. I worked him over for you. Anyway, he'll keep until daylight. Relax.'

He kept Whit in the chair by wrestling him down as fast as he stood up, until Whit wore himself out. Larson kept talking, describing his fight, such as it was, with Lorenzo, his search for Whit at the Club, his scrimmage with the waiters, and his vain hunt for Pete Weston. Whit's fury finally wore itself out. When he gave up struggling and looked as if he could be trusted not to make a break for the door, Larson got back into bed.

'I'm glad I haven't got a temper,' he said. 'What I can't figure out is that Gladys tootsie-frootsie, Whit. Is she a lame-brain or isn't she?'

'Sure she's a lame-brain.'

'Well, maybe you're right. But when the trouble started, all of a sudden she began giving orders like she was used to it – and I took them. I never even thought about it until we were out of that joint. Then Mrs Whitney wanted to get the cops to look for you, and Gladys said no, just like that.'

'*She* gave the orders?'

'She sent me off to find Pete Weston, and she said she was going to bring Mrs Whitney back to the hotel. I never thought about it until the last minute, but she was pushing me and Mrs Whitney around like a traffic cop. I can't figure her out.'

'She didn't want to get help?'

'Not from the police. She wanted me to go after Pete Weston. She said she knew what she was doing, and I believed her. But I don't know what it was she was doing.'

Whit said, 'Neither do I.'

So Gladys, like everyone else in town, was more than she seemed. Maybe he hadn't been so smart in dismissing her as a round-heel with too much time on her hands. From what Larson had to say, she wasn't the rattlepate she appeared to be. Whit had developed a suspicious turn of mind in the past few days. Gladys' anxiety to stay clear of the police meant something. And besides, why all her eagerness to get in touch with Pete Weston when Whit was picked up? He wasn't too confident of Pete Weston. Of course he had known Pete a long time, but not for the past few years. People change. And Reno was no place for a Pulitzer prizewinner in wartime unless he had more to do there than gather vital statistics. Whit was going to have to find out a few things before he played around much longer with people who had so much interest in him and such nasty ways.

He stood up.

'Put on your clothes, Swede. We're going for a walk.'

Larson groaned. 'Now, listen. It's practically morning, and that Lorenzo tramp won't even be able to stand up after what I did to him. Why don't you wait until daylight, anyway?'

'I'm not interested in Lorenzo right now. I need some information, and I've got to get it to-night. Let's go.'

Larson dragged himself out of bed, still moaning, and reached for his shoes.

It was half-past two when they left the hotel. Whit had scarcely breathed as he slipped back to his own room to gather his clothes. Not that he was afraid of what Kitty might say. He was *one* married man who was positively going to be the boss in his own household and go where he wanted whenever he felt like it, but just this once it seemed wise not to take any chances. There wasn't anything to be gained by disturbing Kitty, anyway.

He left the room on tiptoe with his shoes in his hand. He had never made an exit of that kind before in his life, but it seemed to come naturally to him, now that he was married.

The Magnolia Rooms smelled just as bad as ever when the two men climbed the stairs to Casey's flea-bin fifteen minutes later. They had not been followed, Whit was sure, and there had been a sufficient number of people on the streets so that he had not felt too conspicuously like a flushed quail. Larson's presence helped bolster his morale. He was cautious without being nervous as they tiptoed down the dingy third-floor hall.

Casey had said that at three o'clock he would be listening-in to make sure that Gates was not able to send his sign-off message. It was too hard to put a finger on Casey unless you knew where he was going to be at a certain hour. Whit felt that the news, if it were news, of the strange goings-on of Pete Weston and the not-so-dumb blonde was sufficiently important to risk disobeying Casey's orders to hibernate for two days. At least it was that important to Whit, since it might concern his skin.

A board creaked under Larson's foot as they approached the door at the end of the hall. Whit whispered irritably, 'Go on, wake the place up!' Larson mumbled an apology.

No light showed through the crack beneath Casey's door. Whit knocked once very gently, then again. There was no response. He peered at his wristwatch in the dim light. Casey had ten minutes to go before the three o'clock deadline. Whit got out his ten-cent passkey and opened the door.

The room was quite dark. By leaving the door partly open they got a faint illumination from the hall behind them. It did not help much, and the glow from the light well was gone. They could see the dim outline of the ancient brass bed near the window, but that was all. Whit felt his way across the room, waving his outspread hands cautiously in the air to catch the hanging light cord. Larson followed at his heels. They were in the centre of the room when a number of things happened.

The door closed softly just as Whit and Larson saw their shadows spring into being in a circle of light on the wall before them. Larson had gone into action with the sound of the door, but the advantage lay too heavily against him. He had his hand on the butt of the gun under his arm when a voice said sharply, 'Don't try it! Put up your hands and turn around.'

It was not Casey who spoke, but the voice was familiar – very much so, although Whit couldn't identify it. He turned with Larson, both holding their hands carefully in sight, to face the blinding glare of a powerful flashlight. The nose of a dully gleaming revolver barrel showed in the light beam.

Neither the flashlight nor the gun moved for a long moment. Then the flash tilted up to light the electric cord over Whit's head. The familiar voice spoke again.

'Reach up with your right hand and turn on the light, Whit.'

Whit reached obediently. The flash went out as the overhead light came on, but the gun muzzle did not move. Pete Weston had them covered and he clearly intended to keep them covered.

CHAPTER 16

IT seemed to Whit that an awful lot of people had been pointing guns at him lately. He didn't like it. He particularly didn't like it when a pal he had begun to suspect of double-dealing held the gun and gave no indication of thinking about pointing it somewhere else.

He tried lowering his hands.

'Keep them up.' Pete jerked the gun muzzle. 'What are you doing here?'

Whit struggled with a lame grin. 'What's the idea, Pete?'

'What are you doing here?' Pete repeated. He was very serious.

'Just visiting. What are *you* doing here?'

It was then that Whit saw the brass knob of the bed-post lying on the faded counterpane of the bed, and he needed no answer. His note was – or had been – under that brass knob. The note itself meant nothing, but the fact that Pete was there to look for it meant a great deal. He was not dismantling beds in a cheap flop-house at three in the morning in search of a human interest story to beguile the readers of to-morrow's newspaper.

They all heard the loose board creak faintly as someone came down the hall. Pete motioned for silence and stepped back so that he would be screened behind the door when it opened.

There were a hell of a lot of things Whit didn't know just then that he would have liked to know. He wasn't sure that it was Casey coming, he wasn't sure that Larson was going to co-operate properly when the fireworks started, and he wasn't sure that he could move as fast as he would have to move in a moment. But he did know for certain that he wasn't going to keep still while Casey walked into a trap.

Pete saw Whit shift his feet for the jump. Larson wasn't looking at Whit, but he heard shoe-leather scrape on the bare floor. As Pete gestured menacingly with the gun in Whit's direction, Larson slid his own foot cautiously forward. The gun muzzle swung towards him. At that instant Whit dropped to the floor, and with a desperate stretching kick brought one leg around in a sweeping hook behind Pete's ankles. Pete had brought the gun back to bear on Whit as Whit moved, but it did not go off. Pete's arm, with the gun, swung wide in an instinctive struggle for balance as his feet were swept from under him, and Larson was on him like a panther. His long round-house punch cracked on Pete's chin. Pete's head and shoulders hit the floor together, and he was still.

The first thing that Whit saw when he looked up was another gun pointed at him. Casey, standing in the doorway, said, 'Everyone keep quiet till I see what's going on here.' He shut the door behind him and put his back against it.

Whit got to his feet and brushed the seat of his pants. 'Nothing's going on now. It's all taken care of. That was nice work, Swede.'

Larson said, 'Yeh. But I wonder why he didn't shoot.'

Casey examined Larson carefully. 'Who's this?'

'Swede Larson, the bodyguard I was telling you about. This is Casey Jones, Swede.'

Casey decided at last that everything was in order. He put his gun away, shook Larson's hand, and went over to the bed, where he sat down as if his bones ached. He picked up the brass ball that had decorated the bed-post.

'What happened?'

'I wanted to talk to you. About Weston. We got here a couple of minutes ago expecting to wait until you showed up, and found him here looking for the note I had left for you in the bed-post. When we heard you coming I didn't want to take a chance that you'd walk into something, so we ganged up on him.'

'I wouldn't walk into my own room without finding out why the light was on,' Casey said. He turned his head towards the newspaperman on the floor, who was beginning to show signs of life. 'What do you mean, you wanted to talk to me about him?'

Whit told him what Larson had said about Gladys and Pete. Casey listened with interest. Afterwards he motioned towards the revolver that still lay near Pete's hand.

'Did he have you covered?'

'Yep. But he couldn't watch us both. We were too fast for him.'

Larson said, 'We weren't too fast. Either he forgot to take the safety off or his hand was paralyzed. He could have dropped one of us, maybe both.' He shook his head dubiously. 'I don't get it.'

'Well, he didn't shoot,' said Whit. 'So we got him instead of him getting us. Now, what do you want to do with him?'

'I guess we'd better wake him up,' Casey said. 'The F.B.I. isn't supposed to sleep on the job.'

He went to the wash-basin in the corner of the room and came back with a handful of water. He dashed the water in Pete's face and bent to massage the back of his neck.

'Come on, Pete. Snap out of it.'

Pete muttered. His eyelids twitched and his arms moved.

Whit felt like a football player who had just made a magnificent ninety-yard run in the wrong direction. He said unbelievingly, 'Oh, my God. Not Pete!'

'He's my right-hand man.' Casey dragged Pete to a sitting position. 'Come on, come on. Wake up.'

Pete said distinctly, 'Ow.' His eyes opened, and he put his hand to his jaw. Casey took him under the arms and heaved. Still holding his jaw, Pete got to his feet.

Whit could think of only one appropriate gesture. Words were useless. He turned his back to Pete and bent over.

'Go ahead,' he said. 'Make it good.'

Pete took his hand away from his chin, opened his mouth, and quickly put the hand back. 'Ow.'

'You all right?' Casey asked.

'I think so.' Pete wiggled his jaw and squinted at Whit, who was waiting patiently for the kick. 'I'll save it until I feel stronger. Which one of you hit me?'

Larson said, 'Me. I'm sorry.'

'Don't ever do it again, that's all. One of us won't live through it.'

Larson grinned.

Casey was back sitting on the bed. He said, 'You're a hell of a watch-dog, Pete. Letting someone slap you silly while you had a gun in your fist.'

'I didn't want to shoot,' Pete explained around his hand. 'I knew they were all right. But while I was trying to figure out whether or not I ought to explain what I was doing here myself, we heard someone coming. I figured it was you, but I didn't want to take any chances that it might be someone else. So I got behind the door and they jumped me. Boom.'

He let go of his jaw and wiggled his chin experimentally. Nothing fell off.

'Well, nobody's hurt,' Casey said. 'Now that the whole convention is meeting in my room, we might as well get down to business. What did you say you came to see me about, Whit?'

'Oh, nothing. Nothing that won't keep.'

Casey said to Weston, 'Whit's bashful. He came here to tell me that you were acting suspicious and I'd have to watch out for you.'

'I'll be damned,' Pete said. 'What got into you, Whit?'

Whit explained.

'It was Gladys. Larson told me she wouldn't let Kitty go to the cops when I was snatched at the Club to-night. But she did send Larson to find you, and from what he told me, she was acting pretty strange. I wasn't there so I didn't know what was going on and I thought that – well, nuts, Pete. I just didn't know, and I wanted to be sure that Casey wasn't overlooking something. So we came here.'

'Expecting to learn that I was a saboteur.'

'Well, no. But I didn't expect to learn that you were a G-man.' A horrible thought struck Whit. 'What about Gladys? Don't tell me *she's* one of you.'

Casey answered the question. 'She is.'

'I'll believe anything now.'

Larson said incredulously, 'You mean that blonde twirp is a G-girl?'

Casey nodded. 'She's valuable because she looks and acts like a dummy and isn't one. And now you know that much, I'll tell you something else. You go right on believing that she's a blonde twirp, Weston here is a newspaperman and I'm a bum from the skid-row. Get it?'

Larson said, 'Yes, sir.'

'You'd better bring me up to date on a few things now,' said Weston. 'What was that you said about being snatched at Lorenzo's Club to-night, Whit?'

Casey interrupted before Whit could answer. 'You'll have to wait. It's nearly three.'

He reached into an inner pocket and took out a watch – a thin expensive timepiece in a chamois bag, much too fine to be carried by a skid-row bum. It marked three minutes before the hour. He showed the watch to Pete, and the newspaperman nodded his understanding. Together they picked up the heavy suitcase that stood in the corner and heaved it up on to the table.

While Whit and Larson watched, the two men did what they had to do, without waste motion. The suitcase was unlocked with a tiny key that Casey produced from another of his mysterious pockets. It opened like a portable phonograph, one section flat on the table, the other at right-angles vertically, locked in place by a pair of metal arms. The case actually seemed to be a phonograph, in part; the horizontal section contained a small turntable, several regulating knobs, and a movable arm holding a recording stylus, all much smaller than regulation size. The rest of the space was filled with radio equipment, built solidly and compactly into the case. A length of rubber-covered electric cord extended from the bowels of the apparatus; this Pete uncoiled and connected to the room's single light fixture hanging from the ceiling. The operation involved un-screwing the light-bulb and replacing it with a plug, so that for a moment they all stood in the dark. Then Pete said in the blackness, 'O.K.,' Casey clicked a switch, and a small hooded light came on to illuminate the interior of the suitcase. Whit and Larson moved in closer.

When the entire apparatus was finally set up, it consisted of the phonograph arrangement, a headset with a pair of ear-phones, and a compact radio surmounted by a broad metallic ring possibly eighteen inches in diameter. The ring, mounted vertically on its diameter like a large doughnut about to be dunked, could be turned freely around its vertical axis by means of an insulated arm which protruded from the base of the strange contraption and served as a pointer to indicate direction on a compass card marking the circle through which the ring revolved.

There was also a map, which Casey spread out on the table-top where the hooded light would fall on it. Whit looked at it curiously over Casey's shoulder. He recognized it as a detailed chart of Reno and the surrounding vicinity. Two straight heavy red pencil lines had been drawn across the face of the map. They intersected at a spot at the centre of town, which Whit identified as approximately the location of the Magnolia Rooms. From the intersection the lines were projected in a general north - easterly – south - westerly direction, making a figure on the map like a tall emaciated X.

Larson muttered in Whit's ear. 'I give up. What is it?'

'Stick around. I think we'll find out in a minute.'

Casey was ready to go now. He put on the earphones and crouched on his heels in front of his apparatus. The shaded light gleamed on his intent face. From a compartment in the suitcase he took a small shiny aluminium record blank the size of a pancake, wrote the date and hour in its paper centre, initialled it, and handed it to Pete. Pete initialled it as well, and

143

squatted beside Casey to put the disc on the turntable of the phonograph.

Casey looked again at his watch and held it out for Pete to see. Pete nodded. With his free hand, Casey flipped first one switch and then another on the panel in front of him. The phonograph turntable began to revolve silently.

Larson whispered hoarsely, 'What the —'

'Quiet!' Casey spoke without taking his eyes from the watch.

The next twenty seconds dragged by. On the twenty-first, Casey said, 'Now,' and put his hand on the pointer controlling the doughnut contraption. Simultaneously, Pete set the stylus of the weighted recording arm in the outer groove of the record blank.

There was absolutely no sound in the room but the faint scrape of the needle cutting into the revolving disc on the turntable. Casey's hand on the pointer swung the metallic loop of the direction-finder slowly through a narrow arc, left, right, left, right. His eyes were closed, and the effort of his concentrated attention showed in his intent face.

Pete watched Casey. The needle on the turntable moved gradually closer to the centre of the spinning disc. Casey's hand continued to swing the pointer through its arc, widening the swing as the seconds went by. There was no other movement. At the end of what must have been about a minute, the record ran out and the needle of the stylus began to scrape loudly on the inner groove of the aluminium disc. Casey opened his eyes.

'Forty-eight hours to go,' he said.

He took off the earphones and snapped switches on the panel in front of him. Pete lifted the needle from the record.

Whit did not know how long he had been holding his breath, but it could have been a week. He let the air out of his lungs and practised breathing normally again. At his elbow he could hear Larson wheezing like himself.

Pete said, 'No soap?'

Casey shook his head. He was making a note on the paper centre of the disc he had removed from the recorder.

'I didn't think he'd try to get to the transmitter to-night. It gives us two days before he can send another message. If we don't find it in that time, we might as well give up.'

It was all Larson could stand. He considered that he had put up with enough mystery for a lifetime. He said pleadingly, 'Look, guys. A tease is a tease, but you can only go so far. What is it?'

Casey looked up. 'What is what?'

Larson pointed at the apparatus on the table. 'I know it's a radio-phonograph because I've got one myself, but right there I'm lost. If you weren't trying to get Bing Crosby, what *were* you doing?'

'Everyone else in Nevada seems to know what we're up to, so I don't see why you should be discriminated against,' Casey said. 'This is a direction-finder. We're trying to locate an illegal radio transmitter that's relaying important information out of the country. We know it's around here somewhere, but not its exact location. In the last four days we've established that it's within a radius of fifty miles north-east or south-west of here, more or less, and that's all. For about two months we've been trying to run it down, and just when we started getting hot we slipped on a banana peel and gave ourselves away. So now we know that the transmitter will be moved as soon as the operator who runs it can get a last message to the men on the other end. That will be forty-eight hours from now. After that we can start all over again.'

The sense of defeat was apparent in Casey's bald words, and Whit winced inwardly. He was grateful that Casey had not been more explicit. The reference to a banana peel had been for Whit's benefit.

Larson said, 'I can follow that. What's the phonograph business for?'

Casey reached into a compartment at the back of the phonograph and fished out a record similar to the one on which he had just written his note. He put the second record on the turntable, adjusted a thumbscrew on the stylus arm, and touched a switch on the panel inside the suitcase. As the turntable began to revolve, he pried one of the earphones from its headband and handed it to Larson. The other he held out to Whit. They listened to the record play back.

It sounded like a bad attack of static to Whit. The noise in the earphone was the finest assortment of whistles, squeals, bubbling noises, and rusty hinges he had ever heard in his life. Only one sound in the din seemed to bear a faint resemblance to radio messages, as he knew them; it was a clear high-pitched

145

whistle which sounded for eight or ten seconds on one uninterrupted steady note and then ceased abruptly. The record burbled for a while longer and ran out.

Whit said, 'Does it mean something?'

'It's static, mostly,' Casey explained. 'That whistle you heard was the message. I told you how Gates speeded up his code. It's a trick they carried over from the last war, and it's a good one if someone doesn't stumble on to it and get it on a record.' He turned a knob on the instrument panel and set the phonograph needle once more in the outer groove of the revolving disc. 'Try it now.'

This time the turntable barely moved. The sharp scratches and squeals of the static in the earphones had dropped several octaves and were now low growls and mutterings in the bass register. In the middle of the medley, where before there had sounded the steady piercing whistle, a staccato message in the rapid stutter of Morse code was clearly audible.

Whit and Larson returned the earphones. Casey screwed them back in their headband and stowed it away in the suitcase.

Whit said, 'Is it any of our business what the message was?'

Casey was dismantling his apparatus. He shrugged. 'It doesn't matter a hell of a lot, I guess. Read them the last one, Pete.'

Weston waited until Casey had disconnected the electric cord of the direction-finder from the light fixture, and the glaring overhead globe replaced the dim glow of the hooded light in the suitcase. Then he read from a notebook he took from his pocket.

'This is after it was decoded,' he said. 'Message 42. Expect one or two B's in SF, six to ten days with escorting vessels, C's and D's. Indications continue of large convoy sailing ex Pugs in two weeks, as reported 39 40 41. Message 43 on schedule G.'

'I get that part about ex-pugs,' Larson said. 'I'm one myself. What's the rest of it mean?'

'Pugs is Puget Sound,' Casey translated. 'G is Gates' signature. He says one or two battleships with accompanying cruisers and destroyers will put into San Francisco Bay in the next six to ten days, and a convoy will be leaving Puget Sound in two weeks.'

146

'He says,' Whit repeated. 'Is he right?'

'How do I know?' Casey answered wearily. He snapped the lock on the suitcase and heaved it from the table to the corner of the room. 'I don't control shipping on the Pacific Coast. I know that ships have been sunk because of those messages – too many of them. If Gates is guessing, he's doing a good job.'

'Well, my God, man. If you know that there will be Jap submarines waiting for a convoy to leave Puget Sound in two weeks, you're going to stop the convoy, aren't you?'

'I haven't got anything to do with it.' Casey sat down on the bed and began to remove his shoes. 'I haven't got anything to say about ship movements. Somebody – and I don't envy him his job – has got to decide whether it's more important to try to get that convoy by the submarines that will be waiting for it, or to take a chance that we'll lose half of the Pacific Ocean because we aren't delivering planes and munitions. All *I've* got to do is find a radio transmitter in forty-eight hours that hasn't been found in two months.'

No one had anything to say to that.

Casey dropped one runover shoe and pulled at the laces of the other.

'Now if you will all beat it the hell out of here and let me get a few hours sleep for a change, I'll appreciate it. But before you go, I want to say this for your benefit, Whit, and yours, Larson. Maybe I sounded to-night as if I didn't give a damn about what you heard or saw here. Well, that's not so. I trust you, Whit, or you wouldn't be here now; I trust you, Larson, because Whit speaks for you. But remember that everybody in this mess is playing for keeps, and one little leak, one little tip-off that Pete and Gladys and I are not what we're supposed to be, can ruin everything we've done and whatever prospects we have of completing the job, besides probably getting us killed. So bear this in mind: don't talk to anyone, don't trust anybody with what you know, whoever it is; look out for trouble and keep your mouths shut. You've got only two days to worry about, and then it's over with. That's all. Good night. Pete, stick around for a couple of minutes.'

Whit and Larson took the hint.

They left the Magnolia Rooms and their un-magnolia-like smell of disinfectant and stopped around the corner where Pete

147

had told them his car was parked, near the entrance to the gambling joint with the gauntlet of slot machines. Larson, who had done a full night's work, should have been tired but wasn't. He thought it was too late to go to bed anyway, and he wanted to get some exercise with a pair of dice. But Whit was thinking of Kitty and how she would feel if she awoke and found him gone. They waited at the kerb until Weston showed up.

There were a number of things for Pete and Whit to discuss during the brief ride back to the hotel. Pete confessed that up until that afternoon, when he had made his first contact with Casey in three days, he did not know that Whit and Casey had got together. He had been greatly disturbed by Whit's apparent connexions with Lorenzo and Jess Caldwell, as well as by Whit's knowledge that Casey was in town and by the strange business of Pop Foster's death. Now that the cause for their mutual distrust had been removed, they fell back into the old familiar groove again.

'I've been in it for a couple of years,' Pete said. 'I was sent out here as an undercover man three months ago, when we knew there was a leak somewhere in the neighbourhood but didn't know about the radio set-up. Then when we got wind of the transmitter, Durham – the agent who disappeared – was sent out to run it down. He could operate more freely than I could, because I was known around town by then. After they got him, Casey came out to take over. That was less than a week ago. You know where we are now.'

'In the soup,' Whit said. 'And it's my fault, I guess. Did Casey tell you what happened to-night?'

'Not all of it.'

So Whit, with Larson filling in the gaps, rehashed the evening's events. He still felt guilty about being the banana peel that had caused Casey's plans to go to pieces, and he put himself in a worse light than he deserved. Pete tried to cheer him up.

'It's one of those things, Whit. It's too bad Casey had to pull you out of a jack-pot, but it was only because you had done what you were trying to do and what Casey had agreed you ought to do. I wouldn't kick myself around too much if I were you.'

'Sure, sure. I'm a hero. It doesn't change the fact that you've got only two days left to do your job.'

'Two days here. Then they'll move on and we'll pick up the trail all over again. Don't think we won't get them sooner or later.'

'In the meantime there'll be more ships sunk, more men killed, more equipment sent to the bottom.'

'They'll do damage as long as they're loose. I can't argue with you about that.'

Larson said, 'Pete, I could be just dumb, but if you know who these monkeys are that are sending the messages, why don't you haul them in? That would stop the bedtime stories.'

'Casey may decide to do that,' Pete said. 'He's the boss. We were talking about it after you left his room. But there are a couple of drawbacks. One is that while we've always been able to keep an eye on Lorenzo and Jess Caldwell, because they're always around town, Gates and Kohler come and go. We've tried to trail them to the transmitter several times, but they've always been too cautious and we've been afraid of giving ourselves away. Now that we've spilled the beans we may never see them again. And just picking up Lorenzo or Caldwell or both won't do any good. Gates is the man. So long as he's free we'll have the same trouble.'

'The way you tell it makes me feel real good about my part in it,' Whit said gloomily. 'What's the other drawback?'

'Casey wants to get hold of the transmitter and send a few messages himself. So far everything has been against us; the Japs have known when and where to expect our ships and we've only known that we can expect torpedoes. Casey's idea is to turn things around. It would probably work, too, for a while; long enough to pay for part of the harm that Gates has done. Casey won't give up the idea as long as there's a chance. But we've got to keep up the regular message schedule if we once take over. That means we've not only got to grab the transmitter but we've got to haul in the mob all at once so no one is loose to give us away. The transmitter is no good to us unless we have the mob, and the mob is no good without the transmitter.'

Larson said, 'You boys have bit yourself off a tough assignment.'

'We're finding that out.'

It was nearing dawn when Pete stopped his car in front of the hotel to let them off. Whit did not get out immediately. He

149

had been doing some deep thinking during the drive.

'Pete, is there any way to find a radio station besides stumbling over it or following someone there?'

'Casey's direction-finder would work in time. The messages are so brief he can't get an accurate fix without at least eight to ten different angles, and he hasn't had time for that.'

'How else can you go about it?'

'Use a crystal ball. Consult a fortune-teller. Run down the power source.'

'Say that last part again.'

'Power. You've got to have electricity to run a radio station. Gates' set is pretty powerful, and with the equipment he must need to speed up his messages he's using a lot of juice. Find where he's getting it and you'll find the station.'

'Haven't you tried that?'

'We've tried everything. The difficulty is that there are ten thousand consumers of electricity in the Reno area alone, and the whole state is dotted with farms and ranches and mines using industrial power. Gates moved his transmitter at least three times while Durham was hunting him; that was before we had the direction-finder out here, and we never had a chance to get warm before he'd pack up and move along to the next place. Too many possible locations. We know that he isn't using a portable generator because the generator isn't made that's big enough to give him the power he needs and small enough to let him jump around the countryside with it every time we get close. Wherever he is, he's getting his electricity through a meter just like any farmer with a milking machine or a housewife with an electric range. But it would take two years to cover the field, and we'd have to start all over again each time the transmitter was moved.'

'It sounds like a hell of an unscientific way to go at it,' said Larson.

'It is. The direction-finder is a better bet – or would be, if we had time to use it properly. It's not much use now.'

Whit said thoughtfully, 'Well, I'm no Edison, but I still think something could be done with the power angle.'

'In forty-eight hours,' Pete reminded him. 'Go sleep on it and see if you get a brain wave. I've got work to do before the night's over.'

They got out of the car. Pete waved as he drove away.

150

Whit and Larson were too occupied with their respective thoughts to notice the hotel clerk make an unobtrusive note of the time as they came in. They were worrying about different things, but their worries both stemmed from what they had learned that evening. Whit was mulling over problems of electric power, regretting his lack of experience with the subject; Larson was thinking of Gladys and feeling substantially the same regrets.

'That blonde, now,' he said when Whit left him at his door. 'I never would of believed it.'

'What blonde?' Whit said. 'Oh, Gladys. What about her?'

'A G-girl! What a break. And I thought she could be had.'

'Maybe she can. Why don't you try it?'

Larson shuddered. 'It'd be like trying to make J. Edgar Hoover.'

'She isn't put together like J. Edgar Hoover.'

'She's a G-girl just the same,' Larson said. 'It'd be too much of a handicap for a plain cop. G'night.'

Whit entered his own room as he had left it – on tiptoe, with his shoes in his hand, as was proper for a married man sneaking in late. He made no noise as he hung up his clothes and put on his pyjamas, but Kitty stirred when he cautiously sat down on the bed to take off his slippers.

'Wha's time?' she mumbled sleepily.

'Five or six. Go to sleep.'

She opened one eye. 'Wha' you g'tting up s'early for?'

'Force of habit. I always get up early.'

'Aw, g'back t'sleep.' Kitty wrapped a warm, fragrant arm around his neck and pulled him down beside her. 'This 'sa vacation.'

Whit didn't argue.

CHAPTER 17

THE fat man with the straw hat took up his stand in the hotel lobby next morning where he could watch people getting out of the elevators. He would have gone about his job in a different manner if he had been in a hurry, but he wasn't, and he had a chaw of tobacco to help him pass the time. After he had exchanged a few words with the clerk at the desk he leaned comfortably against a pillar and enjoyed his chaw. It had just reached the spitting point when the elevator gates opened and Kitty, Whit, and Swede Larson emerged, in that order. The fat man reached out and clamped down on Whit's arm as he passed.

It wasn't any particular type of grab; just a firm clutch indicating that he wanted Whit to pull over to the kerb. But Whit's nerves weren't what they might be, after the hard night he had been through, and any clutch on the arm meant that the gremlins were about to get him if he didn't watch out. Kitty, a step in front, noticed nothing. But Larson, directly behind Whit and ready for trouble from any angle, saw the fat man's grab and Whit's nervous jump.

The fat man was not entirely a green pea at his business. When Whit immediately slugged him in the paunch with his free hand, the fat man saw it coming in time to push Whit off balance enough so that the blow didn't paralyze him. He didn't take any steps after that, however, literally or figuratively, because something hard was prodding him in the kidney and he didn't think it was an umbrella handle. The fat man didn't know Larson, he hadn't been warned against him, and he wasn't expecting quite such a reception. When Larson said coldly in his ear, 'Go nice and easy, guy,' he went nice and easy. He wasn't dumb.

Kitty came back towards the elevator when she found that she had lost her escorts. By that time Whit and Larson were crowding the fat man into a corner, and the fat man was becoming more and more unhappy every moment. Kitty had never seen him before, but she could tell from the expression on his face that something was up and that it was not a social gathering.

She said anxiously, 'What is it, Whit?'

'I don't know,' Whit answered, grimly eyeing the stranger. 'I don't know, but I'm going to find out. Who sent you here, fat boy? Gates?'

The fat boy shook his head dumbly and unhappily, looking around for help. He made an effort to move away from the wall. Whit pushed him back.

'Come on, talk!' Larson jabbed viciously with the gun muzzle hidden in his coat pocket. The fat man groaned without opening his mouth. His eyes flickered wildly around the lobby. Sweat began to glisten on his face.

Whit doubled his fist and put it under the fat man's nose. 'You and your pals have been bouncing me around long enough. Now will you talk or will I do some bouncing of my own?'

The fat man took a long chance. With a desperate twist he freed himself from Whit's grasp, ducked away from Larson's clutching arm, and at the risk of being shot in the back, plunged across the lobby and unloaded his mouthful of tobacco juice on a potted palm before it drowned him.

Whit had a new and firmer hold on him by the time he straightened up, but the fat man was ready and eager to talk. 'Now take it easy, boys,' he said, uneasily eyeing the pocket where Larson's gun poked its unmistakable nose at him through the covering fabric. 'Take it easy. You've got me all wrong. All the sheriff said was that I was to ask you to come see him this morning. If you don't want to come, why just say so. There's no need to get nasty about it. I'll tell him you were —'

'Wait a minute,' Whit interrupted. The fat man shut up immediately. 'The sheriff sent you after us?'

'Yes, sir. But he didn't say you *had* to come. So if you don't feel like it, just forget the whole thing.'

'My God, man, why didn't you say so instead of leaping at me? I thought —' Whit didn't say what he had thought. 'What does the sheriff want?'

'I don't know. He just said I was to bring you – I mean, ask you to come see him. If you want to.'

Whit looked at Kitty first and at Larson second. Neither one wore a helpful expression. He said, 'Why, sure. We'll come. Anything to oblige the sheriff.'

The fat man had a cup of coffee with them while they breakfasted in the hotel grill. Kitty was extra nice to him because of his fright, and what with the coffee and the effect that Kitty had on men when she wanted to be extra nice, he turned out to be a pretty good guy after his nerves stopped jingling. His name was Strong, and he was deputy sheriff of the county. That was what he claimed, although he didn't pretend to know much about much. They could not get anything out of him concerning the sheriff's reason for sending for them. Deputy-sheriff Strong didn't know and didn't care. His job was to bring them in – if they didn't mind, of course – and the sheriff would talk to them.

They had no chance to discuss the situation among themselves during their ride in deputy-sheriff Strong's official car (one block and a half, with the siren going) to the sheriff's office. But he left them cooling their heels in an ante-room while he reported to the boss. The minute he was gone, Kitty whispered, 'I smell trouble.'

'What kind of trouble?' said Whit.

'I don't know. Just trouble.'

Larson grunted. 'I know one kind of trouble we can count on. That clown is going to tell his boss I got a gun. I told you I should of reported as soon as I got here.'

'You're a police officer, aren't you? What's the matter with having a gun?'

'I told you before, I'm not even a Boy Scout in Nevada. If Buffalo Bill wants to get tough about it, I may have to talk. Maybe I better show him my letter.'

'If you have to. But let's wait until we see what's up.'

Kitty said, 'He probably wants to know what went on at Lorenzo's Club last night. You can't expect to get into fights with waiters and spies and people without attracting some attention.'

'I didn't get into a fight – not that he knows about, anyway. It was you and —'

Larson muttered, 'Watch it!' The sheriff himself was beckoning to them from the doorway of his office.

He looked a little bit like a hospitable spider hanging out the welcome sign for three visiting flies as they went into his office and sat down on the uncomfortable chairs. Their friend Strong was also there, trying his best to look inconspicuous. The sheriff took his time loading his pipe with the mixture of fertilizer and splinters he seemed to enjoy so much. When the pipe was reeking to his satisfaction, he said pleasantly, 'I hear you go around poking guns at people, Mr Larson. That right?'

Larson coughed. 'Well, it's like this. I —'

'Wait a minute,' said Whit. 'Do you mind telling us why we're here, sheriff?'

'Not at all, son. Not at all.' The sheriff waved his pipe-stem. 'We had a murder around here couple of days back. Maybe

154

you heard about it. I'm supposed to find out who did it, so I thought I'd just ask you folks a few more questions – *if* you don't mind.' The sheriff's politeness was much too elaborate. 'I was figuring to ask you what you know about the trouble at Lorenzo Club last night, for a starter, and what happened to Walter Gates and Sam Kohler. Now I want to know why I shouldn't put you in jail on suspicion of murder and for carrying concealed weapons.'

Neither Whit nor Larson could think of a good answer. When the silence got too thick, Kitty said in a puzzled voice, 'I don't understand, sheriff. Do you mean we're suspected of having had something to do with Mr Foster's death?"

'Not necessarily, mam. But I won't say I don't mean that. You and yore husband and his gunbearer, or whatever he is, are mixed up in that murder some way, and I'm not so sure of yore innocence as I was last time I saw you. You!' He jabbed his pipe stem at Larson, giving up the polite approach. 'Have you a licence for that horse-pistol yore carrying?'

'No, sir. Not in Nevada. But —'

'Hand it over.'

Larson didn't move. The sheriff said, 'Strong, take it away from him.'

Deputy-sheriff Strong got reluctantly to his feet. Larson scowled at him, and Strong hesitated. The sheriff repeated grimly, 'Take it away from him. If you need help, call the boys.'

'I guess you better show the sheriff your letter, Swede,' said Whit.

Larson groped in his pocket and produced Lieutenant Webster's letter. The sheriff accepted it and read it through. He said, sourly, 'So now the San Francisco police department is taking over Nevada. What are you doing in Reno? Why didn't you bring this to me soon as you got here?'

Whit horned in before Larson could answer. 'I told him not to.'

The sheriff turned a cold eye towards Whit. 'Is that so? Why?'

'I didn't want anyone to know who he was.'

'Why?'

'I – uh – can't tell you.'

'Well, that's too bad. That's shore too bad. Then maybe

155

you'd all like to go to jail until you decide you *can* tell me.'

The sheriff swung in his chair to reach for the telephone behind him.

Kitty said quickly, 'We might as well tell him the truth, Whit.' She waved down his pantomimed protest behind the sheriff's back. 'I don't want to go to prison because you're too proud to confess you're scared. His life's in danger, sheriff; a man who – well, who likes me, threatened to kill him if we got married.' She managed a modest blush. 'It wasn't a very nice honeymoon with that hanging over us, so we asked Mr Larson to join us. My husband didn't want to explain why he needed a bodyguard, and we told Mr Larson not to let you know why he was here. That's all.'

The sheriff nodded appreciatively, with his hand on the phone. 'That's pretty fast thinking, Mrs Whitney. Pretty fast. I suppose you could describe this man who is threatening yore husband. Maybe you could even tell me his name.'

'Certainly. His name is Clive Vanderbilt, he's about six feet tall, heavily built, red hair, blue eyes, light complexion. Just average.'

'That isn't average.'

'Isn't it?'

The sheriff changed his approach from one of courteous scepticism to the old business of cards-on-the-table.

'Look, Mrs Whitney. I'll talk to you, because I get mad when I look at yore husband. I'm an officer of the law and I've got a lot of responsibilities. It goes along pretty smooth here most of the time, but last week things began to happen. First of all a stranger name of Durham disappears and can't be found, no place.' He held up his hand as Kitty tried to speak. 'I'm not saying you had anything to do with it; I'm just telling you what happened. Next thing, one of the best-liked men in the county gets shot in the back about the time you and yore husband, along with this man Larson, turn up here pretending to be on a honeymoon, and —'

'But we *are* on a honeymoon, sheriff. We were just married. I mean Mr Whitney and I were. Mr Larson just came along because —'

'Please, mam. I know yore married. But yore doing more in Reno than honeymooning. The first night you got here you went to see Pop Foster at 5 a.m. – you've got to confess that's a strange time of the day for a wedding – and you didn't even have a marriage licence. That looked bad. The next night, Foster was murdered. Maybe it's only a coincidence. But the description I got of the man who did the shooting sounded a lot like yore husband, and even though I don't think he did it, he knows something about it. The very *next* night, one of the men who gave us the description was knocked over the head in an alley. Yore husband hasn't an alibi for that. Maybe it's another coincidence. Then this morning I try to find the men who witnessed the shooting and they've *both* disappeared. You and Larson get mixed up in a brawl at Lorenzo's Club and run out before the police arrive, and don't tell me it was somebody else because I know better. Then at two-thirty this morning yore husband and his pal left the hotel and didn't get back until three or four hours later. I don't know where they went or what they did, but I expect another body to turn up any minute. Then there's that business of pulling a gun on Strong this morning. Now I ask you, mam. What do you expect me to think?'

The sheriff was almost in tears.

Kitty was not listening to him. She had turned to look at Whit, who was staring at the tips of his shoes. Kitty said coldly, 'Where did you go?'

'Huh?' Whit looked up. 'Where did I go when?'

'At two-thirty this morning.'

'Oh, this morning. Why, nowhere in particular. I got a little restless, so Swede and I went out to try the crap tables. I won fifty bucks, too – I was hotter than a pair of red flannel drawers. Isn't that right, Swede?'

'Absolutely. I never saw such a streak.'

Kitty said, 'You're lying.'

Whit spread his arms in a generous gesture, to show how clean his conscience was. 'Kitty, I don't understand you. Why should I lie? Have I ever lied to you?'

'Where were you?'

Whit turned to the sheriff.

'I suppose you had a man watching me. He ought to know that I'm telling the truth.'

He crossed his fingers. It was a reasonably good bluff.

'I didn't have a man watching you, but I will from now on. And don't tell me you went out in the middle of the night just to shake dice. You could have got all the action you wanted right there in the hotel casino. What was the matter with their layout?'

The phone rang just then, before Whit had to think up an answer. It gave him a breathing spell he needed badly.

With Kitty and the sheriff both needling him, he was being crowded into a corner where he might have to say something he shouldn't. He rather liked the sheriff, and he could see how the old-timer might be burned up by all the strange goings-on under his nose. If Whit hadn't had someone other than himself to worry about, he would have been inclined to spill the beans to the sheriff without hesitation. But he remembered Casey's earnest advice: don't talk to anyone; don't take a chance, no matter who it is. Whit was convinced that Casey knew what he was doing.

The sheriff said into the phone, 'All right, put him on.' He scowled as he waited. 'Pete? This is Andy. I've got that pal of yores down here again. Whitney. And his side-kicker, Larson. I'm thinking of putting them in jail.'

Pete had something to say. The sheriff answered, 'I wanted to know if you were still as willing to guarantee Whitney as you were last time I talked to you.'

Pete was still willing, but he wanted to know what had happened.

'Everything. Fights, night-prowling, gun-toting – he's just plain suspicious, and he won't talk. Also, his side-kicker – do you know Larson?'

Sure, Pete knew Larson. Known him for years. Swell guy.

'Did you know he carries a gun, without a licence?'

No, Pete hadn't known that. But Larson was pretty reliable. Pete didn't think the sheriff had to worry about it.

'What do you mean, I don't have to worry about it? I'm the sheriff of this county; I'm *paid* to worry about it. I know they're involved in that killing some way, and I'm getting tired of having them in my hair. I just thought I'd let you know before I locked them up.'

Pete talked at some length. The sheriff said, 'Yes, but —' and 'Shore, I know, but —' and 'Well, all right, but —' At the end, he said bitterly, 'All right. All *right*. But just one more break and I'll run them in. And when I do, I'll hold you responsible.'

He banged the phone down.

Whit said, 'Can we go now?'

'No!'

They waited. The sheriff puffed moodily on his pipe, which would have made a handy smudge-pot for chasing the frost away from an orange grove but was hard to stand in a closed room. Kitty began to wonder if they were getting the Nevada third-degree. Finally the sheriff took the pipe stem from his mouth and pointed it at Whit.

'Now, look here, son. You don't want to get tangled up with the law.'

'No. I mean, that's right. I don't.'

'The law's on yore side. It's on the side of every honest citizen. You know that, don't you?'

'Sure.'

'Then you ought to co-operate with me.'

'I am co-operating, sheriff. I didn't have anything to do with Pop Foster's death. I've known him since I was in knee-pants. I want to see his murderer caught.'

'You aren't helping catch him by holding back information.'

'I haven't any information to hold back. I don't know how you manage to figure that everything happens just because I'm in town, but I think you've got me mixed up with someone else. I came here for a honeymoon, and that's all.'

The sheriff shook his head. 'Yore lying, son. You all ought to be in jail, and if you get into just one more bit of trouble I'll haul you in and put you there – all of you.' He reached for the papers on his desk, puffing hard on his smudge-pot. 'Go on. Get out of here.'

Larson cleared his throat. 'Excuse me. Can I have a licence for the gun?'

The sheriff couldn't grit his teeth with the pipe stem in his mouth, but he tried hard. 'If ever in my life —' He choked. 'Strong, make out a licence to carry arms and get these people out of here. Quick!'

Deputy-sheriff Strong submitted to the indignity of making out a licence legalizing possession of the gun which had bruised his ribs that morning. While Larson answered necessary questions for the record, the sheriff worked grimly at his desk, ignoring the other people in the room. The almost-jail-birds thought it wise not to tease the animals unnecessarily. So when Larson's licence was signed, sealed and safely in hand, they prepared to sneak quietly away. The sheriff stopped them as they reached the door.

'Wait a minute.'

They waited. The sheriff made one last try.

'Whitney, we all know that yore wife's story about Reginald Vere de Vere, or whatever his name was – meaning no disrespect, Mrs Whitney – was a lot of moonshine. But you expect someone to be shooting in yore direction or you wouldn't have Larson sticking so close to you. If there is going to be any shooting in this county, people are liable to get killed, and whether it's you or somebody else, it's still my business to find out who is responsible. Maybe you don't care if yore killed. I do – not because I give a hoot about your hide, but because it's my job to keep peace and I'm going to do it. I'll skip the question of Pop Foster's death right now and talk about yores. Who am I going to look for when they bring yore body in?'

Whit felt Kitty's hand tighten on his arm.

He had to think for a moment before he answered the sheriff. He knew that the tough old man had a job to do, as he had said, which he would do honestly and well to the best of his ability. But if Whit told him the truth, or half the truth, or even a part of the truth, it would endanger Casey's plans. And those plans, for the next forty-eight hours, were more important than anything else.

Whit said, 'I'm sorry, sheriff. I can't tell you.'

'You mean you won't tell me.'

'No. I mean I can't.'

'All right.' The sheriff bit down on his pipe stem. 'You can go. Next time I call you in here it will be for keeps, so keep out of trouble.'

'We won't get into trouble where we're going.'

'Where are you going?'

Whit waved his arm in a broad gesture that was intended to take in a chunk of landscape. 'Horseback riding.'

The sheriff smiled for the first time since they had entered his office.

'Fine. Fine. Maybe the horses will throw you and break yore necks. That would take you out of my department.'

CHAPTER 18

'PLEASANT old bastard, isn't he?' Larson said, when they were out on the street. 'Excuse me, Miz Whitney.'

Miz Whitney wasn't paying any attention. She said, 'I want to know where you went last night, Whit. And don't tell me you were out gambling, because I know you're lying as well as the sheriff does.'

'We had to see Casey, honey. Swede told me about Gladys, how she acted last night when I was snatched by those goons at Lorenzo's Club, and how she shied away from the police and sent Swede to find Pete Weston. I knew from what Swede told me that she had been putting on an act up until then, and I thought I ought to pass a word to Casey about her and Pete, just in case. I didn't want to wake you, so we sneaked out to Casey's rooming house. You won't believe what he told us.'

'You mean about Gladys? I can guess,' Kitty said calmly. 'He probably said that Gladys was helping him. Pete Weston is too, I expect.'

Whit and Larson were both startled. Whit said, 'How did – who told you?'

'What do you mean, who told me? I figured it out for myself. Gladys knew too much about everything that was going on last night, and she kept telling me that you were going to be all right and that we'd find you before you got hurt. The only way she could know anything about it was either because she was one of old fish-eye's confederates – and I knew she wasn't after the way Lorenzo talked to her – or someone who was working with Casey. I was going to tell you last night, only you – only we – I was too sleepy.' She looked cautiously at Larson from the corner of her eye. 'When did you two talk to each other, Swede? I don't remember seeing you last night after Whit came back.'

'No'm. You didn't. We was in my room.'

'Oh.'

Whit winked at his wife with the eye that Larson couldn't see. They walked on.

Larson said, 'Are we really going riding or was that just a gag you cooked up for the sheriff?'

Whit shrugged. 'We might as well. The F.B.I. has told us to keep our noses strictly out of their business from now on, and I don't see why we should stick around town waiting for someone to shoot at us. We'll be safer out in the country.'

'Maybe so.' Larson didn't seem enthusiastic about it.

Kitty said, 'What's the matter, Swede?'

'Nothing. I just kind of hate to walk out on Casey Jones and Pete and the blonde twirp.'

'So do I,' Whit said. 'But what can we do? They don't want our help in anything they're doing, and there isn't anything we can do on our own hook. I haven't even got an idea left.'

'I have.'

'What?'

'We could mouse around looking for the radio station. That power-line angle of Pete's seems like a good lead.'

'You're crazy. Pete said himself he couldn't cover all the possible locations in a year, and we've got two days. There aren't more than three or four places in the whole countryside where you'd be farther than spitting distance from a power-line.'

Larson said, 'Uh huh. Maybe not that many. And if *I* was trying to hide a radio station, I know where *I'd* put it – if I was smart enough to figure that anyone looking for it would be a cinch to try the power angle right away.'

They were trudging back towards the hotel when Larson came through with the idea. Whit stopped dead in his tracks. After a long moment he said, 'Go ahead. I know what you're going to say but I want to hear it.'

'Where there aren't no power lines at all,' Larson said doggedly. 'I don't give a damn how funny it sounds or what Pete says either. And I don't know anything about electricity, either, but I'll bet there are other ways of getting it besides buying it from the gas and light company.'

Whit stared. His mind was working furiously. He said, 'Swede, I take off my hat to you. You are smarter than I am.'

'Rib me all you like if it makes you feel good. I'm just saying —'

'I'm not ribbing you.' Whit's brain wave was so hot it burned him. He took Kitty by the shoulders and spoke to her urgently.

'Kitty, honey, Larson's idea is the best one anyone has had in years, and I can do something with it. I need peace and quiet. You run along with him and entertain yourself until dinner time. I'll see you at the hotel.'

'But —'

'I'll be all right. Gates and Kohler aren't chasing me now; I'm chasing them. Anyway, I'm going right back to the hotel and lock myself in. So be a good girl and beat it. Go lose some money playing roulette. Swede, you take over.'

Whit kissed his wife quickly, as she opened her mouth to object, and ran like an antelope with a hot date.

'What are you going to do?' Kitty shouted after him.

'Dirty fingernails,' Whit yelled back. At least it sounded as if he had said that, although it seemed like a foolish remark in the circumstances.

*

The clerk in the book store said, 'Can I help you, sir?'

'I want about twenty dollars' worth of assorted books on electricity and radio,' Whit said.

The salesman said, 'Yes, sir.' He was used to screwballs. He had been in the book business a long time, and nothing disturbed him any more except customers who wanted to know if the book would be all right for Aunt Mabel, and people who were just looking. 'Do you want elementary books or advanced books?'

'Some of each. Everything available about generators. And have you got anything on the local power system – around Reno, I mean?'

'I think I can find something. Right this way, please.'

The bill came to twenty-seven fifty, but Whit had a good working library under one arm when he arrived at the hotel some time later. Under the other arm he carried a few incidentals he had picked up on the way to help him think, including a bottle, a carton of cigarettes, and a map. If anyone had pointed a gun at him or hit him over the head with a baseball bat during the time he had been away from his bodyguard, he hadn't noticed it. There were more vital things to think about. In his room he locked the door, peeled off his coat, and went to work.

Time marched on. The pile of books moved gradually from

his left elbow to his right elbow, the level in the bottle dropped from the top towards the middle, and cigarette butts piled up in the ashtray. Whit did not move from his chair for five hours, except once to turn on the lights when the room grew too dark for reading. He had scouted through six books, drawn a number of lines on his map, and absorbed nearly a pint of whisky and a million cigarettes when Kitty and Larson banged on the door and demanded entrance. He creaked when he rose to let them in, but he was happy even though his head ached and his eyes hurt. He had done it.

Kitty came into the room, took one breath, and hurried to open a window. She said, 'Have you been in this smoke house all afternoon?'

'Yes'm.' Whit scratched himself complacently. 'I have been cramming. I am now an authority on radio, radio telegraphy, radio telephony, electricity, electro-magnetism, electro-dynamics, and electro-kinetics. Ask me anything.' He yawned and stretched. 'Go on, ask me.'

'Did the idea jell?'

'If you mean do I know where the radio transmitter is, yes I do.'

Kitty and Larson looked at him. Larson said, 'You're drunk.'

'Mildly. But I still know where the radio is. To-morrow I shall take you by your sweaty little hands and lead you to it.'

'You *are* drunk,' said Kitty.

'Yes'm. Any other questions?'

'Where is it?'

'Don't you want to hear how I found it, first?'

Kitty knew there was no way to hurry him. She sat down and folded her hands.

'Go ahead, dear.'

Whit picked up the whisky bottle, drank from the neck, wiped the mouth of the bottle on his sleeve, and offered it to Kitty. When she declined, he handed it to Larson. After those preliminaries he snapped his suspenders. He felt wonderful.

'First I shall give credit where credit is due. Swede, your idea was what started me off. I don't know when you started to use your noggin for something besides growing hair, but you rang the bell for once. So I did a little research work.'

164

Larson shook hands with himself. Whit snapped his suspenders again for attention.

'If you were right, and I believed that you were right, then Gates would pick a spot where there were no power lines at all. That cut down the territory substantially. Then I knew, from what Casey had accomplished with his direction-finder, that the transmitter was roughly south-west or north-east of Reno. That cut down the territory some more. I marked down on my map, as well as I could remember, what Casey had on his map, and then I dug up some dope about the local power system and put that down too. Here's what I got.'

He spread his map on the table so the others could see.

'Here are Casey's lines of direction, fanning out south-west and north-east from Reno. These other lines wandering across the countryside are power lines. Casey's direction lines to the north-east cut through the middle of the whole system; plenty of power for a transmitter. So it isn't there. It's over here south of the river, where there's nothing but uninhabited brush country and not a power line for miles.'

Whit's finger moved across the map.

'I had one big lucky hunch. Do you remember Gates' fingernails, Kitty? And Caldwell's? They had been working on something greasy; machinery, probably. When you said they might be getting their power from something besides the power company, Swede, I remembered their hands. I bought a few books and read up on electricity until I knew the difference between a generator and an egg-beater, and then I made a list of every kind of generator there was and began to eliminate the kinds Gates couldn't use for one reason or another; windmill generators, too conspicuous; gasoline-motor generators, too noisy, and so on. When I got through there was nothing left on the list but a turbo-generator. That's how Gates is getting his power.'

'What's a turbo-generator?' said Kitty.

'A generator powered by a turbine. And a turbine, if you don't know, is a motor that functions because it's got a steady stream of water rushing through it.'

'The river!'

'Sure, the river. That's where the gas and light company gets its power, why not Gates? He's an electrician. He and Caldwell built their own power plant.'

165

Larson said, 'It sounds good. But your pal Casey Jones is an electrician, too. How come he and Pete had it figured out that the power lines were the only answer?'

'Because they're smart. Casey's smart and Pete's smart and I'm smart – and you, Swede, you're dumb. You haven't got enough sense to reason that because Gates always got his electricity from the power company so far, he'd have to go right on getting it from the power company when things began to get hot for him. That, and the dirty fingernails Gates and Caldwell got from installing the machinery the last time the transmitter was off the air, was enough to work on. Take a bow.'

'Thanks,' said Larson. 'So you know it's on the river and you know it's somewhere inside the angle that Casey worked out with his radio doodad. The only trouble I can see is that Casey's angle and the river travel in about the same direction all the way to Lake Tahoe. That leaves you a lot of territory to cover between now and to-morrow night.'

Whit took his mouth away from the bottle-neck.

'Swede,' he said gratefully. 'I don't know what I'd do without you to make me look good. Here, have a drink and I'll show you both how smart I am.'

Larson grinned and had a drink. Whit bent over the map, hiding part of it under the pretence of resting his weight on his hand.

'Look. Here are Casey's lines of direction going south-west. He never caught a message long enough to fix a line right on the nose, but he got enough to set the general direction. On percentage, the right direction lies about half-way between the lines. That would hit right about at the tip of my forefinger, where the river takes a jog towards the south on the other side of the California border. Now, I learned something out of these books this afternoon. One thing you have to have for a turbo-generator is a good solid foundation that you can bolt your machinery to. Another is a shelter. And Gates needs a place to hide his equipment. So wherever it is, there have to be buildings of some kind. He isn't going to build them himself if he can help it, but he can't have people being nosey about what he's doing. He needs a nice quiet place on the river with a house or two he can use and no neighbours. Guess what he finds?'

Whit dramatically lifted his hand. The last-act-curtain effect was spoiled to some extent because he immediately had to put his hand down on the table again to keep from falling on his ear, but it wasn't fatal to the performance. Where his finger had rested on the thin blue thread of the river there was a tiny black dot marked 'Ghostburg'.

CHAPTER 19

AT seven a.m. the next morning Whit and Larson were on their way to Alex Hotaling's stables, half-awake and accompanied by two of the finest hangovers known to man. Whit was burdened with a guilty conscience as well. Before Kitty had folded up the night before, leaving him and Larson alone to hatch their drunken plots over the last bottle, she had made him promise faithfully that he would do nothing reckless until he had talked to Casey Jones. But when a thundering headache woke him at the crack of dawn and he tore himself and his katzenjammer out of bed and struggled shakily into his wild-west riding clothes, Kitty was still asleep. He had crept away without even leaving her a note.

As a precautionary measure in case the sheriff had been serious when he threatened to post a man to watch them, Whit and Larson sneaked out by way of the hotel service entrance and bribed a porter to pick up Whit's car and bring it to the back alley. For a substantial commission he had done some shopping for them as well. They now had a pair of Levis, a denim jumper and a pair of boots for Larson, a quart cardboard container of black coffee, a deck of egg sandwiches, and a small bottle of something alleged to be whisky. It wasn't a bad haul for that hour of the morning. Whit's stomach baulked when he looked at the sandwiches, but he got the coffee down and didn't erupt even when he tried coffee and whisky for the medicinal effect. After a couple of doses he felt steady enough to drive the car while Larson climbed into the Levis. Larson had a few medicinal shots himself, and things began to look up.

'I may be going to live,' Larson said. 'Mind telling me what we're up to? I'm a little foggy about what we cooked up last night.'

'Can you ride a horse?'

'Some – if I have to.'

Whit had brought his map along. He gave it to Larson, and Larson spread it open on his knee.

Whit said, 'Ghostburg sits on the south bank of the river, and the highway comes within about a mile or a mile and a half north of the river at that point. The map shows a dirt road of some kind running from the river to the highway, and as far as I can see it's the only connexion between the town and civilization. But we can't go in that way because even if they're not watching the road there'll be a bridge, and they're sure to be keeping a lookout there. Our only safe approach is to get a couple of horses, cross the river at Verdi, and ride up the south bank, coming down on the town from the rear.'

Larson studied the map. 'Ten miles from Verdi, more or less, and ten miles back. Twenty miles on horseback isn't going to do my head any good.'

'Mine either. But it's got to be done, so we might as well get ready for it. Hand me that coffee.'

Alex Hotaling was glad to see them when they drove into the stable yard. Business had been purty slow lately, what with the cool weather, so he still had the second and third best pieces of hoss-flesh in Nevayda for their use. They could have had the fourth best piece of hoss-flesh in the state as well if they had brung Mr Whitney's missus along. Alex thought Mr Whitney's missus was high-class. Purty as a picture. He'd like to see her on his bay mare some day, after he got the hoss back.

Whit said, 'The missus was too sleepy to get up. No news about the mare?'

'Nope. Not a peep. But I ain't worried. I've got that rustler's description out all over the country, and they'll grab him sooner or later. Maybe he won't git strung up, the way he ought to, but I'll git my mare back.'

'You've got insurance, haven't you?'

'Sure, I got insurance. But it's like having your gasoline stole nowadays, to lose a hoss. The insurance money don't fill your gas tank. There ain't any money that will buy me another mare like that one.'

The bay mare's two nearest competitors were led up just then by Alex's stableman, so Alex branched off into a discus-

sion of the merits of the hosses he still had left, particularly
the two he was letting them take. There was only a bare shade
of difference between either one of them and the bay mare,
of course. He'd go so far as to say that they wouldn't find two
better hosses in a coon's age. They could suit themselves about
making their choice; there wasn't a shade of difference between
the two, not a shade. Anything with the AH brand was tops,
that's all there was to it.

Larson leaned against the fence while the sales talk went on,
watching Hotaling's other horses milling in the corral. He
had given only a quick glance at the two saddled animals that
Alex was bragging about at the moment. Now he said, 'If it's
all the same to you, how about letting me have that buckskin?'

Alex stopped talking in the middle of a sentence. 'Which
buckskin?'

Larson pointed. 'The hammer-headed stallion with the yel-
low tail. Anything the matter with him?'

Alex looked at Larson thoughtfully, examining the new
Levis, the jumper, and the general city-slicker-on-a-holiday
appearance.

'Why, no. There ain't nothing the matter with him. What
made you pick him out?'

'He's the best horse you've got.'

Hotaling looked at the new Levis again and decided that
even the oldest range hand might have occasion to buy new
pants once in a while.

'You ain't fooling. He's my private hoss, as a matter of fact.'

'O.K.' Larson turned away from the corral. 'Just thought I'd
ask.'

'I didn't say you couldn't have him.'

Alex spoke to his stableman. The buckskin was brought
from the corral and saddled, and one of the other horses was
turned loose. Alex handed the buckskin's reins to Larson himself.

'I guess you know hosses, mister. Not many people would
pick that one. He ain't pretty, but he's sure easy on the seat of
your pants. Be glad to let anyone ride him that's got enough
savvy to pick him out.'

Larson said, 'Thanks.'

One horse or another was all the same to an old cable-car
buckaroo like Whit, and if Larson wanted a blue horse instead

169

of a green one, it wasn't an unreasonable whim. But Whit
could see that there was more to the selection than a whim.
He watched Larson estimate the stirrup length on the buckskin's saddle, slip the leathers out a notch, hook an experienced finger under the latigo to test the stableman's saddling
job, and climb into the saddle like someone who knew what a
horse was for. When he was mounted, rider and horse were
immediately on terms of mutual respect.

Whit did a little mild chiselling before he left. He talked
Alex out of a flour-sack and a pair of field-glasses that the
livery man didn't mind letting them use as long as they were
careful. Whit promised that they would be; they just wanted
to look at the scenery across the river. Alex gave them directions about getting across the stream and warned them that the
country was purty wild, but that his hosses would take care
of them if they'd just remember that the hosses knew more
than they did. They said they'd remember.

It was still early morning when they rode out of the livery
yard. Whit had the field-glasses slung over his shoulder, and
the flour-sack, containing the headache medicine and the re-
maining egg sandwiches, was tied to Larson's saddle-horn.
They headed towards the river, letting the horses set their own
pace while they warmed up.

Whit said, 'Where did you learn to ride, Swede?'

'Just picked it up. I worked on a cattle ranch once.'

'That isn't where you picked up the broken nose.'

'I got that when I was a pug. Before I learned not to lead
with my face.'

'What else did you do before you joined the police?'

'Oh, this and that. Worked around.'

'Where were you working around when you learned to do
tricks with a gun?'

'Circus. Used to shoot cigarettes out of guys' mouths.'

'You just picked up a gun one day and shot a cigarette out
of a guy's mouth, huh?'

Larson grunted.

Whit said, 'Come clean. You're among friends. What were
you, a bank robber?'

'Bootlegger,' Larson confessed. 'I used to run the stuff in to
Chicago across Lake Michigan, and what with Canadian cops,
Federal cops, highjackers and doublecrossers, I learned fast.

170

But for God's sake don't tell Lootenant Webster. He thinks I was fresh out of a convent when I got my badge.'

'I'll bet he does,' Whit said. 'Here's the river. Which way did Alex say the bridge was?'

'Upstream.'

The going got considerably worse after they had crossed the river and struck off towards the west. There was no road in the direction they wanted to go, and the country was rough, overgrown with thick scrub that grew higher than their horses' withers, so that they were for ever dodging branches which slashed at their faces. Sometimes they dodged successfully, but not often. The brush grew right down to the river-bank and as far as they could see in the other direction. There was nothing to do but put their heads down and suffer.

They were an hour covering the first third of their trip. It was a long hour for all concerned, including the horses. Then they hit an old railroad track which angled in from the south and followed the river-course upstream. It had been unused for years; the rails were rusty, the ties uneven, and brush had grown through the rock ballast of the roadbed, but it was a racetrack compared to the rest of the countryside. They guided their sweating horses on to the roadbed and had time and breath to talk.

Larson said, 'Hey.'

'Uh?'

'I've been thinking. How are we going to find what we're hunting for after we get there?'

'Look around.'

'We can't mouse over the town looking into houses. The idea is not to let those monkeys know we're around, isn't it?'

Whit patted the field-glasses. 'We don't have to mouse over the town. We'll squat on the hill and peek around a blade of grass.'

'What do you expect to see?'

'An aerial.' Whit gave the word its full four syllables to show that he was really hep. 'It sticks up in the air so that radio waves can get a running jump off of it on their way to wherever they're going. If there's a radio transmitter around, there's an aerial.'

'You hope.'

'I know,' Whit said. 'I read a book. Uncork that bottle, will

171

you? I've got gremlins again.

They rode for another hour, still following the rusty railroad track. The rails turned gradually southward with the bend of the stream, and hills began to shoulder up on either side of the river. They were getting into the mountains now; the river was narrower and more rapid, and the railroad track curved through cuts and wound over fills in the hillside. Some of the cuts had begun to cave in across the track, and the fills had washed away with the rains so that the rails stretched across great gaps, with a few ties hanging in mid-air from rusted spikes. The necessary detours began to slow their progress again.

Whit had brought his map along, and he knew from the way the river-course turned south that they were nearing the end of their ride. They were surely across the border into California by now, and Ghostburg was not far from the state line. Whit kicked his horse in the ribs as they hit a clear stretch of track. The click of horseshoes quickened on the rock ballast.

They came around a bend in the track and pulled up in front of a tunnel before them. The tracks disappeared into the hill. A clear rivulet of water came from the black mouth of the tunnel, wandered to the river-bank, and splashed into the stream below. The hill rose sheer from the river, towering above them, so that there was no way to go on except through the tunnel or by way of a wide detour.

The horses drank from the rivulet while their riders considered possibilities. Larson looked doubtfully at the hole in the hillside.

'What do you think, Whit?'

'I don't know. It's probably caved in.'

'If it isn't caved in now, I bet it would get around to it if we tried to go through.'

'I wouldn't be surprised. But even if we could make it, we don't know where the tunnel comes out. We're nearly to the town now; the tunnel might open out right on Main Street. I guess we'll have to go around.'

Larson agreed. They had one last slug of medicine apiece and a chaser from the stream, after which Larson filled the empty bottle with water and put it in his pocket for future reference. They remounted and turned the horses off into the brush.

172

The going got rough again immediately. They had to beat back half a mile or more from the river before the slope of the hillside was easy enough to attempt the climb, and even then the horses were hard put to make it. They sweated their way upwards, grunting.

The buckskin was the better of the two horses, and Larson kept the lead. Nearing the top of the hill he began to sniff the air and make faces.

'We're getting near something,' he said. 'Catch that fruity odour.'

'Smells like more than a ghost town to me. Something is plenty dead around here.'

'Maybe one of the ghosts.'

Whit held his nose. 'He's a fresh one, then. Smells more like somebody's cow stumbled and broke its neck.'

'I'm not curious. The beef shortage would have to get a lot worse before I'd investigate anything as ripe as that.'

'What we're looking for stinks worse than a dead cow,' Whit said. 'Get going. We're almost to the top.'

Larson kicked the buckskin's ribs. The horses put their heads down and tackled the last climb.

Whit began to feel a premonitory excitement as they approached the hill crest. He was pretty sure that his reasoning had been good, but he needed final confirmation. He wanted to be able to go to Casey and say without a question in his mind, here it is, pal; I've done what you couldn't do. In a few minutes he would know at last, one way or another.

Thirty feet from the top of the hill he said, 'Hold it, Swede,' and reined in his sweating horse. Larson's buckskin stopped immediately.

Larson said, 'Now what?'

'We hoof it from here. I don't want to come out on the skyline. No use taking chances.'

'Good idea.'

The two men swung stiffly out of their saddles. Whit unslung the field-glasses, pulled the reins over his horse's head, and went up the last few yards on foot. Larson was at his heels. At the very crest of the hill they dropped down on their hands and knees, crawling through the low scrub which screened the peak. Side by side they parted the last bit of brush and looked down at the river below.

CHAPTER 20

THEY had stumbled on a perfect lookout point. Half a mile upstream the river poured from a cut in the hills and came straight down the valley to curve around the base of the bluff on which they lay. Below and in front of them the bluff dropped steeply to the water. To their left, towards the west, the hill sloped more gradually in a curve that went back from the river and left a crescent-shaped flat between the river and the hill. The rusted railroad track emerged from the tunnel opening almost directly beneath them, skirted the river side of the clump of ramshackle buildings in the flat, and disappeared through the cut upstream.

Ghostburg, lying in the flat two or three hundred yards below, had been quite a dump in its time. It looked like an old mining town. The diggings were not in sight, but there were the remains of a mill or a smelter near the river. In addition to the mill, the town held a church, a railroad station, a building that might once have been a school, a dozen false-fronted store buildings, and perhaps fifty houses lying back towards the beginning of the hill slope. Once there had been streets dividing the town into neat squares, and board walks along the house fronts. Now brush hid the streets and tall grass grew through the cracks of the board walks where the walks hadn't yet rotted away. Everything in sight looked as if a strong sneeze would knock it over.

The road that Whit had spotted on his map led from the far side of the river and disappeared over a hill in the direction of the highway beyond. The road was mostly ruts, but it still looked passable. A heavy footbridge swung from rusty cables strung across the river. The cables ran from a squat wooden tower in the flat near the wrecked mill to the higher bank across the stream, and on the far side of the river, where the road ended at the bridge-head, there was a good-sized shack made of rusty galvanized iron sheeting. Except for the narrow footbridge and the railroad track, the town appeared to have no connexion with the outside world.

Larson, peering through his screen of brush, said, 'The mountaineers have hairy ears, they live in caves and ditches. I wonder how they got any place if they didn't want to ride the railroad. They must of done a lot of hiking.'

Whit was giving the valley a once-over with his field-glasses. He said, 'There used to be a road running upstream on this side. Look along the hillside where the river comes out of the hills.'

Larson took the glasses.

A road had been there, years back, but it wasn't much to look at now. Parts of it had got tired of hanging on to the hill and had fallen into the river, and what remained was overgrown with brush. Only a shadow in the scrub was left.

Larson said, 'By God, now. If anyone ever *does* get around to raiding that place —'

He let the unfinished sentence end on a thoughtful note.

'It would be a pushover,' Whit said. 'A man at the bridge, one or two up here on the hill, one at the tunnel, maybe one upstream to watch the track. You could do it with less.'

Larson wasn't so sure. 'That's all right for keeping them in, but it wouldn't be no bargain if you had to go in after them. I wouldn't want to search all those buildings for some guy who was waiting for me with a gun.'

Whit didn't argue. He had taken the glasses again, and now lay propped on his elbows intently scanning the cluster of buildings in the flat.

He kept the glasses to his eyes for a long time, covering the town by inches. When he had worked his way from one corner of Ghostburg to the other, he went back to the beginning and started over again. The aerial *had* to be there; his reasoning was too good for it not to be there. He tried taking the town in twenty-foot squares, carefully examining one at a time, but he could see no wires. He did everything except crawl into the glasses in the concentration of his search, and at the end of half an hour, when he was practically blind with eyestrain, he had drawn a complete blank.

He handed the glasses to Larson and dug his knuckles into his eyes.

'You try it. I'm seeing pink elephants.'

'O.K. What do I look for?'

'Wires. They might be horizontal, vertical, or kitty-corner, and they'll be well concealed, but they're there. That dump was deserted long before there was any electricity in the country, so any wire you see is what we're looking for.'

Larson looked until he had pink elephant trouble of his own and had to give up the glasses. No luck. Whit had another try, then Larson took over again, and then Whit. Still no luck. The sun rose overhead, passed the zenith, and started home to bed, and the river rushed endlessly around the base of the bluff below the watchers on the hill. Ghostburg slumbered in the sun and gave no sign that it had ever held anything but ghosts.

Larson said finally, 'You could be wrong, Whit.'

Whit shook his head. 'I could be right, too. I *am* right. That town is absolutely perfect for a hideout. Look at the mill, right down at the river edge with a million places to rig the generator. Look at all those empty shacks. It's *got* to be there. Let me have those glasses. I'm going around the hill and try a different angle.'

They tried a number of different angles, as many as they could find without exposing themselves to view from the flat below. The sun dropped lower towards the mountains. Larson took time out during one of Whit's shifts with the glasses and crept back through the brush to unsaddle the horses and get the remaining food. The egg sandwiches were flavoured with horse-sweat and the bottle of water in Larson's pocket tasted like more of the same, but their lunch was better than nothing. It had been a long time since breakfast.

Larson said, 'What happens if we don't see anything before sundown?'

'We go down the hill and feel around in the dark.'

'You're nuts.'

Whit said angrily, 'All right, I'm nuts. It's there and I know it's there, but I'm not going to try to get Casey Jones out here on my say-so. That town is going to be raided at three o'clock if I have to raid it myself. I'd rather Casey and Pete came along, that's all. Take the glasses.'

Larson took the glasses.

It was the sunshine that finally did it for them. As the sun dropped lower and lower in the west, shadows moved and lengthened, and the light struck objects in the flat below from ever-changing angles. Larson was shifting his sights from mill to railroad station to church to schoolhouse for the ninety-seventh time when he caught a faint glint of something shiny that had not been shiny before. He grunted, steadying the glasses.

Whit said, 'What is it?'

'The church. In the steeple, the what-do-you-call-it where they put the bell. Something shines.'

Whit grabbed the glasses from Larson's hands.

It was a wonderful feeling, after the long hours of increasing disappointment, to have his hunch pay off at last. He felt the thrill all the way to his heels. At two hundred and fifty yards he could barely make out the thread that was a single wire running vertically from the belfry down into the church below, but with the reflected sunlight to help him he could not mistake the glazed porcelain surface of the insulator supporting the upper end of the thread. It had been fastened to the empty bell-hanger, low enough so that it could not be seen from the flat or from the far river-bank, and for that reason visible under the belfry peak to anyone looking down from the bluff – if the watcher were lucky enough and patient enough to wait until the light was just right. Whit's determination had paid off. He held the glasses steady while the light imperceptibly changed and the reflection died. When the insulator was once more only a formless dark spot in the belfry, he dropped the glasses and gave Larson a tremendous whack between the shoulder-blades.

'Swede, we've done it!'

Larson said, 'You don't have to break my back just because I thought you might have been wrong, do you? Let's get out of here before the sun goes down.'

He began to inch his way backward through the brush. Whit waited only long enough to take one last look at the flat below, fixing in his mind the location of the church, the bridge, the wrecked mill, and the approach from the bridge to the town. Then he followed Larson.

The horses were eager to get going again. They were oat-burners, unused to the sparse dry grass that had been their only food for the day, and they wanted to be on their way back to Papa Hotaling and the feed bin. Whit and Larson threw the saddles on and climbed aboard. The horses took over from there.

They had come up the hill by a roundabout path because the climb was easier that way, but going down was, in horse-language, a man of a different colour when dinner was waiting. The horses picked the shortest distance between two points, squatted on their haunches, and slid.

The ripe smell that had been so noticeable on the hillside during the climb was still there during the descent. It was even riper, if anything. A few yards below the shoulder of the hill the stench became so overpowering that Whit and Larson had to hold their breath as they skirted a small ravine cutting the slope down which they rode. Whit was the first to notice the spade marks on the lip of the ravine, and he hauled back on the reins and pointed with his free hand. Neither he nor Larson said anything as they swung down to investigate. Spade marks meant something besides a cow with a broken neck.

Whoever had shovelled dirt from the side of the bank to bury the body of the dead horse in the shallow ravine below had neglected to weigh the dirt down with rocks, and coyotes had been at work. The rotting corpse, or what was left of it, lay fully exposed. It was still saddled and bridled.

After a while Larson said, 'I guess that accounts for Alex's bay mare.' He took a penknife from his pocket and held his breath as he bent to saw at the stiff reddish hide. When he straightened up he held a piece of skin bearing Hotaling's AH brand.

'Might account for something else, too.' Whit pointed at the horse's head. There was a bullet hole in the skull.

'I saw that. But it doesn't mean anything. Even a rustler would shoot a horse with a broken leg.'

'Maybe it had a broken leg and maybe it didn't,' Whit said. 'I'm not going to paw around in that mess to find out. But did you ever know a horse to bleed in the seat of its saddle when it was shot in the head?'

Larson looked at the crusted black stains on the saddle leather.

'You got something. Looks like the horse-thief didn't climb off under his own power. Maybe Alex caught up with him after all.'

Whit shook his head. 'I don't think so. He might kill a horse-thief, but he wouldn't shoot his own horse. I think Alex is telling the truth – as far as he knows. Only he doesn't know the truth.'

'What's your guess?'

178

'I'd say Alex's horse-thief wasn't a thief at all. I think he was a Federal agent named Durham who got the same idea that we did but didn't have our luck. And I think if we look around a little more we might find his body.'

They searched the ravine and the surrounding territory for a hundred yards without finding a grave. The sun had dropped below the mountain peaks before they gave up. Whit was still sure that he had hit on the answer, even though there was no body to back him up. As they rode homeward through the gathering dark, he thought of more and more reasons to support his conclusion.

'Look at the dates, Swede.' The horses were back on the railroad track and their riders could stop worrying about gopher-holes and broken necks. 'That mare has been missing about ten days. Durham's last report went through ten days ago, when he said that the transmitter had been moved again but that he had a hunch he knew where it was. And he wasn't any dumber than we are; he could have hit on our idea. So he rented the mare from Alex and made the same ride that we did. Only he wasn't so lucky. Someone saw him up the hill, shot him out of the saddle, killed the horse so it wouldn't wander home, and lugged Durham's body away.'

'It sounds reasonable. But why lug him away? Why not bury him with the horse?'

'I don't know. Maybe he wasn't dead and they wanted to make him talk.'

'Well, we can find out if you're right, easy enough. Ask Alex what his horse-thief looked like and ask Casey if the description fits Durham. Only I don't think we ought to tell Alex too much right away, if we can help it. You remember what Casey said.'

'I remember everything he said,' Whit answered comfortably. 'I'm going to make the son of a bitch eat his words, too.'

They rode the last few miles in complete darkness. The moon would not rise for several hours yet and the stars were dim, but Hotaling's surefooted horses travelled like homing pigeons. The high brush of the flat lands gave the riders a bad time when at last they had to leave the railroad track to follow the river-bank, but they soon learned to keep their guard up and their heads down. A mile from the bridge they saw a flash-

179

light winking through the blackness, and someone hailed them. They shouted. Alex Hotaling rode up through the brush.

'Hi,' he said. 'Where you been? The missus thought you must of got lost.'

'The missus?' Whit had forgotten about Kitty.

'She came after you. Twicet. Once this morning, couple of hours after you left, and then again a little while back. She was madder than a hornet the first time; wanted to ride after you. I tole her you had too much of a head start, and anyway I didn't know just where you was riding, so she went home. This last time there wasn't nothing for me to do but saddle up and come looking.'

'Is she still mad?'

'Well, not so much. You'll live through it.'

Alex clucked to his horse and took the lead. Over his shoulder he said, 'How was the ride?'

'Swell. Country's a little rough, though.' Whit felt tenderly of his face, where the whipping brush had hashed up his complexion.

'Purty wild on this side. It's all right if you know the country.'

Larson spoke up from his position in the rear of the cavalcade. 'You know the country pretty well?'

'Sure do. Better'n anybody else around here. Like the back of my own hand.'

'You'd be a good man to have around if somebody wanted to do a little night riding and needed a guide.'

Hotaling laughed. 'If there was anyone that crazy. Who'd want to do any night riding in this country?'

Neither Whit nor Larson answered, but they were both thinking along the same lines.

The horses had clattered across the bridge and were loping up the road that led to Hotaling's stables before Whit came out with the questions he had been framing for the last hour.

'There aren't many roads across the river, are there, Alex? Seems to me it would be the best direction a horse-thief could take, but I don't see how he'd get out that way. Where would he go?'

'He could make it all right. He probably headed south and cut back east towards Virginia City. It wouldn't bother a good rider.'

'Did he look like a good rider?'

'No, durn it. That's what gits me. He looked like a slicker – middle-aged fat fellow, kind of bald, talked too much, wore a diamond ring big as your eyeball.'

'He didn't tell you his name?'

'Nope. Wouldn't have been the right one, anyway. He offered to put up fifty dollars on the mare, and I figgered that anyone who wanted me to hold his money when I didn't ask for it wasn't going to steal a hoss. I made a mistake.'

'People make mistakes,' Larson said.

Hotaling only grunted.

A brilliant glare of light illuminated the road as the riders approached the stable yard. When Whit and Larson dismounted stiffly at the corral gate and got the light out of their eyes, they saw that the glare came from a spotlight on the windshield of the touring car which Pete Weston had been driving two nights before. Kitty sat alone behind the steering wheel. As they approached, she turned off the spotlight and gave them a chilling glance.

'Hello,' said Whit.

'Evening, Miz Whitney,' Larson said.

Kitty said, 'Sneaky, aren't you? I suppose you had a nice ride, all by yourselves?'

Whit said, 'Yes, mam. We sure did.'

Kitty knew from his manner that he had news. She said, 'What did you find?'

'Some nice flowers,' Whit answered. Hotaling was only ten feet away, unsaddling the horses. 'They withered before we could bring them back, so we had to throw them away. Swede, take Mrs Whitney to my car and tell her about the flowers while I settle up with Alex.'

Larson got Kitty out of earshot and began to tell her in a low voice all about the flowers. Whit went into the barn with Alex and paid the bill.

Kitty and Larson were sitting in Whit's convertible across the stable-yard when Whit limped back to join them. The seat of his pants was beginning to feel as if he had been well kicked by an expert, his face hurt, and he was dog tired. He hoped Kitty would be reasonable about being left in the lurch that morning. He didn't want to argue.

Kitty had already forgotten her peeve. Larson had finished

telling her about the porcelain flower blooming in the church belfry up the river, and she was too excited over their triumph to remember anything else.

'Whit, it's marvellous! After all the time Casey and Pete spent looking for it, you and Swede found it right away.' She smeared lipstick on his dirty cheek as he got into the car beside her. 'There's a medal for you, smarty.'

Larson sat up and cleared his throat hopefully. No one paid any attention to him. He sighed and relaxed.

Kitty said, 'What are we going to do now?'

'Get back to town. We've got to round up Casey and Pete and whatever help they can get to knock the place over at three o'clock. That's Pete's car over there, isn't it?'

'Yes. He came to the hotel looking for you this morning, after you ran out on me. I borrowed his car to come after you.'

'How did you know where we had gone?'

Kitty pointed at his clothes. 'With that dotted-swiss outfit missing from your closet, where else could you have gone?'

'I never thought of that. You didn't tell Pete anything, did you? What did he want to see me about?'

'I just said that you and Swede had gone somewhere and left me without any transportation.' Kitty's expression was unhappy. 'He told me to tell you that you had better keep out of sight until to-morrow. He said that Sammy Kohler was the type of man who would think that because you had hit him and taken his gun away, he couldn't leave town without – without —'

Whit put his arm around her.

'Never you mind about Sammy Kohler, honey. This is my party now, not Sammy's.'

'But if he —'

'He won't. Now drive me back to town in a hurry, like a good girl. Swede, will you bring Pete's car?'

'Sure.'

Larson got out of the convertible. As Kitty stepped on the starter, Whit rested his head on the back of the seat and went immediately to sleep with the clear conscience of a man who had done a good day's work.

CHAPTER 21

At the same time that Whit laid his head down to snatch a few moments of well-earned rest, Sammy Kohler, moving uneasily in his sleep, rolled over on his back. His adenoids immediately began to strangle him, and he awoke with a start.

Sammy lay on a cot in the small room where Durham had died ten days before. The packing cases which had cluttered the room then were now stacked in a corner, empty, and their contents had been assembled into a compact radio transmitter and two separate receiving sets. The equipment filled a long, roughly-built table standing against one wall of the room. Walter Gates sat at the table, methodically dismantling one of the receiving sets.

Except for a small and carefully screened electric lamp which threw a brilliant fan of light on Gates' work, there was no illumination in the room. It had two windows, one in each of the walls which were the front side of the building, but the windows had been curtained with blankets and underneath the blankets the openings were boarded over. The boards did not fit tightly, however. When Gates knew from the break in the snoring noises that Sammy was awake, he switched off the lamp before he went to the front window and pulled the blanket away to peer through a crack at the blackness outside. Afterwards he turned on the light again and looked at his watch.

'You'd better get going. The moon will be up in three hours.'

Sammy grumbled. He had been awake all last night and most of the day, and, what did Walter take him for? Anyway, there was still plenty of time.

Gates went on with his work. Sammy finally got up grumpily scratching his head.

In the careful manner of a teacher explaining an assignment to a fourth-grade class, Gates said, 'We're getting out of here right after three o'clock. I want you to go pick up Jess and Lorenzo and be back before the moon rises. They'll be watching for us in town, so hide the truck out on the highway before you get to Reno, and thumb a ride in. Go to Jess's apartment first. If he isn't there, he'll be at the Club. Go there, tell him what I've said, and do what he tells you to. Make sure you're not followed before you come back.'

'Ah, hell, Walter,' Sammy said. 'To hear you talk —'

'Do you understand?'

'O.K., O.K. But I bet pretty boy Lorenzo won't come along just because I say so. He isn't going to leave that joint of his unless he's goosed.'

'If Jess needs help, he'll tell you.'

'If Jess asks for help, do I bring the pretty boy whether he wants to come or not?'

'Yes.'

Sammy looked happier.

'I hope the bastard wants to argue.' He patted his coat pocket, put on his hat, and left the room.

The door by which he went out opened into the dusty nave of the abandoned church. It was not a door from the outside, as far as one could see; just weathered pine planks among other weathered pine planks. The clutter and cobwebs of the old church were undisturbed, and there was nothing to show that the building was occupied by anything except pack-rats and the owl that hung out in the belfry—unless you were the owl, and resented the heavy copper wire which ran from the belfry down through the steep gables of the attic into the hidden room where the radio transmitter stood against the wall. Or if you were one of the pack-rats, you might know something of the other wires, heavily insulated, which ran under the floor and through a buried conduit to the mill at the edge of the river, where a turbine hummed quietly in the intake from which the mill had got its water in the old days.

Sammy knew as much about the wires as the pack-rats and the owl, and he cared less. His pleasure at the prospect of pushing Lorenzo around was only temporary. It disappeared as he made his way through the pitch black down to the river and across the footbridge to the shack on the far bank where the delivery truck was hidden. By God, he was getting a bellyful of being ordered around by Walter Gates. He was getting a bellyful of the whole lousy job. What good was all that fancy money without a chance to spend it? Why, he hadn't had a woman or a good drunk or played the races in all the time he had been in Nevada. Things were going to be different when he got out of that dump. And if Walter Gates didn't like it, Walter Gates was liable to get something he wasn't expecting.

Sammy told Walter Gates what was what and what Gates could do about it as the truck, without lights, bumped away over the rutty road towards the highway.

Back in the hidden room Gates went on with his work, fully aware of everything going through Sammy's weasel's head. His plans took Sammy into consideration. When he had finished dismantling one receiving set he started on the other. The work took him about an hour. After the job was finished and the equipment packed away, he looked at his watch. There was plenty of time to code and record his last message and dismantle the recording apparatus before three o'clock. That would leave only the transmitter to knock down. The turbine would have to be left—along with a few other odds and ends which had once been useful but were becoming burdensome.

There was one small packing case which Sammy had never seen opened. The lid was secured by a strong padlock. Gates unlocked the box and took from it a loaded sub-machine gun, which he examined carefully before he stood it in the corner behind the empty packing cases. He knew that Sammy was a good shot. The extra firepower of the sub-machine gun would make up for any lack of accuracy on Gates' part.

*

Whit awoke when the car stopped in front of the hotel. He was still stiff from his ride and his saddle-end felt worse than ever, but his head was clear. Kitty's watch said ten o'clock. Five hours to go.

They held a council of war after Larson had parked Pete's touring car and came to crawl into the convertible beside them. Whit said, 'Did you make any arrangements to return Pete's car, Kitty?'

'He said he would pick it up if I left it in front of John's Grill.'

'We'd better go there first, then. We've got to find Pete and Casey right away. Pete may have left a message with John.'

They were still lucky. Pete was at the restaurant when they arrived. The dinner-time rush was over, Evelyn the critical waitress had gone for the night, and the place was empty except for Pete, John, and a cash customer gnawing at a piece

185

of apple pie. Pete and John were at the far end of the counter from the pie-gnawer, talking quietly. The conversation stopped as Kitty and the two men sat down at the counter next to Pete.

Pete said, 'Hello.' He looked tired and discouraged.

'Any luck?' Whit asked.

Pete shook his head. John still stood there, as if he did not plan to move. After a moment Larson said, 'I'm hungry. How about some dinner, John?'

'Sure, sure. Three blue plates?'

'How about a steak and french fries?'

'No steaks now for two weeks. Hamburger, yes.'

'That'll do. Miz Whitney, how about you? Whit? Make it three hamburger steaks with fixings and a lot of coffee.'

'Sure, sure,' John went away.

Whit said, 'We found it, Pete.'

Pete's head jerked around. 'What?'

'We know where the transmitter is.'

Pete's face turned red, then white. 'Damn you, Whitney. This is no time —'

'I'm not trying to be funny. We located it this afternoon, in a ghost town twenty miles up the river. I looked at the aerial myself through a pair of field-glasses.'

The anger faded from Pete's face. He stared at Larson, then at Kitty, and at Whit again, and all of a sudden he was neither tired nor discouraged.

'Spill it!'

'First I want you to listen to a description and see if it means anything to you. A middle-aged man, heavy, getting bald, talkative, wore a big diamond ring —'

'Durham. Where is he?'

'I don't know. Dead, probably. We found the horse he had rented, buried on a hill back of the ghost town. It had been shot in the head. The saddle was covered with blood that didn't come from the horse.'

Pete said levelly, 'They'll pay for Durham. Go on.'

Whit told him the story, beginning with the idea that Larson had got the day before and ending up with what Alex Hotaling had said about his horse-thief. Pete interrupted several times to ask sharp questions, and the tale had to be stopped for a moment when John arrived with food. But after Whit had finished, there was no doubt in Pete's mind.

186

'I don't know what to say,' he confessed. 'I take off my hat.
You were smart and we were dumb. Casey and I and Gladys
have been spending the last two days on twenty-four hour
watch at the Club, hoping that Lorenzo or Caldwell would lead
us somewhere before it was too late. It was the best we could
think of, and we weren't hopeful. Whatever happens, you and
Larson have done a great job.'

'What do you mean, whatever happens? If Lorenzo and
Caldwell are here, you can pick them off any time. And Gates
will be at the transmitter at three o'clock. Kohler, too. They're
probably there right now, getting ready to haul out. It's in the
bag.'

'Nothing is in the bag in this business. But it looks like we're
in the driver's seat at last. What time is it?'

Kitty looked at the family watch. 'Half-past ten. What are
we going to do?'

'You aren't going to do anything. The F.B.I. will take over
from now on. The rest of it is dirty work, and somebody is
going to get hurt to-night.'

'That's all right for Miz Whitney.' Larson put his oar in for
the first time since coming into the restaurant. 'I'm not being
froze out. Count me in.'

'Count me in, too,' Whit said. 'We ran this thing down for
you and we're going to help button it up.'

'I'm afraid not. We haven't any authority to bring in anyone outside the Bureau.'

'You haven't enough authority to keep us out,' Larson said
flatly. 'Anyway, how many men have you got? If you're going
to make a raid to-night, you won't have time to call in the
reserves. You'll need us.'

'I won't argue. It's up to Casey. He's running things.'

'Let's get Casey then,' Whit said. 'We haven't all the time in
the world.'

The pie-eater had gone. John was waiting behind the cash
register when Whit went up to pay the check. John beamed as
he made his inevitable query about the dinner, knowing that
the answer was always the same. They didn't see how he did
it for the price.

'Small profits, quick return.' John made the cash register
ring. 'I like the customers to be satisfied.'

'I don't think you'll have any more customers to-night,' Pete said. 'Why don't you close up?'

They exchanged a glance. John said, 'Maybe I could at that.'

Pete stopped the others as they moved towards the door. John was already turning off lights, but Pete led them back through the restaurant to the rear of the building where John had his bachelor sleeping-quarters. A minute or two later John joined them.

There were no preliminaries. Pete said, 'You all know John the Greek restaurant man. In the circumstances, I think you ought to meet John Masilikos, special agent for the F.B.I.'

They managed to mumble something more or less appropriate. It was too much of a jolt to carry off without stuttering, but John made it easy for them with his large grin. He said, 'What is it, Pete?'

'The amateurs have beaten us to it. They found the radio transmitter.'

'No!'

'Yes. And we'll knock it over to-night, unless Casey has other ideas. We've got to have a conference.'

John turned to Whit. 'Where is it? The transmitter, I mean.'

'Up the river, in an old church in a ghost town. They've got an aerial slung inside the belfry.'

'What about power? There isn't —'

Pete interrupted him. 'We'll have to go over the whole business again for Casey. Let it soak. I'm going to get him and bring him here.'

He left unobtrusively by the back door.

John couldn't wait for Pete's return. His job of running a beanery as a cover for the local headquarters of the F.B.I. had been the least exciting and most exacting of the local assignments, and at the end it had seemed that they were licked in spite of all their work. Now, at the last minute, they had hit the jackpot and were on top again. John had to know the details.

It took Whit twenty-five minutes to answer all of John's questions, and it took Pete twenty-five minutes to find Casey at his post outside of Lorenzo's Club and bring him back. Whit, for the first time in his life, was getting tired of the sound of his own voice, but for Casey's benefit he told the whole story over for the third time. He hoped that J. Edgar Hoover wasn't going to want an oral report from him.

Casey was silent while Whit talked. Whit said finally, 'That's all. Except that you looked at me the other day when you said you had slipped on a banana peel. How do you feel about it now?'

Casey said, 'You sure want to have your back scratched, don't you? But I guess you've got it coming. What do you want me to say?'

'You just said it,' Whit answered. 'I'm satisfied.'

He went across the room and sat down beside Kitty. He felt good.

Casey wasted no time with water that had gone under the bridge. He said, 'We've got four hours. We know that Gates will be at the transmitter at three o'clock, and he'll probably have Kohler with him, but we can't count on Lorenzo and Caldwell being anywhere in particular when we make the raid. And we've got to cover everyone. Whit, how many men do you think will be necessary to raid the ghost town, allowing for a man to cover all possible ways out?'

Whit pointed at Larson.

'His opinion is better than mine. You tell him, Swede.'

'How many men have you got?' Larson asked Casey.

'Four. Pete, John, myself, and another man, Jackson. But we'll need one man at the radio to catch Gates' last message, so figure on three.'

'Then you've got to use Whit and me. It'll take at least four men for the raid; one at the tunnel, one on the hill, one at the bridge, and one to go across the bridge. You ought to have more. If it takes two men to tail Lorenzo and Caldwell you'll have to have seven at least. You've got six, counting us.'

'I can't use you,' Casey said. He was surprised at the suggestion.

Whit said, 'Why not?'

'You might get hurt.'

'You might get hurt yourself. What has that got to do with it?'

Casey shook his head decisively.

'No. This is work for the Bureau. You've done your share, and a good job it was, too.' He motioned to Pete. 'Get on the phone to San Francisco and tell them we need ten men by two o'clock. We'll meet them at the airport.'

'I hate to be mean,' Whit said. 'But two o'clock will be too

189

late. One o'clock will be too late. Any time after the next hour will be too late.'

'What are you talking about?'

'The ghost town,' Whit said. 'You can't get around to block off the back door except by horseback. It'll take three hours' ride at least, and only if you know the way. Larson and I were over the road this afternoon.'

He had Casey by the short hairs and they both knew it. Whit waited for him to give in.

Kitty had not spoken for a long time. Now, as Casey hesitated, she had her say. Her voice was controlled.

'I don't want Whit to go, Casey. I want him right where I can see him, where he'll be safe. And I don't want to tell you your business, either. But if you need him it's too important not to take him, whatever happens. Or anyone else here.'

Whit took her hand. Her fingers tightened hard around his.

Casey turned his head to look at her. He said, 'Thanks, Mrs Whitney. I guess I need him and Larson and you too, and I'm proud to have your help. I wish there were more like you.'

Pete cleared his throat to break the silence which followed. 'I'd better get the sheriff, Casey. He's reliable, and he's got local authority if we need it. We wouldn't have to tell him too much.'

Larson said, 'There's the old-timer up the river who runs the livery stable. He was nuts about that horse your man Durham rode. You could get him to come along without telling him anything except that he was after the guys who killed his mare. He knows the country across the river.'

'If I can do anything, I'll be glad to help,' Kitty said. She still clung tightly to Whit's hand.

Casey said, 'I've got to use all of you because there's no other way out. You three —' he made a gesture which included Whit, Kitty and Larson '— stand up and raise your right hands. I don't know how much authority I have, but I'm going to try to make it legal.'

They stood up. Casey recited the oath.

'Do you solemnly swear that you will support and defend the Constitution of the United States against all enemies, foreign and domestic; that you will bear true and faithful allegiance to the same; that you take this obligation freely, without any mental reservation or purpose of evasion; and that you will well and faithfully discharge the duties of the office you are about to enter, so help you God?'

'I do.' They spoke together.

'Then you're working for the Federal Government from now on. We haven't any time to lose, so listen to what I want you to do. Whit, you're first.'

*

Whit, with Larson at his heels as safety man, pushed his way through the crowd around the dice game until they were bellied up against the high rim of the crap table.

The dice were getting a heavy play to-night at Lorenzo's Club, and it took two men to run the game. One of them, the stickman who scooped in the dice with his hooked stick after each throw and flipped them back to the dice-shooters, was new to Whit. The other man was the slim blond lad who had won all of Whit's money on his first night in Reno.

The blond man was carrying on the mechanical patter that went free with the dice.

'Coming out! Co-o-o-ming out with – ee-o-leven! A winnah!' Silver dollars plunked down on the green felt. 'Leave it lay and watch it pay, folks. There's a natural passer shooting, a natural passer. Get the money down and climb aboard the gravy train. He's co-o-o-ming OUT!'

Whit began to whistle softly as he watched the game. The tune was 'Casey Jones'. The blond man looked at him once, recognized him, and held up a handful of silver in invitation. Whit shook his head and went on whistling.

The dice finally came to him. He had a handful of small coins in his fingers. He put them on the line in front of him as he picked up the dice.

'I'm shooting a dollar and twenty-seven cents.'

Someone snickered.

The dice man shot a quick appraising glance across the table.

'A dollar twenty-seven cents he shoots. Who'll ride with the shooter who risks a dollar twenty-seven? A new passer, friends. Get your bets down, because he's co-o-o-ming out with – a natural seven! Fifty-two, wins the glue. A dollar twenty-seven to the new passer, and it'll be more next time. Let it ride, mister. Can't accumulate if you don't speculate.'

The blond man paid off with a dollar and a half-dollar, the

smallest coins in the rack in front of him. Whit picked up his winnings and rattled the dice once more. The dollar twenty-seven remained on the line.

He collected twice more before he lost his bet and the dice, and then he left the crap table with Larson and wandered away. Their wanderings did not take them so far that they couldn't keep an eye on the slim blond dice man whose name was Jackson and whose identification number was 127.

Five minutes later Jackson motioned to a relief man to take his place. He left the crap game and walked in the general direction of the gents' room. Larson, at a word from Whit, parked himself where he could keep a general watch on the casino. Whit followed Jackson. The hair over the sore spot in his scalp bristled slightly as he passed the corner where Jess Caldwell had slugged him, but there was no attempt at a repeat performance. In the gents' room, Jackson was washing his hands. No one else was in sight.

'Hello,' Jackson said. 'The dollar-twenty-seven man. That was a pretty heavy bet you chunked on the table.'

'I'm a gambler,' Whit said. 'Bet 'em big, win 'em big. That's my motto.'

'Good enough if you win. Where does a man get that much to bet?'

'I got mine from Casey Jones.'

Jackson's manner changed. He said, 'O.K. Who are you?'

'My name's Whitney. I've got a message from Casey. We've located the radio transmitter.'

'We?'

'Me.'

Whit told enough to establish that he knew what he was talking about.

Jackson said, 'You aren't from the Bureau.' It wasn't a question.

'No.'

'Army?'

'No.'

'Navy?'

'No. I'm just trying to give you guys a hand.'

'Why?'

'What difference does it make? I haven't got all night to stand here shooting the bull.'

192

'Don't get sniffy,' Jackson said. His nerves didn't seem to be in good shape. 'I'm just trying to find out what it's all about. If you're good enough for Casey you're good enough for me. What does he want me to do?'

'The raid starts at five minutes after three. There are seven men available: Casey, Pete, John, you, me, a friend of mine, and the sheriff. We may pick up another man on the way. It'll take four men at least to make the raid, and Casey wants Pete to catch the radio message at three o'clock. That means Pete will have to be somewhere near an electric light plug, so he's no good for anything else. You and the sheriff will have to cover Caldwell and Lorenzo if they leave the Club. Pete will send the sheriff here, and he'll handle Caldwell. Your man is Lorenzo. At three-five exactly, you take him. The sheriff will haul Caldwell in simultaneously, and we'll knock over Gates and Kohler at the transmitter.'

'There's one hole in it,' Jackson said. 'Lorenzo and Caldwell aren't here.'

'Oh, God! What happened?'

'I just got the word from Gladys. She saw them leave ten minutes ago with Sammy Kohler. We both thought Casey was waiting for them outside, so we didn't do anything about it. And you'd better tell Casey that something funny is going on, because Gladys swears Kohler was nudging Lorenzo along with a gun.'

CHAPTER 22

CASEY, squatted on the floor in John's back room with John and Kitty helping him clean gun-grease from a nasty collection of shooting irons, listened to Whit's hasty report without interrupting his work. He looked like a shabby but competent spider polishing his mandibles in the middle of a web. When Whit finished relaying what he had heard from Jackson, Casey made only one comment.

'Good.'

Whit hadn't expected such a reaction to the bad news. He said, 'How do you figure it's good?'

'It makes things easier for us. We know that if Kohler came after Lorenzo, Gates sent him. Gladys' report makes it even more certain; Kohler wouldn't rough Lorenzo around unless he did it on orders. Gates is calling in his men for the getaway.

Maybe Lorenzo wanted to stay behind. I don't know, but I'm certain that Gates is going to hand out final orders to-night, and he'll want all the help he can gather to move his equipment. We'll get them all in one place, instead of having to pick them up in instalments.'

Larson was admiring one of the weapons, a tommy gun which had been cleaned and put together ready for business. He said, 'We'll get them in a lot of places all at once if we use this on them. How many of these choppers have you got?'

John, another tommy gun in his big paw, said, 'Four. And two riot-guns.' He gestured with the weapon in the direction of a cavity in the wall where a three-foot strip of baseboard had been pulled away. 'Get some more shells out of there and start filling clips, will you?'

'Sure.' Larson began hauling small wooden cases of ammunition from the hole in the baseboard.

The guns were all clean now. John finished assembling them and laid them in a neat row on the bed, where they gleamed dully in the light; four ugly sub-machine guns and two short-barrelled twelve-gauge pump guns. Everyone went to work loading magazine clips. Kitty, a half-dozen empties beside her and a pile of ·45 cartridges in her lap, mechanically pushed shells into the clips as she had been instructed. Just for a moment she looked at Whit sitting across the room in his preposterous cowboy costume, intently occupied with his own pile of cartridges. Her greasy hands began to tremble. She looked away quickly and went on with her work.

John said, 'Casey, how do you want these guns parcelled out?'

'I'll need one. You'll need one. There ought to be one at the bridge and one up on the hill. Have you ever shot one of these things, Whit?'

Whit shook his head. Casey said, 'Larson?'

'I can handle one. But I've got a gun. Better show Whit how to work it.'

John picked up a tommy gun in one hand, took a clip of shells in the other, and held them out for Whit to see.

'This goes here. Like this.' He clamped the magazine in its place under the breech. 'This lever is the safety; this other one turns the gun into a single-shot rifle if you push it this way. You won't have to worry about that, but leave the safety on until you're ready to shoot. Then turn it around like this, pull

194

this lug back to here' – he pantomimed with the cocking lug – 'let it back, and you're ready to fire. You've got twenty shots in a clip, and I'll give you five or six spares. When you pull the trigger, don't hold on to it too long because the clip will empty itself in two seconds. Just touch the trigger and let go. Got it?'

Whit nodded, taking the heavy gun from John. It felt awkward in his hands.

John said, 'Shooting down hill, hold your sights low and watch the line of fire or you're liable to overshoot. That's all you need to know, except to be sure to jam the butt hard against your shoulder if you don't want to bruise yourself.'

Whit nodded again.

Casey said, 'Don't kill anyone if you can help it. Aim about at the kneecap if you have time. But if somebody points a gun in your direction, don't take a chance. Let him have it first, wherever you can hit him. I'd rather he were killed than you. That goes for you too, Larson.'

Kitty made a small inarticulate noise.

Everybody except Whit turned to look at her. He had been afraid to look for some time. He said loudly and quickly, 'I don't expect anyone to get close enough to me for anybody to point guns, one way or the other. Anyway, this damn thing is too impersonal. If I had my way I'd rather smack somebody in the nose.'

Casey said, 'Maybe you would. But don't try to punch noses with Walter Gates. He's bad medicine.'

'I owe him a punch in the nose.' Whit was trying hard to turn the conversation away from shooting. 'And Lorenzo, too. Everybody gets a crack at him but me. John, you threw him out on his ear once. What happened?'

John grinned, remembering the happy day. 'Nothing happened. Gladys was in a booth out in front with Pete one night, passing along a message for Casey, and Lorenzo came in with a couple of girls who wanted hamburgers. Gladys and Pete weren't supposed to know each other then, and they were about ready to come out of the booth. I didn't want to take a chance, so I asked Lorenzo how he liked his sandwich. As soon as he opened his mouth I threw him out.'

Whit laughed, much more loudly than the joke called for. While he tried to think of something else to direct Kitty's thoughts away from the business ahead of them, there were

195

faint footsteps outside. Pete Wilson came in with the sheriff and deputy-sheriff Strong.

The sheriff had been yanked away from a peaceful evening at home, and he was in a bad mood. He picked out Whit as the person present who had given him the most trouble.

'Goldarndest story I ever heard in my life,' he grumbled. ''Scuse me, Mrs Whitney. What's all this moonshine Pete has been telling me?'

'Talk to the head man.' Whit nodded in Casey's direction.

The sheriff scowled at Casey, taking in the frowsy clothes and the stubble of beard. Casey said, 'Whatever Pete has been telling you is on the level. We need your help. We're going to make a raid to-night, and we haven't time to get enough of our men. Pete says you're reliable. That's why you're here.'

'Who's we?'

'The Federal Bureau of Investigation. I don't carry my credentials with me, but I can get them if you want to see them.'

The sheriff grunted. 'I saw Pete's. I'm not questioning them. I just can't make head or tail of what he tells me. Sounds like a wild-west story.'

'It isn't.'

The sheriff looked around the room. 'These all yore men?'

'They're all Federal agents, yes. I'm prepared to deputize you as well. Can you and your man be trusted to keep your mouths shut?'

'I can keep my mouth shut when I got a reason for keeping it shut,' the sheriff answered. 'Strong here will do what I say. He isn't smart, but he can be trusted.'

Deputy-sheriff Strong smiled in a friendly way. The sheriff had said something that sounded like a compliment.

'That's fair enough.' Casey took out his beautiful watch and checked the time. 'We've got to get started. Whit, you and Larson know your job. Mrs Whitney, you'll have to take a message to Gladys at Lorenzo's Club, and Strong will pick up Jackson. The rest of you are coming with me. Before we start, I'll tell you all exactly where we're going and what we're going to do, so there won't be any slips.'

*

Whit and Larson got into the convertible and drove away.

Larson was at the wheel. Whit held in his lap a large news-

196

paper-wrapped package containing the tommy gun and a canvas sling holding five spare clips of cartridges. Counting the magazine already in the gun, there were a hundred and twenty instalments of concentrated trouble he could shoot at Gates and Gates' men if the necessity arose. He hoped it wouldn't arise. He wasn't particularly afraid of what might happen before the evening ended, but the parting with Kitty had been difficult. It made him feel morose.

She hadn't wept. He would have felt better if she had. Always before, when they quarrelled or when he had done something foolish which frightened her or made her mad at him, she had cried quickly and angrily, not from weakness or feminine pettiness but because she blew off steam that way as he did by cursing. To-night had not been the same. She had been like a log of wood when he kissed her good-bye. All he had of her now was the wrist-watch she had given him at the last minute because his own was still at the hotel. It made a small lump in his shirt pocket.

He moved the package on his knees to a more comfortable position.

Larson said, 'You act like that chopper is going to bite you.'

'I expect it to. I don't know why Casey turned it over to me. You're the one who ought to have it.'

'I don't need it.' Larson took one hand from the wheel and touched the bulge below his armpit. 'I feel more at home with my own iron.'

They reached the Verdi crossroads in less than twenty minutes, and came to a stop a few moments later under the oak tree near Hotaling's corral. The house was dark when they drove into the stable-yard, but a horse whinnied from the barn as Larson shut off the engine, and a light came on immediately in the house. Alex opened the door to see what was going on.

He wore nothing but a suit of old-fashioned long underwear. When he saw the two men in the light shining from the doorway, he said, 'Come in, come in, durn it. What are you doing out here this time of night?'

'We can't stop, Alex,' Whit said. 'Anybody around?'

'Jest my stable man. He's out with the hosses. What's the matter?'

'How would you like to go hunting for the men who shot your bay mare?'

197

'How would I like to —' Alex peered at Whit. 'Say that again.'

'The horse is dead. We found it buried near the ghost town ten miles up the river. The man who rented it from you didn't steal it; he was a Federal agent, and the horse was shot after he was murdered. We're going to get the men who killed him, right now. We need your help.'

Alex came out on the porch to see them better. 'You're giving me a straight story?'

'Yes. We haven't much time. I'll tell you all about it on the way, if you're coming.'

'I'll come,' Alex said. 'What do you figger to do – ride in?'

'We've got to get across the river and up on the bluff back of the ghost town before three o'clock.'

'We'll ride, then. It don't give us much time, but we'll make it.' Alex turned to enter the house. 'Go roust out my stable man and tell him to saddle up. It'll take me about a minute to git me a gun and a pair of pants.'

*

Deputy-sheriff Strong wasn't smart, but he was reliable. He strong-armed his way through the crowd until he got within reaching distance of the crap table where Jackson was still exhorting the suckers to leave it lay and watch it pay. Jackson was going to be needed elsewhere before long, and he wasn't due to finish his shift behind the table for several hours.

Strong got him by the arm first and flashed his badge afterwards. 'You're under arrest. Come along quiet.'

The crapshooters calmed down immediately. One or two of the nearest moved away from the two men behind the table.

Jackson had a stack of silver coins in each hand. He carefully put the money back in the rack in front of him before he spoke.

'What's the charge?'

'Draft dodging. Your number is one two seven and it's been called. Come along before I get tough.'

The muscles of Jackson's arms relaxed in Strong's grasp. He said, 'I guess you've got me. Can I finish out this shift?'

'No.'

Jackson turned apologetically to his stick-man. 'Sorry, Joe. Check my bank in and explain it to the boss, will you?'

'Sure thing. Hope you come out of it O.K.'

Jackson shrugged. 'You know how it is with the draft board.'

Strong let the prisoner take off his green apron and get his hat and coat. They left the Club, got into Strong's car, and drove away in a hurry.

*

'This place we're going to is across the border,' the sheriff said. 'I got no jurisdiction in California, if it makes any difference.'

Casey said, 'You can forget about being sheriff for to-night. You're a Federal deputy now, and you've got jurisdiction all the way from here to the Pacific Ocean and three miles out.'

'Makes no never-mind to me, just so long as I'm legal. Wouldn't want to break the law.'

They were all together in Pete's big touring car, driving out the highway in the light of the pale quarter moon which had just risen over the mountains. Casey was with the sheriff in the back seat, Pete drove, and John sat beside him. Casey and the sheriff had less room than the men in front, because of the gunny sack full of weapons and Casey's huge suitcase on the floor at their feet. But the ride would not be long.

The sheriff said, 'So Sammy Kohler killed Pop Foster.'

'Either Kohler or Walter Gates. Probably Kohler.' Casey fished inside his coat and pulled out a heavy automatic. 'This was his. I lifted it from him a couple of nights back. Did you recover the bullets from Foster's body?'

'Yes.'

'Check one from this gun against them. I think you'll find they match up.'

'I guess you were the one who slugged Kohler the other night. I would have swore it was Whitney.'

'He had a hand in it,' Casey said.

'Will I get Kohler for Pop's murder?'

'I'm afraid not. The government wants him first. But you check those bullets and give me a report, and we'll hang a murder charge on him along with everything else. It won't make any difference in what he gets, but it will close your case.'

The sheriff stowed the gun away in his pocket. 'That's better than nothing. But I was kind of hoping to close the case myself. Foster was a friend of mine.'

Casey made no answer.

They drove for several minutes. The car was still some distance from Verdi when Pete turned off the highway, took a rough back road for a mile or two, made another turn, and pulled up. He had been driving with dimmers since turning off the highway, and now he switched off his lights altogether. Except for the faint moon and one or two spots of light from the few houses scattered along the roadside, the darkness was complete.

'Foster's house is a hundred yards up the road,' Pete said.

Casey said, 'Sheriff, you've got the keys to the house. Go let him in, take a look around to see that everything is all right, and come back. Pete, let me check the time with you.'

He lit a match in the shelter of the back seat. They compared watches. As the match went out, John heaved the big suitcase from the back seat to the side of the road. Pete got out of the car.

'You know what to do,' Casey told him. 'We'll pick you up on the way back. If anything happens to me, you're in charge.'

Pete did not move.

Casey said, 'What's the matter?'

'I ought to be in on the clean-up, Casey. I don't see why we can't skip the last recording. They'll pick the message up on the coast.'

Casey shook his head.

'We can't take a chance now. It's too important. I'm sorry it's got to be this way, but you're the only one who knows what to do.'

Pete said evenly, 'You know best. Good luck.' He picked up the heavy suitcase and disappeared in the darkness. The sheriff followed.

Casey and John waited. There was no conversation between them. In a few minutes the sheriff materialized beside the car.

'Everything's set.'

'Let's go, then,' Casey said. 'You know the road, so you drive. We've got forty-three minutes.'

CHAPTER 23

WALTER GATES finished making his last recording before Kohler returned. The record was longer than usual this time. When he played it back at high speed the squeal in his headphones lasted nearly twenty seconds. He did not like to send such long messages. A direction-finder wasn't much good when a message lasted only eight or ten seconds, but twice that time would give a good operator a fairly accurate fix on the transmitter. To-night it couldn't be helped, and it didn't matter much. He was signing off the air for some time.

He had begun to dismantle the recording apparatus when he heard pebbles click in the darkness outside. He switched off the light and went to the curtained window to listen. There was a murmur of voices outside, and he heard Sammy Kohler laugh as Lorenzo cursed violently at the darkness and the poor footing. Gates turned on the light as the footsteps sounded on the steps of the church outside.

Sammy was grinning as he came into the room where Gates waited. Lorenzo, hatless and without a coat to cover the evening clothes in which he had been taken from the Club, followed Sammy, and Caldwell came last. Lorenzo's face, purple and swollen from Larson's beating, was made even darker by rage. His pent-up fury burst out when he saw Gates.

'Look here, Walter. What do you mean by sending your gunman after me?'

Gates said, 'I wanted to be sure you came.'

'What for? Why should I be dragged out to this God-forsaken hole in the middle of the night?'

'I wanted you here.'

The cold blue eyes chilled Lorenzo's anger. He was still popping with frustrated rage, but he knew better than to pop too much in Gates' direction. He said, 'You could have told me why you wanted me, instead of sending this – this —'

He glared speechlessly at Sammy. Sammy grinned.

Gates did not bother to answer Lorenzo's complaint. He said to Caldwell, 'We're pulling out to-night, Jess. I've knocked down everything but the recording set and the transmitter. We'll take the recorder apart now and dismantle the transmitter as soon as I send the message. We'll leave the turbine.'

'Where are we going?'

'Back to the coast. It's getting dangerous here. The waterfront isn't as good a source of information as the ammunition depot, but we can't operate safely in Nevada any more. They're too close on our heels.'

Caldwell nodded. He took off his overcoat and dinner jacket, folded them carefully, laid them on the cot, and rolled up his sleeves.

Gates said, 'Sammy, you go take up your lookout. Jess and I will pack everything we want to take. I'll call you when we're ready to move.'

For a change, Sammy didn't argue. He was still enjoying Lorenzo's sullen anger. He said, 'Right,' and left the room, grinning insolently at Lorenzo as he went out.

There was no more talk in the hidden room for some time after Sammy had left. Gates and Caldwell worked silently at their job of dismantling and packing the recording apparatus. Lorenzo sat on the cot and watched them. At the end of five minutes he said, 'I'm not going with you.'

Caldwell stopped his work. Gates was disconnecting a wire from the recorder, and he went on with the job. When the wire was free, he said, 'What?'

'I'm not going back to the coast.'

Gates put down the screwdriver with which he was working and turned around.

Lorenzo said, 'I'm no good to you if you leave here. The only reason I was ever any help was because of the Club, because people came there and lost their money and Jess could buy whatever information they had to sell. I'm no use without the Club; I can't take it along, and I'm not going to walk out and leave it.'

Gates said nothing. Lorenzo swallowed. He wanted to look away from the pale eyes, but he dared not. If he wavered now he was licked. He went on.

'I've got a big investment in Reno, Walter. You can't expect me just to give it up. Maybe if you'd let me have a little time —'

'Who has a big investment?'

'I'll pay you back. Every cent. I can pay you back right now, if you'll give me a few hours to raise the money. To-morrow morning. To-night.'

'You're coming with us to-night.'

'But, Walter —'

'That's all.'

'You can trust me.' Lorenzo was pleading now. 'My God, you don't think I'd talk, do you? I couldn't say anything without getting into trouble myself. And I wouldn't talk anyway,

202

whatever happened. You know I wouldn't.'

'No.'

'Walter, listen to reason. I —'

Gates said, 'Start nailing up those packing cases. We're all leaving here in fifteen minutes.'

Lorenzo could not meet the cold eyes any longer. He moved to carry out his orders.

*

Alex Hotaling brought Whit and Swede Larson to the tunnel mouth in the hillside with twenty-five minutes left to get up on top of the bluff.

It had been a tricky ride in the dark, with only the thin moon for light. Alex had used a flashlight continually as the horses picked their way along the railroad track, but the flash was not enough. The horses had been forced to travel faster than was safe and they stumbled frequently. Once Larson's horse – not the sure-footed buckskin this time – went down, and Larson ploughed up the gravel ballast of the railroad track with his hands and knees. But the horse was not injured, and a little unrestrained blasphemy salved Larson's wounds as he remounted. They were all grateful when at last they reined up at the tunnel mouth which marked the end of the worst part of their ride. Whit himself was grateful enough for three men. The tommy gun slung across his back was beginning to feel like an anvil with spurs.

'Here we are,' said Hotaling. 'Now what?'

Whit said, 'Could anyone get through here from the other side?'

'Could, I guess. She's caved in a little here and there, but she wasn't blocked off last I knew. I couldn't say for sure.'

'Then your job is to camp right here and wait. If anyone comes out of that tunnel, you've got to stop him. Don't kill anybody if you can help it, but don't take any chances.'

Alex grunted. He pulled his rifle out of the long holster under his saddle leather and swung to the ground.

'Where do these hoss-killers hang out?'

'In the old church on the other side. They probably won't make for the tunnel, but it's a bare chance we've got to cover.'

'What's to keep me from going through and laying for them at the other end? I'll be mighty handy when the shooting

203

starts.' Alex slapped the rifle butt with the flat of his hand.

'Nothing, if you want to try it.'

'I'll try it.'

That was all. Alex tied his horse to the nearest bit of scrub, switched on his flashlight, and entered the tunnel. Whit and Larson watched the beam of light as it bobbed away into the blackness.

Larson said respectfully. 'He sure must of loved that mare.'

'I guess he did.' Whit shifted the tommy gun to a new position. 'Let's go.'

They guided their horses off into the brush and began to climb.

*

The turn-off from the highway to the river was only a faint track marked by a dim and weatherbeaten sign, but the sheriff knew the country well. He let Pete's car loiter for the last few hundred yards of highway, until approaching headlights had passed and were out of sight. Then he made the turn, pulled ahead in second until the car was safely away from the main road, and cut his lights. They waited in the darkness.

Several cars went by on the highway, most of them going towards town at a patriotic thirty-five miles per. Eventually a pair of fast-moving headlights came into view far down the road towards Reno.

The sheriff grunted. 'That's Strong. Hope the durn fool don't use his siren before he gets here.'

The siren was quiet. Strong's car slowed, made the turn, and bumped over the rough road towards the watchers in the first car. The sheriff switched his lights on and off quickly, and the lights of the second car went out. The car stopped. Two dark figures left it and approached the car in front. The leading figure said cautiously, 'Casey?'

'This way.'

Casey opened the door of the touring car and stepped into the road as Jackson and Strong came up.

Jackson said, 'Who's here?'

'John and I and the sheriff. This is Harry Jackson, sheriff.'

Harry Jackson and the sheriff said hello. Jackson said to Casey, 'You'd better bring me up to date. All I've heard is what my pal here told me on the way out and what I learned from Whitney. Is this the clean-up?'

'This is it. There isn't time for me to go over everything with you, but I'll give you the highlights. John, break out those guns.'

John groped for the gunny sack in the back seat. There were muffled metallic sounds from the car while Casey's low voice spoke in the dark.

'We have two men across the river, possibly three, and five on this side. Strong, you know what to do. I don't think shooting can be heard by anyone driving by on the highway, but if it is and someone comes down this road to investigate, stop him. Use your badge. If there's trouble, fire a couple of shots to warn us. Give him one of the riot-guns and some shells, John.'

Strong said, 'Yes, sir.' He took the sawed-off shotgun that John handed him and tucked it under his arm.

'You know your job, sheriff,' Casey said. 'Remember that the timing is what counts. It's absolutely essential that you throw the spotlight on the church belfry immediately the shooting starts, so that Larson can get a clear shot at the aerial. I don't think we'll have to worry about messages going out after three o'clock, but we've got to play safe and put the transmitter out of commission. You're the key-man for that.'

'Don't worry about me.' The sheriff's voice was solid with assurance. 'Better let me have one of yore scatter-guns so I can keep an eye on the bridge, too. It'll be better than a revolver in the dark.'

John handed out the second riot-gun. The sheriff put it under his arm as Strong had done.

Casey held his watch out and tilted it to the moon, but the light was too dim. He lit a match in the shelter of his coat and checked the time.

'We'll start in two minutes. Now, Harry. There's an abandoned mining town on the other side of the river, a mile or so down this road. Gates, Kohler, Jess Caldwell and Lorenzo will be there. There's a footbridge across the river – check me on this, sheriff – about twenty-five or thirty yards long, then some steps down to the flat. Fifty yards downstream, to the left, there's a stamping-mill, and fifty yards back from the mill, directly away from the river, is a church. The transmitter is in the church. Gates and the others should be there too.'

'Maybe a little over fifty yards from the mill to the church,' the sheriff said. 'Not much.'

'If it's fairly close we won't go wrong. Harry, you and John and I are going across the bridge. You'll take a tommy gun, go to the right – upstream – get around behind the church, and wait. If there's any shooting, open up. If anyone tries to break away upstream or back through the hills, he's yours. Don't kill anyone if you can help it. John will be downstream, we've got a couple of men on the bluff back of town, and the sheriff will be at the bridge. That's all. Any questions?'

'Where are you going to be?' asked Jackson.

'I'm going into the church.'

'You're a damn fool. You'd better take me and John with you.'

Casey did not answer. He had lit another match in the shelter of his coat and was looking at his watch for the last time. The match went out. He said firmly, 'Now.'

The sheriff tramped on the starter. Casey and Harry Jackson swung up on the running board as the touring car started. Deputy-sheriff Strong, the riot-gun under his arm, stood in the middle of the rutted road and watched the lightless bulk of the car lumber away in the darkness. When the noise of its motor died away, there was no sound but the far-away rushing murmur of the river.

*

Inside John's restaurant it was quite dark. The lights were off and the blinds down over the big plate-glass windows. Some illumination came from the street through the small ventilating windows high up on the side wall, but it was not enough to read by. Gladys used a tiny purse-flashlight to examine Whit's map as she relayed Casey's message by telephone to headquarters.

Kitty had brought the map to Gladys with Casey's instructions. She was grateful that Casey had given her something to do. It had kept her busy for a while; getting the map, finding Gladys at Lorenzo's Club, bringing her back to the restaurant where the telephone was safe to use. Kitty's head had been so full of the details Casey had given her to pass along that she had been unable to think of other things. But now her job was done and she had time to think. Too much time.

Gladys said into the phone, 'Twenty miles west of Reno on the river. It's about a mile from the highway. . . . Yes . . . . Yes. . . . He didn't have time; everything happened too fast. He wants men sent to Tahoe and Carson City right away so that they can close the roads if anyone gets away, and he

wants the man at the ammunition depot arrested immediately.
. . . Yes. . . . . What time is it now? . . . Then it will start in
thirty-five minutes. . . . That's all I have for you now. Do you
want — . . . I'll call you as soon as I get word. Anything else?
. . . I will. Good-bye.'

She hung up and the tiny beam of her flashlight winked out.
She said, 'Now we wait. Let's go in back where we can have a
light.'

'No.' Kitty's voice had an edge to it. 'I'm going, Gladys. I
can't stand it. I've got to be there.'

'You couldn't do anything, Kitty. How would you get there?
There's only half an hour left and we have no car.'

'I don't care. I'll walk; I'll run; I'll do anything. I've got to go.'

Kitty was at the door before Gladys caught her. She
struggled blindly to break free. Gladys said sharply, 'Stop it.
I'm not trying to hold you back. If you're going I'll have to
go with you, but we can't walk. We'll see if we can get a car
at the garage.'

They were lucky. The garage had a car for rent. It was an
old coupé, but it was in good condition and it moved along.
As soon as they were out of town and on the straightaway,
Kitty pushed the accelerator to the floorboards and held it
there. There was room for only one thought in her mind now;
twenty miles, thirty minutes; twenty miles, thirty minutes. She
held tightly to the wheel and watched the white line of the
highway streaming down the path of her headlights.

Neither girl had anything to say during the wild ride. They
roared through Verdi, the half-way mark, when the minute
hand of the clock on the coupé's dashboard stood between two
forty-five and ten minutes of three, but then the highway began to climb and the curves of the road were sharper. Kitty
had to slow the car to stay on the road, and although she
rode the accelerator hard whenever a clear stretch opened before her, they did not make such good time.

After they passed Verdi Kitty began to watch her mileage.
She was going by her memory of Whit's map, and she knew
only that the turn-off was about ten miles out and that it
would not be well marked. As it was, she missed the weather-
beaten signpost that marked the side road. But Gladys saw it
and shouted over the roar of the motor, and Kitty braked the
coupé in a scream of skidding tyres, slammed into reverse, and

went backward at full speed. At the signpost she punished the tyres once more as she shifted into low and yanked the car around into the side road. They bumped forward fifty yards and found their way blocked by another car.

Kitty was not to be stopped now. She jumped from the coupé and ran forward. As she came into the beam of the headlights the distinct click of a cocked gun-hammer sounded from the brush. A voice said, 'Stand still, lady.'

Kitty stopped. Her heart pounded furiously.

There was no further sound for a moment. Then the click came again as the hammer was lowered, and the plump figure of deputy-sheriff Strong stepped out of the brush.

'Sorry, Mrs Whitney. Didn't recognize you at first. You'd better shut those lights off.'

Kitty motioned to Gladys in the car. The lights and the sound of the idling motor died together. Gladys left the coupé and came towards them, holding up her long skirt and picking her way carefully because of her high heels.

'Who's that?' Strong brought the gun muzzle around to bear on the approaching shadow.

'Gladys – Gladys —' Kitty could not remember if Gladys had another name. 'She's Mr Jones's assistant. Where is my husband?'

'Why, he's across the river, I guess. Don't exactly know myself.'

'I've got to see him.'

'Afraid you can't right now. The fireworks are about ready to start. Mr Jones and the others just went down the road a few minutes back.'

Kitty said desperately, 'Then I'm going —'

She stopped as Strong held up his hand.

The first shots in the distance were muffled. They sounded like a short burst from a machine gun. There was silence for a moment, then three or four louder reports answered, fired quickly but not with the rapidity of the first shots. They were drowned immediately by the heavier rapid chatter of a second machine gun, this time nearer and sharper than the first. After that there was sporadic general firing, faint but clear on the still air.

Without a word Kitty turned and ran in the direction of the river.

Strong yelled, 'Hey, come back here!' and took two or three

208

irresolute steps before he remembered his orders. While he hesitated, unable to make up his mind, Gladys dodged past him and ran after Kitty. She had gone only a few yards when one spike heel turned beneath her. She stopped long enough to take off her shoes and ran on, calling Kitty's name. The sound of gunfire swelled in the distance.

CHAPTER 24

THE first shots were fired by Walter Gates.

Lorenzo, silently obedient, had nailed up all the filled packing cases during the time it took Gates and Caldwell to complete the dismantling of the recording apparatus. They finished their job at a few minutes before three o'clock. Jess, idle for a moment, shot a quick look at Lorenzo, but Lorenzo was staring at Gates' broad back as Gates, one eye on his watch, prepared to send the last message. The power tubes underneath the rough table glowed as Gates cut in the current and let the transmitter warm up. He put his watch down on the table and used both hands to set his recording on the high-speed turntable of the transmitter. The second hand of the watch ticked around. At five seconds before the hour he turned the power full on and placed the needle of the pick-up arm on the revolving record.

No one in the room moved or spoke during the time it took the record to run out. When the needle reached the inner groove, Gates cut off the power and stopped the turntable.

'Let's not waste time, Jess, you pull the tubes out of the transmitter and take care of them yourself. Lorenzo, you pack the other parts as I hand them to you, and be careful to wrap everything well. I don't want any breakage.'

Lorenzo did not move. He said, 'Pack them yourself. I'm leaving.'

'I told you that you were coming with us.'

'I'm going back to Reno.' Lorenzo's face was muddy beneath the bruises, but this time he looked Gates squarely in the eye and stood his ground. 'I'm through. I don't care where you go or what you do, but I'm not going with you, now or any other time.'

He turned on his heel and walked towards the door.

He was out of the room before Gates got to the corner where the sub-machine gun was hidden, but he did not try to run and Gates had plenty of time. As Lorenzo reached the threshold of the outer entrance, Gates stepped through the doorway of the inner room, stood to one side so he would not block his own light, and lifted the gun. It roared and bucked against his shoulder. Lorenzo, knocked off balance by the impact of the heavy slugs, fell forward through the door and died with his battered face resting on the weather-beaten planks of the church steps.

It was then two minutes after three o'clock. The sheriff, watching from the rest of the slope across the river, heard the shots and saw the light coming from the church. It was his cue. The motor of Pete's car was warm and started immediately. The sheriff switched on headlights and spotlight and drove over the brow of the hill, careening wildly down the slope with one hand on the wheel and the other busy with the spotlight.

The slope of the hill was just right for the beam of the headlights. They carried across the river and lit the buildings in the flat like a ray from nigger-heaven. But the swivel of the spotlight was stiff, and when the sheriff wrenched at it the powerful pencil of light carried clear across the town and picked out a circle of brush on the hillside two hundred yards beyond the church. The swivel had to be oiled with some old-time western profanity before the sheriff could jockey the beam back to the church belfry where it belonged.

Sammy Kohler was keeping a bored lookout on the flat roof of the railroad station when things began to happen. He had heard the roar of the shots in the church and was peering nervously in that direction as the lights came on across the river. When he whirled around to see what was creeping up on him and stared directly into the glare, the wavering beam of the spotlight looked to him like the punishing finger of God searching for Sammy Kohler. He followed his instinct and blazed away.

Sammy's judgement of distance was poor because he was hurried. The bullets from the station roof did not come close to the car on the far river-bank, but they did give Sammy's position away and that was bad for Sammy. John Masilikos had already crept across the footbridge with Casey and Jack-

210

son and was moving down the river-bank to take up his assigned position. He was not more than thirty yards from the railroad station when Sammy started shooting. He emptied half a clip of shells from the tommy gun, and Sammy's body slid off the roof and fell into the darkness.

By that time Gates and Jess Caldwell had just put out the light in the church and were shooting at gun flashes through cracks in the boarded windows of the inner room. The mill building blocked the line of fire from their position at street level so they could not aim at the source of the lights across the river, but they were able to return the shots coming from Jackson upstream and from John near the railroad station. Casey, who had worked his way to within a few feet of the church when Lorenzo's body tumbled down the steps, held his fire and dropped back to the point from which John was giving the church occasional short bursts from the tommy gun to keep its occupants busy. Casey whispered a few instructions, slapped John's beefy shoulder, and skirted around the railroad station and the mill on his way upstream to see why Jackson had suddenly stopped shooting.

Up on the bluff, Whit and Larson were still panting from their last-minute dash to get into position as the battle started in the flat below. They threw themselves down on the hillcrest while the car across the river wobbled down the slope with its headlights glaring into the ghost town.

'We just did make it,' Whit said, puffing hard.

'This is what I call a reserved seat,' Larson said. He lay on his belly at the edge of the bluff, gun in hand, waiting for the beam from the spotlight to pick out his target. 'Hurry up with that spot, sheriff. Time's a-wastin'.'

'Somebody doesn't like the lights,' Whit said. Sammy had just fired his three or four shots at the automobile across the river.

'Yeh. I wonder who is – wow! Somebody doesn't like whoever it is that doesn't like the lights!'

A colourful stream of fire had spewed up from the river-bank towards the man on the roof of the railroad station. The shooting from the roof stopped immediately.

Larson said, 'That guy down there has one of those choppers you're lugging around. See what they'll do if you treat them right?'

211

'Uh huh.' Whit rubbed his sweaty hands together and took a new grip on the tommy gun.

The beam of the spotlight flickered jerkily down the hillside and came to rest on the church belfry. Firing continued from the church and from the river-bank. Whit said, 'There it is, Swede. I hope you're as good as you think you are. It's a long shot.'

'I won't know how good I am until I start working on it,' Larson answered. 'I can barely see the damn thing. Make me a bet and I'll do better.'

'You're going to use that?' Whit gestured at Larson's automatic.

'Sure.'

'Take this thing. You ought to be able to do better with a longer barrel.'

'I know my own sights better. It won't be any tougher than shooting at cigarettes. Make me a bet.'

'Four to one. Twenty bucks to five on the first shot.'

'Give me three shots and I'll take the twenty at even money.'

'Start shooting,' Whit said. 'You've got a bet.'

Larson rested the automatic on his bent forearm and squinted through the sights at the faint shine of the insulator in the belfry two hundred and fifty yards away. The muzzle kicked sharply upwards as the gun roared.

Whit said, 'Missed. It's an impossible shot, Swede.'

'I've still got two left. Looks like I woke one of the ghosts, anyway.'

A grey shape soared out of the belfry, flapped its wings in two or three slow movements, and disappeared in the dark. Whit said, 'That's Gates, taking off in his private plane.'

Larson grinned, squinting through the sights again. He took a deep breath and exhaled slowly. When his lungs were empty, he squeezed the trigger.

Even from that distance they could hear the sharp crack of the porcelain insulator through the roar of the gun. The faint reflection of light in the belfry winked out. Whit reached for his wallet and silently handed Larson a bill.

'Thanks.' Larson folded the money and tucked it away. 'That's that. I wonder what happens next.'

'Casey said to wait and see.'

They waited. The lights shone steadily from the automobile

on the bank across the river, and intermittent short bursts came from the tommy gun at the riverside near the railroad station. No answering fire came from the church.

*

Walter Gates did not know that his aerial had been shot down, although the knowledge would not have bothered him much. The radio was of no further value; he had signed off the air at three o'clock, and no one would be listening for any further message now even if he were able to send them. But his plans would have changed if he had realized that two of the shots aimed at the church came from the hill back of town.

He crouched behind the heavy planks of the boarded-up window and peered through a crack, watching the periodic winking flicker from the muzzle of the tommy gun near the riverside. The heavy bullets were coming through the clapboards of the church as if the walls had been paper. Neither he nor Caldwell had been hit so far, but only their hurriedly constructed bulwark of packing cases kept them alive. Caldwell, at the window in the side wall with only a small-calibre automatic, was neither as well-armed nor as well-protected as Gates against John's cross-fire. Caldwell's shoulders hunched instinctively every time the tommy gun chattered outside.

After one long burst from the river-bank had sent splinters flying around the small room, Gates said, 'We can't stay here.'

Caldwell kept his eye on the spot upstream from which Jackson had fired last. 'How are we going to get away?'

'I don't know that we are, but we've got to try it. Are you ready?'

Caldwell did not answer.

'They'll hang you if they take you alive.'

Caldwell cleared his throat as if he were about to speak, but he said nothing.

'I'm going to try to get over the hill and into the brush,' Gates said. 'The mill casts a shadow that will cover me until I reach the slope, and after that I'll have to take my chances. You can stay here or come along, whichever you like.'

The tommy gun hammered again briefly from the river-bank. Gates put the nose of his own weapon through a crack and pressed the trigger. The noise was terrific in the closed room; empty cartridge cases spun in a steady stream from the gun's breech. When the magazine was empty, Gates dropped behind the packing cases to reload as John's answering fire slammed in through the side of the building. Caldwell shuddered as he felt his own bulwark of packing cases jerk from the impact of the bullets. Gates stuffed a double handful of cartridges into each pocket, waited until the slugs stopped thudding through the wall, and ran for the doorway, crouching low. Caldwell followed him.

*

Kitty ran until her breath gave out, then walked, then ran again. Twice she missed her footing in the dark and fell, but except for a bruised knee she did not hurt herself. Several times she heard Gladys calling behind her, but she paid no attention. Gladys, handicapped by her lack of shoes, fell behind, and Kitty hurried on, driven by her need to reach Whit. If she could find him she did not care what happened afterwards.

The noise of the fight grew louder as she approached the river. She was badly winded when she reached the crest of the last slope and saw the scene below, flooded by the lights from the automobile on the river-bank. She stumbled down the hill, sobbing for air. Her shoes scuffed the rocks of the road, and the sheriff, waiting near the bridgehead with his scatter-gun ready for action, very nearly shot first and asked questions afterwards. But he held his fire long enough to see who it was. He stopped Kitty at the bridge.

'Hold on there, mam. Where do you think you're going?'

'Where's – Whit?' Kitty gasped. 'Is he – all – right?'

' 'Course he's all right.'

'Where?'

The sheriff pointed.

'Up on the hill there, safer than a babe in arms. No call for you to go getting yourself excited. Why aren't you back in Reno where you belong?'

'I – was – scared.' Kitty leaned against the sheriff for support, panting. He patted her shoulder.

'Nothing to be scared about. You just set down on the ground over there behind that shack where you won't stop a stray bullet, and we'll smoke these rats out in no time. Now —'

He swung around and lifted the riot-gun as pebbles clicked at the top of the slope. 'Who's this coming?'

'Gladys,' Kitty said. 'She came with me.'

'Who's Gladys?'

An unusual burst of fire from across the river interrupted before Kitty could answer. They both turned to look.

John Masilikos, suspicious at the lack of response from the church and ready for trickery, had been the first to see the two dark figures escaping in the shadow cast by the mill building. It had been Jackson's job to get to a spot where he could close in on the church from the rear if necessary, but Jackson's luck did not carry him beyond his first position. Casey had found him bleeding badly and half-conscious from the shock of a bullet which had ripped his arm from wrist to elbow as he fired at Caldwell's window from the corner of a building in the flat. Casey was busy with a tourniquet when Gates and Caldwell made their break. He awoke to the danger when he heard John's tommy gun hammering in repeated bursts from the railroad station, and looked up to see the stream of fire directed at a spot a good hundred yards back of the church. Casey hurriedly fastened the tourniquet, picked up his own weapon, and ran to head off the fugitives.

The sheriff had also seen what was happening. He cursed the additional responsibility Kitty's presence brought him. As Gladys came limping down the road to the bridge, he thrust Kitty at her.

'Here, miss. You two get behind that shack and stay there. Hurry.'

'What's happening?' Kitty clung to his coat. 'What is it? Is Whit all right?'

'He's fine, dammit. Let go.'

The sheriff pulled away and ran for the automobile on the river-bank. The two girls watched from the bridgehead as the sheriff reached the car and swung the beam of the spotlight to the hill-slope back of the buildings across the river.

Crouching on the crest of the bluff, Whit and Larson waited tensely as the fight came their way. Whit clutched the tommy gun in his sweaty hands and pulled like a hunting dog on a leash against Larson's restraining arm. Larson whispered over and over again, 'Take it easy. Take it easy. Wait until they come up over the hump. They'll get here. Take it easy,' and Whit answered mechanically, 'O.K. O.K. O.K. O.K.' His entire body was tight with strain.

Both John and Casey were shooting up the hill now. The twin streaks of flame from the flat played back and forth across the slope beneath the shoulder of the bluff where Larson and Whit waited, but the shots were at random and no answering fire came from the brush to give away the position of the fugitives. They were above the range of the headlights. If they could work their way up the hill in the shadow for another few minutes without being seen, only Whit and Larson stood between them and escape.

The sheriff's alertness with the spotlight precipitated the final action. John and Casey had both run out of loaded cartridge clips and were hastily reloading with loose cartridges when the bright beam swept up the hill and picked out the two men in the brush. They were near the top, but not near enough to run for it, and if the spotlight held them for the few moments it would take the men below to load up in the dark, they were finished. Gates dropped to one knee, lifted his sub-machine gun, and sent a stream of bullets down the path of light.

The slugs of the first burst got one of the headlights, pierced the radiator, and ricocheted off a fender in a scream of jagged lead. The sheriff winced at the vicious whine of the ricochet, but he stuck to his post at the spotlight, ready to follow the targets up the hill when Casey and John began shooting. They were dangerously slow in reloading. Gates' second burst, higher this time, thudded through the engine hood and sewed a spangle of stars in the windshield, still without finding the spotlight. The air filled with the strong odour of gasoline pouring from a broken feed line. The sheriff dropped his ineffectual short-range riot-gun and yanked a long-barrelled revolver from his belt, but Gates' next shots caught him in the arm and shoulder before he could pull the trigger. He fell against the running board as a spark flickered in the wreckage of the battered engine and blossomed immediately into a roaring flame of burning gasoline. The spotlight continued to send its steady beam of light across the river.

The automobile was blazing by the time Kitty and Gladys reached it. The fabric car top had ignited immediately, and flames shot high into the air, lighting the whole river-bank. The two girls were dragging at the sheriff's heavy body when Gates, still trying for the light, emptied the last shells in his gun at the burning wreck. Kitty gasped, staggered a few steps, and collapsed. Gladys, her skin blistering and her eyebrows and eyelashes already gone, tugged and hauled until the sheriff was clear of the flames. She was beating at his burning clothes with her hands when one of the tommy guns in the flat across the river began to hammer at last.

Whit saw the whole thing from the hill-top. When the two girls appeared in the circle of light cast by the burning car, he had sprung to his feet and bellowed inarticulately, half in warning, half from the shock of seeing them there. He was running along the crest of the hill, still shouting at them to get back, when the final stream of fire sprang across the river from Gates' gun and Kitty went down. Larson caught up with Whit then but could not hold him. Whit brushed him to one side and plunged over the shoulder of the hill that hid him from the men below. The unfamiliar weapon in his hands weighed him down. He threw it away as he ran. Larson cursed him and followed at his heels.

The first answering shots from the flat had finished Gates. He was sitting on the ground with half a dozen bullets in his chest when Whit came plunging down the hill. Gates struggled to raise his empty gun to meet the attack, but Larson was taking no chances. He shot Gates between the eyes, and Whit found the body dead in his hands when he took it by the throat. Caldwell, with blood seeping through his white shirt and one arm dangling at his side, had plenty of time to aim as Whit leaped towards him. The men in the flat below could not fire safely at such long range, and Larson was blocked from a clear view of Caldwell by Whit's charging body. He tried a risky snap-shot over Whit's shoulder and missed. Caldwell's first bullet hit Whit in the belly. Whit stumbled, recovered his balance, and kept coming. Caldwell took aim again.

Alex Hotaling had been a long time making his way through the tunnel beneath the bluff. The passage was much worse than he had expected, and at the end he was blocked by fallen timbers which barred his way without shutting off the sounds of the fight outside. He broke through at last, wet and muddy, in time to see the last act played out in the circle of light on the hillside above. Until Whit came charging down the hill to spring at Gates, Alex did not know which of the actors was friend and which enemy, and he was not quick enough to beat Caldwell's first shot. But he had the rifle-butt cuddled against his cheek and Caldwell's shirt-front clear in his sights when Caldwell aimed the second time. Alex muttered, 'Hoss-killer!' and squeezed the trigger.

Up on the hillside, Whit stared stupidly as Caldwell's body fell at his feet. It was difficult for him to think. He heard Larson say something from a long way off, and then his knees buckled and he toppled loosely forward on his face as the spotlight in the burning automobile failed at last. Everything went black on the hillside.

CHAPTER 25

THE nightmare went on for hundreds of years, while Whit struggled and sweated with his terror. He could not conquer it because he did not know what it was he was fighting. He knew only that somewhere Kitty needed him, and that he was being dragged farther and farther away from her. But he fought on interminably, and at the end he battled his way up to the brink of consciousness and opened his eyes.

Kitty was there, watching him. At least her face was there, although it was blurred around the edges. It hung over him like a toy balloon, dirty, tearstained and haggard, but it was real. Whit tried to lift his hand to touch it and found that he had neither arms nor a body. He was just a head himself, attached to nothing. He moved his lips with an effort.

'— 'll right?'

'Yes. I'm all right. Go to sleep, honey.'

'— scared. Don' g' way.'

'I'll be right here. Please go to sleep.'

He felt a vague pressure where his hand might be if he had a hand. His fear was gone now, and his disembodied head felt light and comfortable. He smiled at Kitty's blurred face and went to sleep.

A long time later he opened his eyes and looked around. By moving his head – not too much, because it took a lot of energy – he could see that he was in bed in a room with pale green walls and ceiling. A bright patch of sunlight came in beneath the lowered blind of the window at his bedside, and there was a vase of flowers on a white-topped table across the room. It was very nice and peaceful.

He rested for a while, letting memory come back to him.

218

There had been a hell of a fight. Kitty was hit —

His belly muscles screamed as he tried to sit up, so that his ears rang with pain. He lay quite still, feeling the sweat pop on his forehead. His body was back with him, all right. He could feel every inch of it, weighing him down like an anchor, and there was a pressure on his chest that held him to the bed. He waited until the pain went away before he carefully lifted his head to look around.

Kitty slept soundly in a chair at the bedside. She had leaned forward so that her dark head rested on his knee, and she held his hand in both of her own. He closed his fingers and squeezed gently.

'Hey.'

Kitty stirred, turning her head towards him in her sleep.

'Hey.'

She opened her eyes.

'You look terrible,' he said. She had washed her face and put on fresh make-up, but her eyebrows and the hair over her forehead were singed away and dark circles shadowed her eyes.

Kitty smiled and moved her head so she could put his hand to her cheek.

'So do you. How do you feel?'

'Pretty good. I had a bad time for a while. I thought you were shot.'

Kitty said nothing.

Whit's memory was pretty good now. He said, 'You *were* shot.'

'Yes.'

'Where?'

'In the leg.'

Whit twisted his head to look over the edge of the bed. Her legs, as far as he could see, were as perfect as ever. He frowned at her.

'I want to see.'

She stood up, hiked her skirt, and let him see the prettiest pair of gams west of the Mississippi. One smooth thigh was marred with a patch of gauze and adhesive tape. He whistled in the best drugstore-cowboy manner, but his whistle lacked the old fire.

'It wasn't much, really,' Kitty said. 'I'd never been shot before and I thought I was killed. Gladys had to pull the sheriff

219

out of the fire by herself. I don't know how she managed it. She burned herself badly.'

'Serious?'

'No. Blisters on her face and arms, mostly, and some hair gone. Worse than mine.' Kitty touched the short hair at her forehead. 'The sheriff has a broken arm, but Gladys kept him from burning to death.'

'Anyone else hurt? How's the Swede?'

'He wasn't hit. Mr Jackson, the dice man, was shot in the arm. Casey and John are all right.'

'What about Walter Gates and the others?'

'They're all dead.'

The conversation was making her unhappy. Whit pressed her fingers.

'Forget about them. How am I doing?'

'I'm not supposed to talk about you.' Kitty took one hand away from him and pushed the call-button pinned to the coverlet. 'The doctor says you have to lie still and keep quiet and not worry.'

'I'll worry if I feel like it. How long have I been here?'

'This is the third day.'

Whit was startled. 'I must be in a bad way.'

'Not now. The doctor says the danger is over. But you bled so much before we could get you here —' Kitty swallowed and shook her head. 'I thought you were going to die. You needed blood and I wanted to give you mine but they wouldn't take it. I yelled and made a pest of myself until they had to give me dope to put me to sleep.' She pressed his hand. 'It didn't make any difference. Everyone wanted to give you blood.'

'Who won?'

'Casey. He said it was his fault for letting you get shot, and he was going to pull you through if anyone did. He had the right blood-type.'

' "Pull me through" is a good way to put it. I feel like I've been through a meat chopper. Or a Caesarian operation.'

Whit put his free hand on the coverlet and felt the thick pad of bandage beneath the blanket. His hand went to his chest where the pressure was, and he found that a wide band of heavy cloth had been tied across his body to hold him down. He was experimenting with his legs and feet when the doctor came into the room.

The doctor wore a white coat with a stethoscope bulging one pocket, and he was like all other doctors Whit had known – full of sweetness and light and cheerfulness and no information. He had been told to keep his mouth shut about the sudden flood of battle-casualties in the hospital, and he was obeying his orders literally. All Whit could get out of him was that everything was hotsy-totsy.

'What happened to me?' Whit asked.

'You were shot.'

'I know I was shot. What did the bullet do to me?'

'It made a hole in your abdomen.'

'A big hole?'

'Not too big.'

'How long am I going to be laid up?'

'Some time. Not too long.'

Whit didn't have the strength to keep trying. He said, 'I give up. Can we talk about something else?'

'What do you want to talk about?'

Whit stopped to think. It wouldn't do to discuss the raid with a strange doctor even if he knew anything about it, which wasn't probable. Kitty wouldn't have much information either, and didn't want to talk about it, anyway.

Whit said, 'Is there anyone I know around here?'

'You've got quite a collection of visitors and fellow patients waiting outside. You can see them for fifteen minutes if you lie still and don't get excited.'

'If I lie still,' Whit said. 'Doctor, I haven't got the strength to kick my way out of a paper bag. Herd them in.'

It was old home week in Whit's room when the visitors arrived. Larson was there, beaming all over his battered prize-fighter's face and staying close to Gladys. It was the first time Whit had seen Gladys in anything but an evening gown. She seemed very small and young in a blouse and short skirt. Both of her arms were bandaged to the elbow with stained dressings, her face was covered with patches of dirty dark salve, and the blonde hair was very short on the front of the head. But she smiled at Whit through the dirty mask as she came into the room, and Larson watched her as if she were a queen in ermine. He seemed to have forgotten his worry because she was a G-girl and he was only an ordinary cop.

Jackson was the other walking casualty, with one arm in a

221

sling. Pete Weston came last, showing none of the marks of battle. They all stood around the bed and looked at Whit. The doctor said 'Fifteen minutes' and left the room.

Whit said, 'I hear you're a heroine, Gladys.'

'Oh, I am not.' Gladys' dumb-blonde training still showed in the way she spoke.

'I'll bet the sheriff thinks you are. How is he?'

'He's fine. He's in the next room. He says he'll come to see you as soon as they let him get out of bed.'

'How are Casey and John? And Alex and deputy-sheriff Strong? What about Gates' last message?'

Pete answered all of Whit's questions.

'Casey and John are out salvaging the radio equipment right now. Casey – I mean Gates – goes back on the air in two weeks from San Francisco, and this time his information will be coming right from the feed-bin. Strong is having the time of his life acting as sheriff, and Hotaling is back with his hosses. Did you know he saved your life, Whit?'

'I knew somebody did. I thought it was you, Swede.'

'I shot Gates,' Larson said. 'Caldwell plugged you once before I could do anything, and then Alex got him with his deer-gun from the tunnel. It was a good shot. Caldwell would have killed you sure if he'd of had time to pull the trigger.'

'Kitty says you got them all,' Whit said. 'So I guess I didn't mess things up too much by running down the hill like a damn fool. But I'd sure like to know what my wife and Gladys were doing across the river. Whose idea was that?'

'Mine,' Kitty said. 'It was all my fault. I couldn't stand waiting. Gladys tried to stop me, but when I said I was coming anyway she came along. I'm to blame if anyone is.'

'I don't know that anyone is to blame for anything,' Pete said. 'It's lucky for the sheriff you two were there. No one got away, and no one was around to hear the shooting. I'd say it was a successful raid.'

'How does Casey feel about it?'

'Well, he's got the transmitter. That's what he was after. He thinks you were a chump to jump Gates and Caldwell bare-handed, but he says any man with enough guts to do it is good enough for him.'

'I went off my head when I saw Kitty go down,' Whit said. 'It didn't take guts.'

'That's what you think.' Larson grinned as he held his hands up, two feet apart. 'They cut a piece of sausage-covering out of you that was long enough to —'

'Swede!'

Kitty glared at him. He shut up immediately.

Whit put his head back on the pillow and closed his eyes. After a while he said faintly, 'I thought I felt a little empty. What happened to you, Jackson?'

'I stopped a lucky shot,' Jackson said. 'It's sore, but it isn't bad. It'll be all right.'

'You won't be banking any crap games for a while.'

Jackson laughed. 'I've been aching for a chance to get out on the other side of the table ever since I came to the town, and I've still got one good arm. I'm going to take some of these house-games apart, if I can find someone to help me rake in my winnings.'

He looked sideways at Gladys, and Larson glowered at him. Gladys smiled to herself.

'Once a sucker, always a sucker,' Pete said to no one in particular. 'Well, we've got to get out before we're thrown out. Casey said he'd be in to see you to-morrow, Whit, and I'll be back in a day or two. If you want anything at all, just ask for it. It's on Uncle Sam.'

'Thanks.' Whit flopped his hand on the bedcovers. It was the best he could do in the way of a parting wave. 'Thanks for coming in. I'll be seeing you. Swede, stick around for a while, will you?'

The others said good-bye and left the room. Larson watched Gladys uneasily as she went out with Jackson, but he stayed.

Whit said, 'I guess your job is over, Swede. I'm still alive, and it wasn't only Alex that kept me that way. As far as I'm concerned you're still on the pay-roll. Do you have to get back to the city or can you stick around until I get out of here?'

'The Lootenant said I could have as much time as I wanted,' Larson answered. 'I'll stick around until you're out. Never mind about the pay-roll.'

'I'll be laid up for some time.'

'That's all right. I got things to do.'

Whit said, 'So you've decided to try it after all, even if she is a G-girl. How come you changed your mind?'

Larson grinned at him. 'Well, hell, I was swore in as a G-

223

man and I haven't been swore out yet. That puts us in the same class, doesn't it?'

'I guess it does. You've got to look out for Jackson, though. He's in the same class, too.'

'Yeh. I know it. I better get along.' Larson turned to Kitty. 'I'm sorry I sounded off about the – about Whit, Miz Whitney. I didn't know that he didn't know.'

'You big dummy,' Kitty said. 'Go chase after your blonde. And I wouldn't worry too much about Jackson. If it were up to me I'd take you any time, even if you are dumb.'

'Say, thanks. Tell that to Gladys next time you see her, will you? So long.'

He hurried out of the room.

After a while Whit said, 'Did that talkative doctor tell you how long I'd be here?'

'A couple of weeks. Then you have to live the clean life for a few months.'

Whit sighed.

Kitty left her chair and lay down on the bed alongside of him, being careful not to bump any of the sore spots. He didn't have quite enough strength to get his arm around her by himself, but she helped him and they were settled at last, cheek to cheek and very comfortable. They lay quietly that way for several minutes.

Whit said, 'This is a hell of a way to spend a honeymoon.'

'Mm.'

'What do you mean, mm?'

'I'm satisfied.'

'With your husband in this shape?'

'At least I've got a husband. And I'll keep him, too. You're a 4-F now. The draft board wouldn't even let you in the door.'

'I hadn't thought of that. I wonder if I ought to tell them.'

'I already wrote them a letter.'

'Oh, you did, huh? What did you say?'

Kitty turned to put her face in the hollow of his shoulder, where it fitted best, and put her arm around his neck.

'I said you weren't going to be good for anything for a long time, but you'd do as a husband before you'd be good enough for a soldier. Now go to sleep and start getting your strength back. The honeymoon isn't over yet.'